What Went Wrong?

Book Four

Enjoy!

kgcummings

[signature]

Bless our Vets!!!..

authorHOUSE®

AuthorHouse™
1663 Liberty Drive, Suite 200
Bloomington, IN 47403
www.authorhouse.com
Phone: 1-800-839-8640

First published by AuthorHouse   12/5/2008

ISBN: 978-1-4389-2345-1 (sc)

Printed in the United States of America
Bloomington, Indiana

This book is printed on acid-free paper.

It was the encouraging and prompting of many friends, and readers across the country that sprung this novel into being. It's no secret that there were six books written in the series, but the third book, with it's typical *Gone With the Wind* ending, may have been the last had it not been for old and new friends alike asking, *What Went Wrong?* Thank you Becky for the title! To each of you that urged me along, I say thank you. Because when I make friends, I keep friends, the thank you list here could go on for pages. So, once again "thanks" to all of my friends that are named in previous novels. Thank you to Ada and Jerry Forney, and Claire and John Ellis who have opened doors to new opportunities for me. Thank you to Wandalyn Ure who has a beautiful heart and soul, and helps with her unending prayers for me. Thank you once again to Nam Vets, Mike, Phil, Tony, Bob, Sam, Steve, and Bill who gave of their time, and their stories. I love you guys. Without the strength and support of my mother, Gertrude Kathryn, my daughter, Krista Bella, and my dear "Jimmy McHaelik", things would fall down around me when I'm off in Cyberland typing day and night. Thank you, and big hugs. A special thank you goes to Kelley Bracken-Rainey of KBR Photography who wow'd me with the cover photograph on this novel. She is a dear lady I met on MySpace who has an artist eye for photography. When I saw the picture on her page, it "spoke" to me, and I knew at that time Book Four had to be published. Thank you Kelley for your friendship and generosity, and please keep that camera at work!

Without further ado, find out What Went Wrong.

kgcummings... *Kathy*

$$Chapter \ 1$$

The gentle spring breeze blew softly, blending the aroma of freshly mown grass, and the sweet scent of lilacs through the open window. A playful pair of squirrels were chasing each other, leaping unhindered through the tree tops without a care in the world. The branches swayed, and little birds were chirping while their parents fluttered about in a never ending search for worms to bring back to their nest. A small child like voice could be heard singing, *"I am a pretty little Dutch girl, as pretty as can be. All the boys on the baseball team are crazy over me. My boyfriend gave me peaches, my boyfriend gave me pears. My boyfriend gave me twenty-five cents to kiss him on the stairs. I gave him back his peaches, I gave him back his pears. I gave him back his twenty-five cents, and pushed him down the stairs."* The giggles suddenly stopped.

Beth Ann gazed out the window wondering, *what's the meaning of this?* She glanced down at her hands on the window sill, and began to shake. Her eyes darted quickly back toward the open window, the bars were very frightening. She looked at her nightgown, and started to cry. Back in bed, terrified, she covered her face with her hands. On her pillow, she shook her head back and forth crying, "No, no, no!" Something wasn't right. It was springtime. The open window, and pleasant scents attested to that. She should be outside playing with John. Beth Ann suddenly sat upright, screaming, "JOHNNY!" She began singing between her sobs, *"When Johnny comes marching home again, hurrah, hurrah!"* Beth wondered aloud, "Why doesn't John come to visit me? He's twelve. They let big boys visit the hospital." But, it seemed like she was just outside playing. She knew she had just been singing while she jumped rope. And, she didn't even miss, while Mary Lou and Trudy stood at each end twirling the rope. At least she thought she was just singing while she jumped... Everything was so confusing. *Why? Why, why, why are my hands so big... like Mommy's?* She ran her large hands over her chest, and stopped at her breasts... "No, no, no!" She cried harder. That chubby woman in the white dress and white stockings, and ugly white orthopedic oxfords came in again. With pity in her eyes, she gave Beth another needle. Soon, very soon Beth Ann went back to sleep.

Drug induced sleep was good. It kept the patients quiet. The afternoon passed more quickly, and peacefully, when they could be sedated.

Before long, it was time to get ready for dinner. Beth Ann brushed her long red hair, and put it up in a pony tail. She could do it without a mirror and in fact she could put it up better and faster without the mirror. That woman frightened her. *How can this be?* This place was strange. Even the mirrors were odd. She was still little, and that lady looking back at her was a total stranger. Well, not total, she did resemble Aunt Dorothy more than a little bit. That was foolish. *Who ever heard of a little girl seeing an old woman of, oh maybe twenty-six, or twenty-seven in the mirror?*

Beth Ann sat eating quietly at the round table in the cafeteria as she always did. One lady ate with her fingers, and another threw a temper tantrum every night insisting that she didn't get any food even though the soiled plate was always empty in front of her. Those ladies didn't understand that

Beth wasn't as big as them, and couldn't talk about the things that big people talk about. They asked her questions like, did she ever "do it" with a man. She hated it when they teased her about the things young girls only whisper about at pajama parties. Beth Ann started to tremble, then she spilled her milk when she reached for it with her big clumsy hands. She left the table crying when all those silly mean ladies laughed at her again for having another accident.

Maybe tonight her daddy would come to visit with her again. She liked it when Daddy came. He'd talk to her, and sing to her, and tell her she was his little doll princess until she went to sleep. But, Daddy didn't look very much like Daddy anymore, at least not in the daytime, or when the lights were turned on bright. When it was dim, his hair still sparkled like a shiny, new copper penny. She knew she filled her daddy's heart with love. He always said so, well, he always said so when she was a good little girl. When she was naughty, he'd give her such a look, it would break her heart. She didn't understand the look he gave her sometimes now. It was kind of sorry, like when Jerry… *Oh, never mind*, she stopped herself from thinking about that, and only thought of how she loved her daddy very, very much.

Beth Ann loved her mommy, too. Mommy was firmer with her, and was always reminding her to grow up, and be responsible. In her heart, she knew mommy was right. Daddy said Mommy couldn't come at night because she was busy helping with the kids. She guessed he was talking about Johnny and Jerry. Brothers were such a bother. She was very angry that John didn't come to visit, but maybe it was because when Jerry went to the hospital, he never ever came home again.

Before she had time to worry if she would never go home from the hospital, too, Beth Ann's face broke into a big grin. She hugged her daddy's neck until he sat down in the big wood and vinyl chair.

"Daddy, your belly is getting too fat!" Beth patted her fathers paunch. "Look at you, I can hardly sit on your lap anymore! And, don't you start teasing me again about how I'm a big girl now, or I'll bop you on the bean! I think that chubby lady took the big chair, and brought in a littler one. She needs a big, big, BIG one for her seat!" Beth Ann giggled, then yawned, as she snuggled in her daddy's embrace. He softly hummed in a low undertone, *"Hush little baby don't say a word…"*

Jack wiped a tear from his cheek with his shoulder as he continued to hum with his grown daughter in his arms…

****

Nights melted into days, into weeks, into months.

"Mom-meee!" Beth Ann excitedly yelled when she saw her mother enter the activity room.

"Hello, sweetheart." Nancy held her daughter close to her heart as she stroked her pony tail. "How's my big girl today, Beth?"

"I feel really good today, Mommy. I ate all my breakfast, and lunch, and I didn't spill a thing either time! Not one drop." She looked extremely proud of herself.

"I'm very happy to hear that, honey. Doctor Young told me that you are opening up and talking more freely with him now. That has earned you more privileges. Beth, would you like to go out for a nice walk to get some fresh air?"

"Outside?" Beth's eyes sparkled as she thought of being out in the sunshine. Nancy nodded her head yes. They walked hand in hand toward the gazebo.

"Beth, I'd like to ask you something serious," Nancy began. "Beth Ann, do you know where you are?"

"Uh huh. I'm in the hospital."

"Do you know why you are in the hospital?"

"Ummm, 'cause I was bad and, and did what I wasn't suppos'tuh do…"

"Beth, you aren't going to get in trouble. Tell Mom, what it was that you did that you weren't supposed to do." Nancy watched her closely as her daughter twirled her hair, and kicked at the dirt with her toe. Beth gazed up at the clouds, and bit at her lips. "Beth, it's okay, you can tell Mommy anything. I won't be mad, and you won't be punished."

"I, uh, I, ummm… I went over to the Quiver's when you told me not to, and ummm, me and Davy and his sister Linda and his cousins were playing pirate ship on the wood pile like we were told not to and… ummm, I had to walk the plank, and, and when I did, the board flipped and I fell hard and the board had a rusty nail in it and it went in my leg and, and all the kids were standing around scared like 'cause I was screaming really, really loud and nobody would touch me, or help me and I had to grab the board and pull on it to get the rusty nail out of my leg all by myself. Mommy, it hurt so bad and his aunt yelled at me to quit my screeching." Beth's eyes were filled with tears. "I'm so so sorry I did what you told me not to do."

They each took a seat inside the shade of the gazebo. Nancy took a deep breath. "Beth, shhh, honey, it's okay, you aren't going to get in trouble. Beth Ann, I want you to look at your leg, look where the nail went in… Look at it Beth. Do you see an open wound?"

Beth shook her head no. "Didn't it really happen Mommy?" She tearfully wondered if this memory was another of those strange incidents that happened at this place all the time.

"Yes, dear, it really happened. Look close, really close. See? There's the scar. Right there." Nancy and Beth both examined where the nail had pierced Beth's leg. "It's very faint because that happened a long, long time ago. You took a bad tumble when you fell, and you hit your head, too. You were in the hospital for the head injury, and they also cleaned your leg wound, and gave you a tetanus shot."

Beth looked very thoughtful. "I remember. And, I did go home. Little time later, my baby brother got sick. Jerry went to the hospital. He didn't ever come home. Mommy, did Jerry die there?"

Nancy sadly nodded her head yes.

"Mommy, I don't wanna die here." Beth cast her eyes down, and took a deep breath. "Johnny... he *never* comes to see me..."

"Beth honey, he, he can't..."

"Mom! He's old enough! He's twelve."

"Beth, John went to war..."

"...Laos." Beth stated, then looked surprised that she'd said that. "John is bigger than twelve, he's gone..."

Nancy's heart began to pound, and it pounded hard. "Yes! Beth, that's right. Laos, do you remember?"

"Yes, yes. Uh huh, Johnny went to Laos. I remember Grandpa sitting in his ugly green recliner watching the news saying, 'Laos... the name suits the place. You mark my words, Beth Ann, that place is going to louse up the whole world.' Then, Grandpa went to the hospital, and he died. When is Johnny coming home?"

"Beth, John's been gone for nearly ten years now."

"Ten years? That's a real long time. Seems like Grandpa was right again. Why can't he come home yet? Isn't the war done?"

Nancy shook her head no. "There is still war in Southeast Asia. Beth, I think we've talked about this enough. Try to remember this Beth. It hurts to remember, believe me I know, but try. Tell your doctor about where John is. It's very important. Dr. Young wants to help you. He wants to help you grow up again, and be responsible." Nancy picked up her purse.

"Mama! Mama! Don't go! I'm sooo scared!!!" Beth's face had paled, and she was trembling more violently than previously. She turned and hugged her mother tighter than she ever had before. It somewhat startled Nancy.

"I know you are honey, but…"

"Mom, Mom… Shhh… Listen to me, I'm sooo scared… I've never been this scared in my whole life."

Nancy could hear the urgency in Beth's voice, and saw the look of total terror in her eyes. "What is it, dear?" Nancy held her daughter as she slightly relaxed.

"I ummm, did something else bad… and please, please don't be mad… But, Mommy… Oh, and please, please don't tell Daddy… Mom, I'm, I'm ummm, I'm gonna have a baby… I, I, I did it with that Fly Boy from Florida and, and, and he left me. He just went back to the Base, and he didn't call, or come back after that Thanksgiving… I'm so so sorry I did what you told me not to do." Beth's voice had faded into barely a whisper.

"Shhh… Beth, it's okay, honey. You are a good girl. Everything is just fine. Shhh… Don't cry, your baby will give us all joy. Babies are a blessing, Beth. Mommy loves you very much. Shhh… Please don't cry. Everything will work out for the best. Shhh…"

"He did exactly what you and Daddy always said guys do if you do it with them before you get married. I, I gave him my virginity, and then he disappeared. He left me, Mom. He left me. He's gone… he left me… I gave him my body, and he left and didn't come back. They'll call me a bitch and a slut and a whore. He left me… he's gone… No note, no phone call… He left me… We did it and he left me like trash on the side of the road. I'm trash, nothing but trash! That's why he left me… all alone, and pregnant. I'm so scared. Alone, and pregnant, and no husband, and I'm a bitch and a slut and a whore!"

No amount of talking could calm Beth down. Someone on the grounds' staff called for a nurse, who came quickly with a sedative. Nancy accompanied them back to Beth's room all the time assuring her that she was loved, and that she was still a good girl. She stayed with her only living child, holding her hand until the shot put her into a deep sleep.

Beth had confirmed what Nancy had always suspected. She thought of her beautiful seven and a half year old grandson, and was very grateful that Jason was in their lives irregardless of the circumstances of his conception. She wiped tears from her eyes.

Nancy also respected Beth's wishes, she wasn't mad, and she didn't tell her father.

****

More months passed…

"Beth, you've made wonderful progress. Your weekend visits at your parent's home seem to be going very well. Your children, according to your folks, have adapted marvelously to living with them part time while your husband-"

"Excuse me! EX husband, thank you." Beth snapped.

"He's not your ex husband yet. All we need to work on now is your anger toward Mr. Madison."

"Nothing to work on Doc. He chose to take a hike in the middle of the night. Gone, poof… like steam from a coffee cup. He can stew in his juices now. I gave him everything I had, and he still chose to go back to his hippie chick."

"That's not the way he tells it and you know it, Beth. You've been in here together, you've heard his side of the story."

"Oh, yeah, yeah, yeah… Haven't we all heard that one before… 'I needed someone to watch the kids while you were in the loony bin. So, I asked the tramp I've been sleeping with since we got back from Okinawa to give me a hand.' Hey, Doc, wanna buy a bridge? I just wonder who's watching my kids while she's giving him a hand." Beth made an obscene hand gesture. "Besides, two can play that game. I've renewed my friendship with a man I know from church. At least he's faithful, and moral. His wife died, and he chooses to remain celibate until he remarries." Beth sat with her legs crossed firmly at the ankles, and her arms folded tightly across her chest.

Doctor Young knew there would be no further progress on this day with Beth Ann. Once she slipped into that mind set, she seemed to get more stubborn, and it became increasingly impossible to work with her.

However, overall Beth had made an excellent recovery. As soon as it was decided where she would go after her release, Beth could go "home".

Chapter 2

Many months ago, soon after Jason had called his Nana to tell her that he hadn't seen his daddy in a few days, and that something was wrong with his mom, the apartment on 150 East Fourth Street had been given up. Frightened, and frantic Jason told Nana that the night before last, he and Mommy, and Rianne drove by where daddy worked, and saw his Camaro and Jodi's hippie van in the yard. Nancy couldn't believe her ears as she listened to Jason's ramblings. "When we got home, Mommy told us to go play... No, she didn't even put us to bed... Right now? ...She's still sittin' in the corner huggin' a teddy bear an' her knees are under her chin. I told her Rianne an' me was hungry, an' she told us to go home an' eat an' leave her alone. Nana, she won't stop playing that stupid game, an' the baby's crying an' has poopie pants... Uh huh... Since night before last... After supper when we got back from driving by my Dad's. ...Nope... *Nana*, I *couldn't* go to school... who would take care uh Rianne?"

When Jack and Nancy arrived, they were aghast at what they saw, but maintained a calm demeanor as to not upset the children any further. Nancy hugged Jason, and praised him for the good job he did taking care of his baby sister. The kitchen was in shambles, but at least they had eaten something. Nancy pulled a thirty pound wet, soiled diaper off of Marianne, shoved it in an empty bread wrapper, rolled it in newspaper, then put it outside in the garbage can. She wouldn't even attempt to wash, and reuse it again. Nancy asked Jason to put some clean clothes, shoes, and toothbrushes in a suitcase for both he and his sister, and not to dawdle. She went to work straightening up the kitchen as quickly as possible after sponge bathing her granddaughter. No way could they have emergency personnel inside with the house looking like that. Nancy knew Beth could lose the children if they saw the condition of the place.

As Nancy busied herself with the baby on her hip, and answering Jason's questions about how many diapers to pack and what kind of dresses Rianne would need, Jack attempted to get a response from his beloved Beth Ann. He finally told Nancy to get the kids out of there, "Now." He didn't want them there when they came to take their mother away. Jack's heart wrenched. His little girl had always been his perfect little doll princess. In disbelief he stared at her stringy, messy, unwashed hair, and crumpled clothes. The smell of stale urine told him she'd not even gotten up to use the bathroom, he turned his head quickly when he got a whiff of her breath. She was dehydrated, and hadn't eaten a thing for days.

Jeff was distraught, but as cooperative as any man could be under the circumstances. It was agreed that the kids would stay with Jack and Nancy rather than Jeff having to make arrangements for full time care for the baby, and getting Jason to school during the week while he worked. Jeff was grateful that his in-laws were willing to help. All agreed the kids needed as much stability as possible during this time. Jeff could offer no clue as to why Beth collapsed the way she did. He said, "I'd moved back home, and thought all was well. Then she…" Crying, he never completed the sentence.

****

Upon her release from the hospital, Beth moved into her parents tri-level home in Centerville. Beth refused to go to the apartment that she and her husband had never shared above the auto repair shop. *Let the hippie bitch be the queen of that castle,* she thought.

Beth continued weekly sessions with a new doctor outside of the hospital, and was adjusting to life on her own quite well. Beth began classes at the local business college, and soon would have her certificate as a Key Punch operator. She continued her friendship with the widower she had met in church a couple of years ago while she was pregnant with Marianne.

Life wasn't perfect, but it was good.

Life was good, except for when the nagging question was rolling around in Beth's mind. The question that she never asked, so she was never given the answer to while she was still in counseling with Jeff.

Life was good, except when Marianne cried when she had to leave her mother to go with her father for the weekend.

Life was good, except when Jason cried when he had to leave his father to go back home to her after the weekend with his dad.

Life really was good when she was in the company of the handsome, wealthy Tom Ericsen. She got to know him better as they rode his horses every Sunday after church while her kids were with their father. Tom leaned over, after their picnic supper, and kissed Beth very passionately. He was a nonsmoker, his mouth tasted so good. His hands aroused much passion within the center of her being. Bruce never touched her like that, he wasn't allowed. Only Jeff, only her husband knew the intimate places that she loved to have touched… until Tom Ericsen. She wanted sex, but Tom stopped short of gratifying himself, and her, with his body. Beth remembered how angry Jeff got when she "begged" for sex. She took the pleasure Tom gave with his hands, and tried to be satisfied with it. It was good, actually, it was very good. For the first time since she met Jeff, she wondered what it would feel like to have another man's private part thrusting deep within. She opened her legs to Tom, as his hand explored, and she fantasized.

"Enjoy, Babe, enjoy. Let me help you through this. You like it don't you? Tell me if you like it."

"Uh huh! Uh huh! Yes, yes! I like it. I love it!"

Tom never took his eyes off her body. "You don't want me to stop, do you Beth?"

"No, please, don't stop! Don't stop! I like it, I like it very much. You make me feel sooo good!"

Tom intensified his fondling. "Let it go Babe, let it go, let it go. Don't hold back. There she goes, there goes my little honey dripper." He enjoyed watching her as he made her melt around his erotic touch. Vocally, she voiced her pleasure, silently, she wanted more. As she lay there, he spoke, "You want it, Beth. You miss it. I've never seen a woman want it as badly as you." Tom eyed her up and down. "You would like it if I did it to you right here, right now, wouldn't you? Do tell, am I correct?"

Though fully clothed, Beth felt naked and exposed. Unable to hide her yearning, she nodded her head yes. His handsome face smiled down at her, as he softly stroked her silkiness. "Babe, I can make you come like you've never come before." He kissed her hand, then placed it on himself. Beth had only touched Jeff, and he was nothing to complain about, however, her eyes grew wide as she first explored the manhood of the second man she ever touched. Tom smiled as he watched her. "You want it don't you Babe? But, this is what you get." He barely touched her with his fingertips.

Beth was begging unashamed, "Take me… Please, I'm so ready for you. I want you, Tom. Please."

"You know what you have to do first."

Closing her eyes, she pondered what it was that he wanted from her as Tom watched the rise and fall of her breasts. They were much larger than he preferred. *This gal is different*, he thought. He was happy that she shared his passion for horses, and for riding. He was impressed that she, unlike others he'd met since his wife, didn't seem overly influenced by his money. He was also pleased that she truly loved her children, and that she was a God fearing, church going woman. His shoulder twitched slightly as he thought about God, and the way he enjoyed how Beth begged for him, how she wanted him to satisfy her sexually. He liked her because she only took what he was willing to give, without throwing a tantrum. He didn't give a damn whether his family liked her or not, they didn't like his first wife either. His beautiful wife, his child bride, oh how he longed to be one with that woman's body again. He had promised her, "Til death do us part." And, it was death that parted them. He never did to her what he did to Beth, he made love to his wife before they wed. Beth would get what she wanted, *if* she made the right choice. If not? He'd see her again next Sunday at church. But, she was going to have to comply with his wishes if she wanted to have sex with him. He knew if she didn't, he was going to have to break it off with her. He hadn't been caressed by any of the other women he'd dated the way he allowed Beth to touch him. He adjusted himself. He needed to send her home so he could finish the job, as tonight he came close to breaking his own rule. He continued to watch Beth, he couldn't help but notice how beautiful she was. If only she was blonde, if only her eyes were blue, if only she was a little taller, less busty, slimmer, if only she was…

Renée.

****

Jack and Nancy continued to enjoy their grandchildren during the week. They were always polite to their father when he came to pick them up on Friday while Beth was still in school, and when he'd bring them back on Sunday evening before she returned home from her riding dates with Tom Ericsen. Jeff missed the good old days, but his priorities were maintaining his relationship with Jason, and trying to develop one with Marianne. Beth's parents were still as confused as ever as to what had happened to cause the break up of the marriage. All they whispered about behind closed doors was how Jeff and Beth were at one time so much in love. Each confessed to the other, that neither of the two had ever confided anything personal to either of them.

Beth managed to maintain good grades in her business classes, do the kids and her own laundry, help Jason with his homework, and potty train Marianne. She enjoyed having Saturday to herself, then on Sunday it was off to church, and riding and romancing with Tom. In her parents home, when her kids were tucked in bed sound asleep, and her homework was completed, Beth would lie in bed, and think. In the dark, alone in her solitude, Beth still continued to have that nagging question to ask Jeff lingering in the back of her mind.

When she was stronger, she would ask...

Chapter 3

"Jodi, for the last time, I don't want to go. If you and the boys want to go that bad *GO*, just go without me!" Jeff yelled as Jodi slammed out the door. The last thing Jeff wanted to attend was a rock concert. He hid the fact that he was hurt that Jason wanted to go with them.

There was much to do since he bought Seth's Auto & Repair. He did like the looks of Madison Motors on the building's sign, though. There were piles of paper work to be attended to, between bookkeeping, and tracking inventory, tax reports, and payroll. It was one thing to let it slide when Jason, and Marianne were there, but letting it go just so he could attend a rock concert in a park was a waste of time.

A knock came on the door that totally annoyed him. Nine chances out of ten, it was Jodi coming back inside one more time, in a last ditch effort to try to get her own way.

"You know it's unlocked, so just come on in so I can tell you NO for the last and final time!"

"Well, you've sure changed your tune since I slept with you, Fly Boy."

His heart skipped a beat, and he dropped his pencil as he recognized that voice.

"Beth, it's you! I'm sorry, forgive my rudeness. Come right in. Can I get you something to drink? I have some soda in there for Jason, but he wouldn't mind, or I've got beer, or I could make coffee…" He realized he was rambling. "Beth what did you do to your hair? It's so, so, so straight. Oh, would you like to sit down? Where is Marianne? What brings you this way?"

"Jeff, which question do you want me to answer first?" Beth laughed.

This was the most they had talked since Beth was released from the hospital. Jeff would call to tell her what time he would be there to pick up the kids if something came up at the shop. If she was going his way, she'd sometimes offer to drop them off. There still was an occasional grumble between them, sad to say.

"Again, I apologize. It's just I'm surprised to see you here." Jeff struggled to keep from jumping up and kissing her.

"I should have called ahead, I'm the one who should apologize. A beer would be nice. I quit teasing my hair, and grew out my bangs. I'd love to sit down. Marianne is with my parents. I felt like a drive, I ended up here. I'm sorry, I hope I'm not interrupting."

"No actually, I just finished going over the books. I'm surprised that you haven't asked about Jason."

"Jeff you're right. He's your son, too, and just as I don't have to account to you for every minute of his life, you shouldn't have to either. But, if you'd like to tell me, I wouldn't mind…" Beth smiled.

"He went with Jodi and her kid to some concert in Waynesboro. As much as I wanted to be with him, I didn't want to be at the concert. When you came, I thought she was back nagging at me again to go."

"She must have some kind of a spell over you. You can't seem to get her out of your system." Beth said sarcastically half under her breath.

Jeff heard and knew the look. He let out a long sighing breath. "Beth, she wasn't here that night. Her van broke down, she had her kid with her, after I unhooked the tow, I ran her and the kid home. Look, don't get all worked up over this, okay? It was no big deal."

"Well, why didn't you return Jason's phone calls? He says he must have called a dozen times while I was off in la la land."

"I've explained all that to Jason, and took care of the situation. Didn't he tell you what happened?"

"Nope. Must be a male communication flaw in the Madison bloodline."

"Beth, the secretary took the message, but never told me he'd called. When I asked her about it, she reminded me that the rules were no personal phone calls and figured that that went for me too, as an example to the others. I gave her a warning, and have since let her go for... umm... improper relations with a coworker in the office on company time." Jeff's jaw tightened.

Beth wasn't pleased, but nodded her head as she sipped on her beer. She thought to herself how bad it would look if people knew she skipped church, and was drinking before noon on Sunday. She glanced around the apartment. "So this is Versailles?" she commented with a playful grin.

Jeff shrugged his shoulders. "I don't spend much time up here. I'm down in the garage most of the time." Beth walked around, and stopped to look at the deer head. Jeff continued, "In Versailles they have chandeliers in some of the rooms made completely out of deer antlers. I guess the old rulers couldn't afford the whole buck head like me."

Beth snarffed her beer, and Jeff half expected to get smacked with a pillow. He didn't, but he grinned, as she continued to laugh. Walking over to the window, she looked across the lot, "You know, if it wasn't for all the cars, and all the other junk scattered around, the view is incredible from this window."

Jeff got up and stood behind her, looking at the same view. "I guess I never really noticed. It could be that beauty is in the eye of the beholder." He could smell her freshly shampooed hair.

Beth could feel his breath on her neck. Her head went back to that hollow place below his shoulder blade where it fit so well. After a few more minutes, she walked away, and sat on the couch.

"So, Beth, are you working? You got your certificate didn't you?"

"Yeah, I did. I'm key punching at the bank now officially, but that's only the half of it."

Jeff laughed, "What's the other half, bringing coffee and doughnuts to the boss?"

"Oh, Mr. Barker would love that! The arrogant male chauvinist pig. Unofficially, I'm a computer operator, sort of. I love it, but the working conditions stink. Don't get me wrong, I haven't turned into one of those new women's libbers out there making a lot of noise. I think they just want to keep stuff stirred up. They haven't done much for equality in the work place as far as I can see. While they're busy flag burning protesting the frickin' war, they just toss in their bras to keep the fires hot. Dumb. Like I'd want my twins hanging on my waist before I'm thirty!"

"So what's your gripe then?" Jeff chuckled at her sense of humor, as he eyed her chest.

"They won't give me the title of operator, and they don't give me the pay for no other reason than I'm a woman. Jeff, you know the feeling ya get working with powerful monster machines?"

Jeff grinned, "Have you ever listened to, or smelled a Hemi?"

Beth shook her head no, "But, you know what I mean. I was hired as a key punch operator. You've seen the cards that have holes in them. The machine I went to school to learn to operate, punches the holes in the cards when you type on the keyboard. Each hole in each column represents one digit, either alpha, or numeric. I punch the information on the cards about each customer, and each vehicle to finance it for three years. If you multiply that by the number of vehicles sold in a day, you are talking about some big bucks. I do my job, watch, and observe. One day the 'golden boy' computer operator couldn't make it in to work on time. The supervisor, showed me how to stack the cards, run them through the card reader, and print out an edit report. I already knew how to balance, verifying that payments equaled face. I made a few necessary corrections. I'd made one transposition error, it was obviously my error, so I fixed it. I rejected the others, and sent them back to the departments that made the errors. I ran another edit report to be sure that the batch balanced, then put the cards in the tray to update live later. The supervisor was amazed that I ran that second edit with no assistance, since I'd only been shown how to operate the computer once."

"I've never had any doubt that you're smart. What's the problem?"

"Problem is, I got called in the front office. Seems the 'boy' computer operator wanted 'his' hours changed so 'he' could continue 'his' education. They asked me if I would consider running edit reports in addition to my key punching duties until he came in. 'Sure!' I told them, thinking it's going to be a hefty increase in my salary. HA! I got told that they don't hire women as operators, 'Sorry'. I'd already said that I would do it, so if I was to go back on my word, I could kiss off any future promotion to any department where a woman is allowed to advance."

"Beth, that really does stink. So why don't you quit, and find another job?" Jeff suggested.

"Because, even though they're getting a computer operator for key punch operator wages, what they pay me is far better than anyplace else around. As much as it stinks, it's still the best game in town. My only consolation is, I really do love the work. My ear is so tuned to the printer, that I can tell what report is running by the sound of the hammers hitting the ribbon. The speed is incredible. The flashing lights indicate that each component is doing what it's supposed to do. What can I say? I love computers."

"Who ever would have guessed?" Jeff shifted in his chair wondering what they would talk about next, as he looked at his watch.

"Jeff, when do you think Jason will be back?"

"My guess is around 6:00, I told Jodi that he needed to be home by 7:00 so that you could debrief him, and make sure his homework is correct."

"Wise guy!" she grinned. "I really need to talk to you, and I don't want to argue in front of him any more. The pop shots we occasionally take still cause him grief."

"I know, and I'm sorry."

"Yeah, me too." Beth's body was trembling, then she continued speaking, "I, I'm so confused."

Jeff concealed how fearful he was that Beth was going to have another breakdown.

"I, I've wanted to ask you something for a long time, but, but the words get caught in my throat every time I start. Then something mean comes out of my mouth."

"Relax angel eyes, I don't want to argue with you either. Let's just talk, and see where it goes. When you're ready, just ask me. I nibble a little, but I don't bite." Jeff grinned. "Do you think Rianne will ever warm up to me?"

"Marianne is a different kind of kid. Jason was always willing to please, he always wanted to be a part of the fun. We did have fun..." Beth's eyes trailed off thinking of happier days. "Marianne wants to go her own way. If you remember, I couldn't nurse her. I don't think she would have if she could have. She didn't even want to be held for her bottle. She likes me, my folks, Tom, and tolerates Jason."

"Tom?"

"I've been dating him for a while now."

Jeff remembered, but felt like he'd been kicked in the stomach hearing her finally admit it. He knew he had no right to feel that way. "Jason never mentions him."

"Jason doesn't like him. Tom is a very nice man. Tom just isn't his Daddy. You know, I used to get jealous when you two would have a guy day. I'm glad that you did, but I felt left out."

"I'm sorry Beth. You never complained. Would you like another beer?"

"When did you say Jason was due back?"

"Probably around 6:00."

"No thanks." She glanced at her watch. "Umm, Jeff... Tom has asked me to marry him."

She looked at her husband. There were tears welled up in his eyes, and one rolled down his cheek. Her heart melted, as no matter what had happened in their lives together, he had never allowed himself to cry. She reached for his hand, and felt the old familiar butterflies.

"Did you say yes?"

"I haven't given him an answer yet."

"Does he, um, rock your cradle?"

"I, I don't know. Tom is... ummm, moral. I'm married, he's a widower..."

"Is he normal?

"What do you mean?"

"Well, unless he's under 14 years old, my guess is he isn't normal if he's not rockin' with a woman as beautiful as you." Jeff licked his finger, wiped his eyebrow, then limped his wrist.

"Jeff, don't be a dog!" She whacked him with a pillow. "Just because we haven't had sex doesn't mean there's anything wrong with him!"

Jeff looked serious. "Do you love him, Beth?"

"Not like I love you." She didn't bat an eye.

"You love me?"

"Jeff," she forced out the question that had tormented her since she woke up in her empty bed, "Jeff, why? Why did you leave me?"

"You didn't say you loved me. We had made what I consider to this day, the most incredible love two human beings in the history of the world had ever made. I would have died for you that night if you would have asked me. Then you got up, washed your body of myself, and turned your back to me... I left, thinking that's what you wanted. I was heartbroken. I just sat in my car. I bawled my eyes out for the first time in twenty years. I couldn't force myself to go back inside to be rejected again by the only woman I've ever loved." Tears began to roll down his cheeks as he swallowed hard.

Beth cried, too. "When you moved back in, I was having a rough period. Sorry, I know you hate that talk. I wanted you so badly, but I have my hang ups. When it was finally over, I had such a bad day. Both kids had been acting up, Marianne with her teeth, and Jason with his crash cars. Dad took the kids, and I went to church, just to get my head together. I didn't know what to do to get, well, rockin' again. I prayed to God that you still found me attractive. It always seemed to me like we just fit, but I've always felt inferior to the... others. Later on, I didn't want the lovemaking to end." Beth sobbed. "But, my folks would be bringing the kids back in just a few hours. I knew if I fell asleep I might not get a shower for another sixteen hours, or more. I didn't want to be scrambling for a night shirt when the door bell rang, so I pulled on a clean one after my shower, and dropped exhausted into bed. I don't remember what position I was in. I only knew that I had totally and completely, given you all that my heart and body had to give. When I woke up you were gone. You didn't come home after work, or at all that night, or the next. You were gone, no note, no phone call, no nothing. When I drove by here, I saw the Camaro, and knew you'd really left me. I lost it. I never knew what I had done."

Each one could hardly believe what they were hearing. They stared into each others eyes, and wanted to come together. Jeff glanced toward the bedroom, Beth nodded yes. They went into his room, and shut the door.

They made beautiful love. It wasn't just the physical act, they truly made love to each other. There was no one else in the whole wide world, but them. Jeff made love to Beth with the tenderness of a man enthralled with his beloved. She felt the fulfillment of completion, with the comfort of being adored. Beth held his handsome face in her hands, looked deeply into his blue eyes, as she told him, "I love you with every breath of life in me, Jeff Madison. I love you, I love you, I love you."

"Yeah? Well, you're going to have to prove it woman!" Jeff taunted, then whacked her with the pillow.

"YOU Brat!!!" She whacked him back.

"I've been called worse." They laughed, they teased, they remembered the fun they shared in the past.

Showered, back in bed, and with the passion of their youth renewed, Beth kissed down Jeff's body stopping to give him a hickey just below his navel. She teased him about his CO not seeing that one. He laughed, then gently suggested, "Beth, you've never kissed me any lower, you could go a little further south, ya know."

Hearing him sigh with pleasure, Beth felt a previously unknown urge burn within. Impassioned by his response, she was more than willing to continue to pleasure until he moaned with release.

"Oh, my Jeff… oh, my dearest, Jeff… Oh, my darling. Nothing I've ever done has made me feel like I could show you how deeply I love you as much as this." She knew he was the man she loved more than life itself.

"Beth, Beth, my beloved Beth. Oh God, thank you, Jesus." Jeff never wanted to be with another woman as long as he lived. Every fantasy he ever had came true with this woman, his Beth, the bride of his youth.

Together, in peace, they napped. They woke up around five. Jeff was on his back. Beth was next to him with one leg over his body, her head on one strong shoulder, and her arm across his chest. She told him what she would like to do to redecorate the apartment. He asked her which drawer they should put their kids in. She smacked him, and he pinched her bottom. They decided to build a house on the lot in front of the garage with an upstairs veranda to enjoy the beautiful view. Passion rising again, they gazed into each others eyes as their lips gently met. Beth moved to mount Jeff...

The bedroom door flung open. Beth quickly rolled off of Jeff pulling the sheet up over her breasts.

"Jeff! What the HELL?"

"Jodi! Where's Jason?"

"Jason!?! That's all you have to say, 'Where's Jason?' Tell me Jeff, just where did this carrot-topped goddess come from? No fucking wonder you didn't want to go to the goddam concert!" Jodi was screaming.

"I asked you a question! *Where is my son?*"

Jodi saw the fury on his face. "Oh, cool it! He's outside showing Rocky some raggedy old car. Who the hell *is* she, and what's *she* doing in our bed?"

"Where do you get off calling this *our* bed? This is *my* bed, and this is *my* wife. If it isn't too much trouble, shut the damn door!" Jeff stated coolly.

Jodi slammed the door shouting, "You are a two timing, low life son of a bitch, and I'll be *damned* if I'll have your baby! I'm going to New York in the morning, and you're not stopping me! *I'm* getting an abortion."

"When I said shut the damn door, I meant shut it with you on the other side. Jodi, I told you from the start I would never be free, and you still pursued me. I promised you nothing. You smoked your joints, and told me all your thoughts about open relationships, and free love. You never asked, or cared what I thought. I think I would like to spend more time with my wife, *alone*. So kindly leave, and shut the door behind you."

They heard Jodi and Rocky drive off. Surprisingly, Beth didn't cry. She looked into Jeff's deep blue eyes, and asked what he thought about the abortion.

"Beth, if she's pregnant, the kid isn't mine. Yours are the only two children I claim, or ever will claim. I know they're mine. Let's get dressed, and go pick up Marianne."

Beth smiled at him. He watched her dress, and made teasing remarks about wanting to see her take it off again. Playfully she jiggled a little before hooking, buttoning, and zipping up. There was a lot of giggling.

Beth followed Jeff out of the bedroom. A not too happy Jason looked at his father, and then at his mother. He should have kept his mouth shut. Instead he looked at his mom and asked sarcastically, "So, are you one of the tramps my dad sleeps with?" Before he knew what hit him, Jeff had backhanded Jason, and had him pinned against the wall.

"Jason Charles Madison, don't you ever talk dirty to, or about your mother again. She is the most beautiful hearted, pure woman I've ever known in my whole life, and I will love her until the day I die."

"I'm sorry, Dad." Jason answered with a mixture of shock, and fear on his face.

"I don't want to hear your lame 'I'm sorry' excuse. Personally, I don't care what you think about the other women that hang around here, but I do care about what you think about your mother. Were you here all afternoon? Were you?"

"No, sir."

"Don't call me sir, call me Dad. Answer me!"

26

"No, Dad."

"If you weren't here all afternoon, then you don't know what was going on, and furthermore, it's none of your business. Your mother and I are separated, but she is still my wife. If I ever hear you being disrespectful to your mother again, this is just the opening act of what you can expect from me. Do you understand me?"

"Yes, Dad. Really I'm Sor-"

"I said I don't want to hear it! I'm not the one that's owed the apology. Just look how you've hurt your mom." Jason flinched as Jeff's hand reached to turn his chin so he could see his mother. Jason was terrified remembering the time his mother had to go to the hospital.

Beth was shaking, clutching her stomach leaning against the doorway. Beth looked at Jeff and said, "Above all, I never wanted our children to be ashamed of me."

Jeff dropped his hand from Jason's shoulder, and turned away from his son. It's hard to say which of the three of them hurt more. Jeff had never hit either of his children in anger, and didn't know if he had permanently damaged his relationship with the child he adored. Jason never expected that his dad would ever lay a hand on him, but he learned his boundaries that day. Beth hurt to the heart, and was struggling to keep her head together.

Jeff walked over to Beth, and took her in his arms. He stroked her soft auburn hair, and told her he loved her. Jason's heart pounded as he quietly observed this tender moment between his parents. He hoped beyond hope that they would be getting back together.

Beth clung to Jeff's body, and rubbed his back gently. When she got control of her emotions she looked into his deep blue eyes and said, "Jeff, I honestly don't think that it can work." She started sobbing again.

"I'm sorry Mommy, please don't cry, and please don't blame Daddy. I deserved what I just got. I'm sorry for what

I said, and I'm ashamed of myself for saying it. Dad is right, lots uh women come here. I'm only eight, but I've got eyes an' ears. They get silly an' giggle when he talks to 'em. Even when he talks to them about serious stuff like fuel lines, and drive shafts, and blowin' engines. They act so stupid. Mommy, I just didn't want you to be one of those kinds of women. I'm sorry for even thinkin' that you could be that way."

"Jason, I never want to risk embarrassing you, or making you or Marianne ashamed that I'm your mother. It would be best if we leave now. Gather up your homework, I want to check it over when we get home."

"Mom, can I be alone with my dad for a few minutes before I go?"

"Sure, baby."

"I'll be right back, son." Jeff spoke low. He felt so bad about hitting Jason. "I want to make sure your mom is safe."

Jeff walked Beth to her car. They slipped their arms around each other, and kissed deeply.

"Beth, it can work. We can go back to counseling. What we have is too good to give up."

"Jeff, you've been with so many women. I can't compete. I've been wildly attracted to you since our first date. Even then I felt that a small hometown girl like me was foolish for thinking that a sophisticated, world traveled, drop dead gorgeous airman could be interested in me. Look, with Jodi pregnant, you need to work on your new family."

"Angel eyes, you have no competition. You're the only one in my heart. Other women mean nothing to me. They just hang around the shop looking to get laid, they only want me for stud service. Beth, I have an appetite that only you can fill. They don't care about me, I don't care about them. As for Jodi, there's no new family with her. I'm not saying she isn't pregnant, but no matter, I'm not the father. I've never told her, or anyone else for that matter, I had a vasectomy after Rianne was born."

A car with two young chicks drove up, they looked at Jeff with his arms around Beth. They both waved peace symbols with their fingers, and blew him kisses. The passenger pulled up her shirt, flashed her bare breasts out the window as they drove off laughing.

"Jeff, I love you, and I always will, but I'm going to marry Tom Ericsen."

"No, Beth, no. Beth, please change your mind. Please, let's go get Marianne, and bring her back here with us like we just planned. Please."

"No, I've made up my mind."

"Please, Beth, please. I want YOU! Please!"

"Oh, stop it! You *never* allowed me to beg!" Beth glared at him.

Jeff knew that look. He gave up. In a weak defeated voice he spoke, "Just know that if you ever change your mind, I'll be free to pick up the pieces, start over, and grow old with you. You will always be my wife, my bride and... I will love you until the day I die."

Jeff insured that she was safely locked in the car, before returning up stairs to face his son. He was sorry he lost his temper, and hit the boy. But, what came out of Jason's mouth could not be laughed off, or overlooked. Jeff meant every word he'd said, and took a deep breath as he opened the door.

Jason started talking before the door was shut. "I know you don't want to hear it Dad, but I really am sorry. I don't remember very well a time when you and Mom liked each other very much. To see her come out of your room... all I could think was she was like the others, and Mom well, she just doesn't act like that. Even when I see her with that Tom."

"Jason, you don't remember our happy family?"

"I kinda remember the three of us running on a beach, and laughing. And you making me suit up and working on Chebby, and Mom calling us grease monkeys and laughing, and splashing rocks in a pond getting Mom's fluffy hair wet, and laughing. She doesn't laugh like that with Tom. I heard laughing in your room. I couldn't hear any jokes, but I heard laughing. I thought she was... someone else, an' not Jodi cause Jodi was with me. When I saw it was my mom I was scared, an' hurt that she maybe was a tram- you know, when I'm not around getting in the way. She don't act happy, an' laugh with him."

"Jason, buddy, I love you, son. I'm so sorry I lost my temper and hit you. Jason, I adore the ground your mother walks on. If there was anything I could do to change this situation, I would do it gladly to bring our family together again. This time we came so close." Jeff hugged his boy, and sobbed.

"I'm really sorry I messed it up for you, Dad."

"You didn't, son, you didn't. Daddy messed it up a long time ago."

Chapter 4

I have seen all things that are done under the sun;
all of them are meaningless, a chasing after the wind.
What is twisted cannot be straightened;
what is lacking cannot be counted.
Ecclesiastes 1:14,15

1971

Jeff felt so much emptiness when he signed his final divorce papers, that he lost faith. So it began, the end of counting. Very little in his life mattered. He drank too much, he smoked too much, the same silly girls still hung around the garage, if they weren't the same they were different. He didn't know, he didn't care. He cared about making his business a success, as that was the way he was able to support his children. And, of course they mattered.

Eventually, Jodi found out that Jeff was divorced, and stopped by the garage to say hello. Even if none of the employees noticed her walk into the office, Jason noticed and seemed happy to see her.

"Look how big you've gotten in just a few months! Are you doing okay, sweetie?" She asked.

"Sure, Jodi, how about you? How's Rocky? Can you bring him by so we can play again?"

"We'll see Jason. I've been doin' okay, so has Rocky. He misses you, too. You're a big boy to him, and he looks up to you. Is your Daddy around?"

"Yeah... He's upstairs."

"Oh, I see. Is he alone?"

"No, he's with a girl."

Jodi missed his rascally grin. She turned to leave when she came face to face with Jeff walking back into the office with Marianne in his arms. Realizing she'd been had by the young Mr. Madison, she laughed, and swore vengeance on him.

"Well Jodi, Rianne *is* a girl!" He laughed hard, and ran to give her a big hug.

"Hey, Jodi, what's up? Van running okay?" Jeff asked her.

"Yeah, groovy. I haven't seen you at the Alibi Inn since, well, you know..."

"Jodi, I needed some space. I don't want to talk about these things in front of my kids, okay? Jason is with me every weekend. Rianne comes too, if and when she wants to. I won't have just anyone watching my kids, so that I can go knock back beer in some dive." Jeff had Marianne sit on the desk so he could tie her shoes.

"You worry too much."

"Maybe I'm old enough, and smart enough to realize the danger."

"So, your ex-old lady gets every weekend free of kids? I should be so lucky. Jason asked if I could bring Rocky by to play sometime. That okay with you?"

"Sure if Jason wants to have him over, it's okay with me, but I can't be responsible for Rocky. I have a business to run here, and it's not a day care center. So make sure you're around to keep him out of the men's way, away from the equipment, and out of the driveway."

"Daddy piggy back Rianne to swing now. Okay?"

"Catch ya later, Jodi. Okay, Baby Cakes, up you goooo! C'mon Jason, I got the tire swings made that I promised you." Jeff lifted Marianne to his shoulders, and she hugged his neck tightly.

Jeff knew a garage was no place for his little girl to be dressed in her pretty clothes, so he always had bib overall's, or some thing to put on her whenever she did decide she wanted to be with her daddy and brother. She wasn't a tom boy, but she wasn't a prissy little girl either. Jeff loved her so, yet she still kept him at a distance. Her eyes were deep blue, but she was the picture of her mother. She did have his black hair, and it was long and straight. Jeff wondered why his boy got the curls.

Jason stood up on his tire swing, and had it going in a spinning motion as he went back and forth. Marianne was content just to swing with her daddy pushing her. Jeff looked around the large open area, and thought of the house he and Beth talked about building there. The mighty oak tree stood tall in what would have been their front yard. The void in his life was nearly overwhelming.

Jason asked his dad if it was okay to go get the picnic basket, and blanket now. He could see the men were breaking for lunch, and realized he was getting a little hungry, too.

They spread the blanket under the tree, and munched on left over fried chicken from a bucket. Jeff told the kids how their Colonel Pop had met their grandmother in France during the war. He worked with Marianne to properly pronounce, "Bonjour, Grande-mère. Je t'aime, beaucoup." Quite surprisingly, she spoke very well considering she was just mastering English.

Jason had run off to ride his bike, and pop wheelies. He was way out back on the bike track Jeff had built for him where the men wouldn't be test driving the vehicles. Jeff sat with his back against the trunk of the tree, and was surprised when his sleepy eyed Marianne crawled into his arms. He wasn't surprised she was tired. She had been chasing butterflies in the field before Jason had come back with their picnic lunch. The surprise was she wanted to be in his arms. Beth kept assuring him that Marianne was just an aloof child, but he never was too sure. His heart melted as he stared down at the face of his baby girl. He started to softly hum, then dozed off along with his daughter.

In his sleep, he felt an adult female body snuggling close to him. He was startled by a familiar voice speaking softly, and low in his ear as to not wake up the sleeping child in his arms. "That was beautiful, blue eyes. I thought you said you couldn't sing."

"Please don't call me blue eyes. And, I didn't say I couldn't sing, I said 'I don't sing'. Furthermore, I only sing to my kids, and only when I feel like it. Isn't she beautiful? I'd really like to be alone with Rianne now Jodi. I need to take the kids back to their mother in a few more hours. Do you have a sitter for Rocky tonight? You could come back around nine or ten, if you'd like, okay?"

Far out, Jodi thought, *looks like getting him back is gonna be easier than I thought.*

All too soon it was time for Jeff to gather up his kid's belongings, and return them to their mother. He asked Jason if he remembered the French lesson from lunch. Before he could answer, Marianne spoke up, "Bonjour Grande-mère. Je t'aime, beaucoup." That totally convinced Jeff that he had fathered the two most brilliant children that ever walked the face of the earth.

On the way home he asked his children to repeat after him:

Douce nuit, sainte nuit !
Dans les cieux ! L'astre luit.
Le mystère annoncé s'accomplit
Cet enfant sur la paille endormi,

After repeating it several times, Jeff told them it was the first verse of a Christmas carol, then he sang it to them. "If you practice that verse every day without singing it, I'll teach you another verse next week, until both of you can sing it all the way through with no help from Daddy. Then, for Christmas you can sing it to your mother, and Papa Jack and Nana as their Christmas present."

"Uncle Tommy, too?" Rianne innocently asked, totally blowing the wind out of Jeff's sails.

As he drove back into his own yard he could see Jodi's car waiting in the driveway. She hopped out with a burnt out joint in her hand, and followed him up the stairs. In a way he wanted to be alone, but being with someone he was at least a little bit familiar with gave him some comfort. She reached in his pocket, and snatched his lighter. She put the half smoked joint in a roach clip, and lit up. After taking three quick hits off it, she passed it over to Jeff. He almost said no as he usually did, but tonight he figured, *what the hell.* He took three long drags, and handed it back. Before he felt any effects, he told her, "Jodi, you are a real nice girl, and I like you a lot, but don't expect anything from me. I can't give what I don't have. And I don't have room in my heart for anyone else. I love my wife, I love my kids… I love my shirt… the color is so intense, don't you think? And the fabric, like it feels like it's made of spun silk. Like what they sold in Chaing Mai. Know what I mean? I have a black silk robe my mom gave me, that she got in Paris or Bordeaux or some damn place over there. I wonder if it's here someplace, or if it's still with Beth's stuff. She got the Chevy. Jason called it Chebby when he was a little guy. I'd trade the robe, and Bucky, and the Camaro, and a kidney to keep my kids. Know what sounds good? Pretzels sound good like even the name just kinda just rolls off your tongue, but Puffy Sugar Bites sound better. Want some munchies now? That old Bucky up there looks like he's stoned, know what? He is! Just look at that glassy eyed stare. Hey ya gonna keep Bogarting that joint?" Jeff took several more deep hits before he realized that the flickering candles that Jodi had lit made the beads around the old buck heads antlers put on quite a light show as they danced in the breeze of the oscillating fan. He stuffed his mouth with Puffy Sugar Bites, and marveled at the sound that the crunch made echoing inside his ears.

Jodi played Zeppelin's *Whole Lotta Love* at full volume. Physically, Jeff was everything that she could want in a man, but she knew his heart wasn't hers.

It was nearly dawn when Jeff woke up to the rhythmic sound of tick, tick, whoosh, tick, tick, whoosh, over and over. He realized that the record had come to an end. It was just spinning around and around, going no where, doing nothing. *Such is life,* he thought. Other than feeling a little spacey, he felt no other ill effects from the previous evenings activity. He looked at Jodi sound asleep next to him on the floor. *She is a good kid,* he thought, but he hoped this time she would keep her promise, no strings, no pressure, no commitment. They'd been down that road before, so he had his doubts. He looked at her tiny body. Other than those large breasts, there wasn't much else to her. Child bearing ruined her chances of being a bikini model, but the right outfits looked great on her. He still hadn't told her about his vasectomy, and decided it wasn't any of her business. Preventing pregnancy wasn't enough though. Since the new morality that developed with the pill, and the women's movement screaming for sexual equality, a whole string of new diseases that were resistant to medical treatment were being passed around much the same as a joint at a head party. Jeff knew Jodi smoked up, and she slept around. Used to be if you didn't wrap your gun, you worried that an unwanted child would result, now you had to worry about your own life as well. He needed protection for himself. He wondered what made Jodi tick, but he didn't wonder for too long. He picked her up, and placed her on the couch. He went to get a comforter to cover her, picked up his cigarettes, and went to bed alone.

Jeff kept his word to Marianne and Jason. Each week they learned a new verse to *Douce Nuit, Sainte Nuit.* He marveled at how quickly they learned. Jason seemed a little uncomfortable this weekend.

"Son, is something bothering you? You don't seem quite like yourself."

"Dad, I don't want you to be mad at Rianne. She's just a little more than a baby, and well, she is a girl, and you know how girls talk all the time."

"Me not a baby, it was an axidint. I was prasticin'!" Marianne snapped.

"Nana was givin' Rianne her bath while Mom was at work, an' she started to sing. We'd been just sayin' the words, and no one noticed that it was anything special. Papa Jack thought it was cool that you're teachin' me'n Rianne-"

"Rianne not mean!" She scolded her brother, sticking out her tongue.

Jason rolled his eyes. "Okay, okay Rianne! Dad, he thinks it's cool that you're teaching us French, and Nana wants ya to call her."

"Rianne! *Don't* stick out your tongue. Did she say what it's about?"

"Christmas, I think."

Jack and Jeff hadn't had a conversation since Beth had been released from the hospital. They each exchanged pleasantries, and shook hands, but the friendly bantering was a thing of the past. Jack was baffled by the situation as Beth still shared nothing about the break up with either of her parents. They knew she was seeing Tom Ericsen from church, and he seemed like a nice enough fellow. Jack saw things he didn't like, but he didn't want to risk upsetting his daughter, so he kept quiet.

"Hello, Jack, this is Jeff. How ya doin'?"

"Hello, son, I'm great. How about yourself?"

"As well as can be expected. Jason mentioned that Nancy wants to talk to me. Is she available?"

"Sure. Hold on. Maggie! It's for you!"

"Maggie?"

"Oh, we were snuggling one night, Jason turned up the radio full blast, and that song was playing. Been calling her that ever since."

Jeff heard a thump, and soon determined that Nancy had socked him. *So that's where Beth got her slap happiness,* he thought remembering the numerous pillow whacks she'd playfully given him over the wonderful years of their marriage.

"Hi, Jeff. How are you, honey?"

"Fine, Nancy, is it okay that I call you that?"

"It's my name, I'd be confused if you didn't. Jeff, Jason was upset with Rianne for singing the song that you're teaching them. Jack and I heard them reciting it, and thought it was a poem until Rianne started singing it in the tub. Jeff, she has a beautiful voice for a child her age. Jason can carry a tune better than most boys, but our little girl has a gift from God. I taught her another children's song, then had her sing it for the music minister at our church. He was very impressed. I wondered if you would mind if the kids sang the song you're teaching them at our Christmas Eve service? There's still plenty of time for Pastor Dwayne to help them sing with the piano. You're welcome to stay for a pot luck supper, and coffee after our darlings make their debut. That is if you don't mind that they perform."

"Nancy, I think I have the two most beautiful, brilliant and now talented children in the world. If they are willing, I'm all for it. What does Beth think?"

"Beth doesn't know. The kids are still trying to keep it a secret from her and T... uh... Umm, Jeff, do you think your parents will be home for Christmas? They're welcome to attend and stay for supper, too."

"I'll be sure to ask them. But, I'm sure we'll plan on just being at the service, okay?"

Jack had hoped that Tom would be away on Christmas Eve. He just had a gut feeling that if Jeff and Beth could be alone with no distractions they could work things out. He'd seen them together before they went to Okinawa. He knew true love when he saw it. In his opinion, Tom saw Beth as a trophy. He knew his daughter was a "looker". Jack never could figure out why she wasn't more popular with the boys in high school, but he felt blessed that he didn't have to deal with that. He was proud to walk his daughter up the aisle, and give her to Jeff. He knew Jeff wouldn't hurt her after their talk. He truly didn't understand their split.

Jack's wish didn't come true. Tom and his grand ego were there taking up two seats in the front row. Beth sat next to him, and nodded with surprise when she saw Jeff and his parents walk in with her dad. Jack insisted that they sit with them at the opposite end of the pew from Tom. Before entering the church, Jack asked Vince if he, or Michelle had a clue what had happened. Neither did.

Blah, blah, blah... *So much talking in these Protestant churches* Jeff thought. In his church, they read scripture, sang songs, received communion, and went home. *To each his own*, he thought. *This is America, thank God we have freedom of religion.* Finally the time came for the grand finale of the evening. It was not printed in the bulletin. Pastor Dwayne turned to the church body, and proudly announced, "We now have a special performance by Jason and Marianne Madison."

It was the most perfect rendition of Silent Night that anyone had ever heard. It was sung totally in French as a duet until the last verse when Jason handed the microphone to Marianne and she lifted her voice to the Lord singing the last verse in English without musical accompaniment.

Jason recognized his other grandparents. He leaned over and whispered something in his sister's ear. Speaking together, they said, "Bonjour Grande-mère and Kerno Pop. Joyeaux Noel. Je t'aime, beaucoup."

Michelle ached to hug her grandbabies. Needless to say there wasn't a dry eye in the house. When service was dismissed, Tom snatched Marianne up into his arms, and had her on his hip. He turned his back on Michelle as he put his other arm around Jason's shoulder and turned him around also.

Vince didn't know what had happened, but he saw the same look of rage in Jeff's eyes that he'd seen in his own father's eyes years ago. Heartbroken, Michelle was whisked out of the church before her crying disturbed other church members. Vince assured her that Jeff would handle the situation, and she would see her grandchildren momentarily.

Tom smiled proudly, and thanked all of his friends as each one complimented how adorable, and talented the children were. Jeff pushed his way through the crowd in time to hear Tom tell the deacons that he planned on adopting them after he and Beth were married. Jeff looked him straight in the eyes bluntly stating, "Over my dead body Mr. Ericsen." He reached over and took Marianne from him, and grabbed Jason's hand.

"Jack, Nancy, I'm terribly sorry. We're leaving now. Beth, this is my night to have my children. I'll have them back to you sometime tomorrow. We'll deal with this problem after the holidays." He spoke with a tightly clenched jaw. Jeff would not physically let go of his kids as they kissed their grandparents, and mother good-bye.

Jeff caught up with his parents in the parking lot with both kids in tow. They all went to a diner across town. After a lovely evening, they made arrangements to meet again in a few hours for Midnight Mass. Jeff buckled Marianne in her booster seat, and insisted that Jason wear his seat belt. He told them although this visit wasn't planned, it was a legal visit, and wanted them to try to take a nap in the car on the way to his home. Marianne stayed sound asleep as he pulled the car around back, but Jason woke up, and looked around sleepily at all the cars. Jeff hid his displeasure, and asked Jason to please stay in the car with Marianne, "Keep the car doors locked, and don't open them for anybody for any reason." After just calming down from the church episode, he was equally as furious now.

"Jeff! You're back! Far out, meet some of the heads from the Back Seat Lounge!" Jodi shouted.

"How the hell did you, and your traveling freak show get in here?" Jeff was seething angry.

"Don't go gettin' all gnarly on me, man. I know where you hide the extra key. We didn't want you to be home alone on Christmas Eve!"

"News flash Bimbo! I'm not alone! I suppose everybody else knows where the extra key is now, too. Get out of here, all of you! Jodi, don't you ever pull a stunt like this again. For crying out loud, what the hell is the matter with you? You've got a kid that you should be spending Christmas Eve with. When are you going to pull your head out of your arm pit?" Jeff heard lots of grumbling, and the word "bummer" repeated as everyone gathered up their stuff, and left the apartment one by one. He opened windows, even though the weather was quite brisk, just to air the place out. Jason commented on the funny smell when Jeff brought the kids upstairs.

"Yeah, son, Jodi's friends smoke a different brand of smokes than your daddy." He tried to sound casual.

"Daddy, me cold." Marianne said sleepily. Jeff wrapped her in a blanket, and held her until she went back to sleep.

Jason looked at the raggedy Christmas tree that he and his dad had cut from out back, and dragged up the stairs the previous weekend. "Dad, don't you have any decorations?"

"No Jason, I don't. I would've bought some, but I didn't think I was going to have you, and your sister tonight. I thought you would be with your Papa Jack, Nana, and mother when Santa came to visit."

"Dad, I'm almost nine and a half. You can cut the Santa crap any time now. I'd rather be with you anyway. You got any popcorn?"

"Yeah, I do! Jase, you just turned nine four months ago, don't rush it son, you're old a long time." Jeff grinned at his boy. He reached up in the cupboard for a bag of popcorn. He found fishing line, a couple of sewing needles, and the guys went to work after popping several batches.

Jason dug around in the cupboards until he found some foil, then folded it to make a silver star to place on top. Still not satisfied with the look of the tree, Jason glanced around the room. A big smile came across his face as he spotted the old buck head. He had his dad take the beads down, then they wrapped the tree with the multi colored strands. That was the finishing touch. Jason was content now. Jeff suggested that he try to get a nap.

"Dad, we don't get that much time together. I'd rather just hang out like we used to. Dad, is it a sin to wish that someone was gone... away?"

"I don't think it would be a good idea to wish someone dead, if that's what you mean."

"No, not dead, just gone." Jason eyes welled up with tears. "Dad, I remember the look on your face when you held Mom when I made her cry, and you patted her hair. I saw her rub your back all nice and soft like, not grabby. I think you two should be together, not that it's any of my business."

"Thanks, Jason. If there was a way to fix it, I'd give it my best shot."

"Dad, you told me I didn't mess it up. You said you messed it up. I don't remember you messing up, but we were happy, then we were sad, then we had Rianne. Did she mess it up?"

"Oh, no, Jason. We wanted Rianne very much. We had a wonderful son, we wanted to add to our family. We planned for Marianne for a long time. Daddy got into a very bad situation, and didn't know how to handle it. I handled it badly, and messed it all up. Let's try to catch a couple of hours nap, son. Remember, we're going to my church for Midnight Mass."

Jeff wrote in his journal as both children slept. At 11:00 Jeff woke up the kids. Marianne was bright eyed and chipper since she had slept nearly three hours. Jason had been to church with his dad before, but never to Midnight Mass. He sat between Vince and Michelle and paid close attention. It was new to him, and different, however, he couldn't help but notice that the Christmas Story was the same. Marianne sat on her Mom-mom's lap, and played with her rosary beads.

When they returned home, Jeff whipped up a batch of crepes, and the five of them ate. They talked about whatever was on their minds, as long as it was cheerful. He asked the kids if they wanted to open their presents now, or wait until morning before he brought them home. He grinned knowing what the answer was going to be. Marianne fussed over the beautiful dresses that Mom-mom and Kerno Pop brought from Paris. Jason liked his new clothes, too, but wasn't nearly as impressed.

Marianne squealed, "Oooh, Daddy! Look!" when she opened a carefully wrapped package containing a genuine Jumeau doll.

Little girls must be born knowing pricey gifts, Jeff decided. She was just as happy with the new "Bowbie Dowl" and the

Rubby Dubby Scrubby doll he bought for her, so that blew that theory. Jason got a model Eiffel Tower kit from his Colonel Pop and Grande-mère. His favorite gift was a radio controlled car from his dad. His dad always seemed to know what a boy would really want for Christmas. The kids were sad that they didn't have any presents for them, but Jeff, and their grandparents assured them that just being together was gift enough. The kids both hugged Jeff at the same time, and gave him kisses. *All that's missing is your Mommy*, he thought. It was going on two in the morning before the Madison's went back to their hotel. Try as he might, Jeff couldn't get the kids to sleep in the bedroom without him. They all piled in the same bed like a family of puppies.

Just as promised, he had the children back in their mother's care Christmas Day. Beth hugged each of her children as they went running in the house. They each had decided to leave their present from their dad at his house, and only bring the "French" presents home. Before he drove off, Beth hollered, "Jeff! Wait up!" She ran out to the car, and hopped in the front seat.

"Merry Christmas, Jeff." She said. "I want to apologize for what Tom said last night."

"Merry Christmas to you too, Beth. Why on earth do you feel like you need to say you are sorry for that arrogant bastard?"

"Jeff!"

"Beth!" he snapped back. "I said we'd discuss this after the holidays, and here you are bringing it up now. Well, since you brought it up, here's the way it is. The answer is NO! Did I say it plainly enough for you? Would you like it in another language? NON! Don't even bother to ask if he can have my children. Those kids are the only reason I live and breathe. Those kids are what keeps me here instead of moving to France where I have family that loves me. Those kids are my flesh and blood. I love them, and will take care of them before my own needs are met. Just in case you don't understand how serious I am about this, you'll be getting a letter from my lawyer with new visitation and custody conditions, if I even suspect that you two are entertaining thoughts of taking MY children, or reducing my time with them."

"Jeff, shhh… Listen, Tom has never discussed adopting the kids with me. I learned about it at the same time you did. I was appalled at the idea. I reminded him that when I told him I was a package deal, it meant that my kids were yours, ours… Not his."

Jeff thought about what she'd said for a moment. "Well, I suppose that does make me feel somewhat better, but don't let him feed that thought. Tell him if he wants kids, I said to quit whacking off, and do it like a man."

Beth playfully hit him, and asked for a Christmas kiss. Jeff puckered his lips, and wrinkled his nose like a rabbit. Beth giggled and leaned into the silly kiss, and was soon lost in the moment. Their lips melted together like butter on pancakes, as she felt the warm playfulness of his tongue dancing with hers.

Jason answered the phone, "Yes, my mom is here… Well, no you can't exactly talk to her right now... She's busy at the moment... Because she isn't really here... Do you want me to go get her, or do you want to wait till she comes back inside? …She's out in the Camaro kissing with my dad."

Nancy grabbed the phone from Jason, and swatted his backside. "Hello? Oh, hi, Tom. That Jason! He's such a little kidder! Beth is outside discussing visitation with Jeff. How about I have her call you when she's finished. Okay. I'm sure it won't be long. Bye"

Jason went outside, and tapped on the car window, startling both of his parents. Beth opened the door, and Jason hopped right in, and sat on her lap. "Mommy, you may have to call Santa Claus to come pick up all my presents."

"Jason Charles Madison, what did you do now? Did you torment your sister or-"

"I told Tom you were in the Camaro making out with my dad. Oh, don't worry about it, though. Nana already hit me, then lied saying I was only kidding."

"Young man, you get in that house, and go straight to your room! You can't know how mad I am at you right now. Move it, buster!" She cracked his fanny hard as he ran back into the house laughing.

"Beth, angel eyes, I love you. Children can be trying sometimes. Let me know how you punish my son for telling the truth, okay?"

Spending the day in his room, even on Christmas, was a small price to pay for being able to lay that news on Tom. Jason was very pleased with himself.

$$Chapter\ 5$$

1972

"TOM SAYS, TOM SAYS, TOM SAYS! I'm sick to death of hearing about what TOM SAYS! I don't give a DAMN what Tom says. I'm not concerned about what Tom thinks or does, let alone what TOM SAYS. If you are leaving on a two week, all inclusive, deluxe honeymoon cruise, good for you. I hope you have a ball, but I WANT MY KIDS. DAMN IT!"

Jack and Nancy heard the outburst from Jeff, and were completely shocked at the tone of voice they heard coming from their usually mild tempered ex-son-in-law. They exchanged glances. "Nancy, go sit with the kids. If we can hear this, you know they must hear it, too."

Jason was sitting on the bedroom floor in the corner with tears rolling down his cheeks. He had a shaking, and crying Marianne sitting on his lap, wrapped in his arms. He remembered the shouting, it was a far and distant memory, but he remembered, and it still made him sad. When they lived together, Dad and Mom would talk about stuff he didn't understand, mostly using those low tones. Sometimes they'd shout, he'd be scared and would hide in his room. One time, Daddy came back for a week, and everything was really nice, but then one day he was gone. They didn't live together ever again after Mommy went in the hospital. Jason's heart was broken.

Marianne didn't remember. Marianne was scared, she loved her Daddy, but she really didn't know what daddies were supposed to do, or what they were for. He was fun to be with, but she didn't like him yelling at her Mommy. Uncle Tommy didn't yell like that at her Mommy. She held her arms up to Nana when she walked in to the room.

Nancy took Marianne from Jason's arms, and held her on her hip. She clutched Jason to her heart, when he rose to his feet. He placed his arms around her waist, and sobbed. She took both kids to her bedroom, and turned on the TV to an old 60's sit com rerun. They all sat up in her, and Papa Jack's big bed. Nana told them, "People shout when they're upset. Try not to worry, both of your parents love you. They want what is best for all of you. Papa Jack will try to help them work out this misunderstanding, okay?" Nana winked at Jason, and smiled. "So, do you think they will get off the island on this episode Rianne?"

Jack reluctantly went into the living room. He'd done his best to stay out of the divorce. Since he was never asked, he never gave any advice.

"Excuse me. Could I talk with the two of you?"

"Daddy, it's really none of your business!"

"I'm afraid that's where you are wrong this time young lady! Your divorce is none of my business. Your decision to marry Tom Ericsen is none of my business. But, turning my living room into a combat zone, while my grandchildren are in my house crying, and upset *is* my business. Now what the hell is the problem here?"

"What's the problem? The problem is standing right in front of you! HE'S the problem!"

"Oh, really? I'm the problem? Let's see now, let's just suppose the shoe was on the other foot... I'm the one getting remarried, I take the kids from you, then dump them off on my parents, while I go away on my honeymoon, and you sit alone night after night wishing they were with you. I'm not asking for permanent custody, Beth. I just would like my kids while you are off on your cruise. And don't worry, I won't short you a red cent for keeping them for two and a half weeks-"

"IT'S TWO AND A HALF WEEKS NOW?"

"Just keep your voices down! Both of you!" Jack growled.

"Yes dear, actually it's exactly seventeen days. The weekends are mine, and your honeymoon slips right in there. What's the big deal anyway? They're my kids, too. You didn't get them at the grocery store, you know."

Beth bristled at his jab, "You listen to me, and you listen to me closely, I won't have my children hanging around your stinking garage, amongst your stable of cheap floozy girlfriends. You had your chance to make the marriage work, and you chose to sleep around-"

"I never cheated until after I learned you were running over here to 'church' every other Sunday to comfort the poor grieving widower Tom Ericsen."

"I went to church. I wasn't sleeping with him!"

"And how the hell was I supposed to know that? You weren't sleeping with me! Do you have any idea how long it took me to figure out the 'Tom' that you told me proposed to you was the same pompous ass that made trips over to see you every Sunday at 'church' when you weren't over here? Then I find out, through the grapevine, he'd been sniffing around you while you were still pregnant with my daughter. It's just a damn shame this has to come out now in front of your father, who did his best to raise you to be decent."

"I am decent! I still haven't slept with Tom!"

"Beth, I'm decent, too. If you would have shut your mouth long enough to listen to what happened that day, you would've known that, and none of this would have happened.

It's all water under the bridge now. I will love you until the day I die, but, if Tom is who you want, go crawl in his bed. Like I said a long time ago, you got my kids, you got my name. Now you can have his name, but I want my kids. All I'm asking for is my weekends, and the two weeks. I can't force the issue now since the wedding is tomorrow, but I promise you this, I will not disappear, or be an absentee father. Those kids are *mine*."

"Beth, your mother and I had no intention of butting into your business. We stood by you through your illness, and we love you, but now you are being totally unreasonable. The kids are yours and Jeff's, not Tom's. When you're married, and the kids live under his roof, he can make all the rules he wants as it pertains to his house, but bottom line is, Jeff is their father." Jack turned to Jeff. "Tonight and tomorrow are yours, but if you allow the kids to see their mother get married, after the ceremony I'll personally drive them over to stay with you until Beth returns. It's none of Tom's business, but if he has a problem with it, he can deal directly with me. I told him off at Christmas, I can do it again. I'll respect him as your husband, Beth, but I don't like the man. I'm sorry."

Beth went crying into her bedroom.

Jeff put his fingers over his eyes, pinched them, gulped hard several times, before regaining his composure. He looked up and saw Jack still standing there. Jeff offered his hand. "Jack I apologize. Please forgive me for losing my temper in your home. When I was a kid, I pretty much had my temper beaten out of me. I just lost it when I couldn't see any logical reason why I couldn't have my kids. It still seems like it's part of a plot, orchestrated by Ericsen, to take my kids, and adopt them. Why, Jack? Do you know? I don't blame him for wanting to marry Beth. She's a beautiful woman. It might not seem this way, but I do appreciate that he likes my kids, but why does he want to possess them? It's not like I don't support them. Why?"

"I don't have the answer to that, Jeff. The man is polite. He has never been disrespectful to my wife, or myself. But, I just can't seem to find an area where we click. It's almost like Nancy and I are extra baggage that he has to put up with just to keep the prize. Marianne and he bonded since the beginning. I don't see a relationship between him and Jason. In all fairness, though, that might not be all Tom's fault. Jason has been a daddy's boy since birth. It's always a joy to me to see the way his face lights up when your car pulls into the yard. I pray that they can find some kind of a link to make my grandson's life bearable. I'm sorry, son. You can't know how sorry I am about all of this." Jack patted Jeff's shoulder.

"Jack, if you don't mind, I'd like to go try to make peace with Beth. She is the mother of my children, and although it breaks my heart, she is getting married tomorrow. It's not good to be parting on these terms. I'll at least want to see my kids before I leave, also."

"I agree, Jeff. I'm going to my room with Nancy, to talk to the kids. Just tap on the door when you're ready, okay?"

"Sure. Thanks, Jack."

Jeff felt more calm, and in control of himself after talking to Jack. He admired the man, and always thought of him as a sailor with a heart of gold. He lightly tapped on Beth's bedroom door, speaking softly, "Beth, angel eyes, can I come in? I'd like to apologize." She didn't answer, but he opened the door slightly, and looked inside. She was sitting up on her canopy bed, the bed they had shared whenever they came to visit her folks. It tore his heart out to not feel free to lie beside her, to take her in his arms like he'd done so many times before. He stood there with glassy, damp eyes. He stepped inside, and closed the door. Again, he was taken aback by her appearance.

Beth had a pillow clutched to her stomach, and tears rolled down her cheeks as she stared through him. "Jeff, you really thought I was having an affair?" Her lip quivered.

"Yes, Beth I did, until the Sunday you came over and told me you hadn't slept with Tom. Angel eyes, it wasn't because I thought you were a tramp. It's just that you were always so passionate. You never said no. We were the hottest couple I knew, and then nothing. I'd been faithful to you until you told me to leave. I knew you were coming over here alternate Sundays. Before long the rumor got back that you were involved with a rich widower. Well, I assumed you were fooling around. So, I slept with Jodi. You said you were willing to forgive me. When we got back together Beth, I tried harder than anytime in my life to make our marriage work. I know the timing was off, but Beth, you seemed so distant."

"Jeff, it wasn't your fault. But, it isn't my fault either. This goes back before Jodi. You didn't see the look in Tamiko's eyes when I caught her with her hands on you. She burned her face into my memory with that smirk. I'd look at you, and she would be between us, her eyes were glaring at me. She had *her* hands on *my* husband's body. Jeff, I still see her. Even now."

"Beth, I was on my way out the door. I wanted my son, she'd left him at the neighbors. She was standing between me, and the door with her hands on me trying to stop me from leaving when you walked in. I didn't see the look, but I don't doubt what you're saying is true. The girl was desperate to get to America. What happened wasn't as bad as what you thought happened. My God knows I wish none of it had ever happened, I didn't initiate anything. I only want to hold you in my arms for the rest of my life, whether it's one more day, or a hundred years."

Beth set the pillow aside, and held up her arms to Jeff. He was there in an instant. Their faces met, and their lips meshed. They were stretched out the length of their bodies, taking comfort in each others embrace. Simultaneously, they let out a heavy hearted sigh. They both wanted, but they couldn't. Beth was getting married in the morning.

Together they stood at Jack and Nancy's door, and asked their children to come out. They both apologized to the kids for upsetting them with their quarrel, and promised to never act like that again. Marianne got off of Beth's lap, walked over to Jeff, and slapped him. His eyes welled up with tears that rolled down his cheeks. When she saw what she'd done, her eyes started gushing tears, too. She crawled in his arms, hugged his neck, gave him baby kisses, saying, "Rianne so so sorry Daddy."

"Daddy's sorry, too, Baby Cakes. It's okay. It's okay. Shhh…" He hugged her close, kissing, and stroking her head. Before leaving Jeff hugged Jason tight, said good-bye, and that he'd see him tomorrow.

Jeff left the Campbell's home without his kids, but he trusted his former father-in-law, and took him at his word that he would bring the kids over after the ceremony.

****

Jack side glanced over at Jason on the drive to Jeff's house. "It's both a happy, and sad day today isn't it, son?"

"What's so happy about it, Papa Jack? That Tom is married to my mom, and she should be married to my dad. Even she didn't look happy. Sure she smiled, and said all the right things, but she wasn't smiling with her eyes. Did you ever watch her with my dad? Her eyes sparkle around him, unless they're fighting."

"You are too smart for your own good Jason Madison. I don't have the answers for you, my boy. I wish that I did."

"So why do you say it's a sad day, Papa Jack?"

"I have the same feelings you do, son, but there's nothing else I can do, but what I'm doing now."

Jack pulled in around by the original two bay doors, he walked around back, and started up the stairs with Marianne on his hip. Jason ran up the stairs two at a time, and hugged his dad who was waiting at the top with the door open. Jeff rubbed and patted his boys back, and wished that Jason was once again little so that he could hold him, and rock him to help him get through this new life adjustment. Marianne held her arms out to her dad. Jeff reached for his little girl with one arm, and kissed her cheek as he tried to get her situated without having her kick Jason in the head. "What do you say we all step inside? Come in Jack, please."

Jason was still teary eyed. Marianne looked sad, but she didn't know why. She knew it would be fun being with her Daddy for a couple of weeks until her Mommy came back, and then they would live with Uncle Tom in a big brand new house.

Jeff asked if they were hungry. They weren't. They changed out of their wedding clothes, and Jason took Marianne out to the tire swing.

"Jeff, I apologize for bringing the kids late. I know I promised to bring them right after the ceremony, but I figured if I brought them after the reception, I could stay to visit with you for a while instead of having to run right back to the wedding party."

"It's fine Jack. I assume that everything went as planned?"

Jack nodded his head with downcast eyes, then looked up, "Yes, son, just as planned." He released a long sigh as he saw his former son-in-law squeeze his eyes tight, and bite his lips. "Are you going to be alright, Jeff?"

"I'll get through it Jack. I have to. For my kids. I wish we'd had more kids. Say, Jack, I didn't offer you anything to drink. I've got juice, soda, water, milk, beer, wine…"

"Anything stronger?"

"Scotch."

"Now you're talking. Got ice?"

"One scotch on the rocks coming up."

"Aren't you going to join me?"

"I'll have a beer with you. I normally don't have hard stuff in the house. Last night was a little rough after I left your place. I stopped by the Alibi Inn. Got halfway up the steps, and couldn't make myself go inside. I went to the liquor store instead."

"I understand. Things got real tough for us after we lost Jerry. Nancy kept blaming herself. She wouldn't let me near her for fear she'd get pregnant again. Sometimes I'd just want to hold her to comfort her. She'd push me away, thinking I was making advances. It wasn't long before I stopped off to knock back a few before going home to a weeping wife, and squabbling kids. Oh, I know now that John and Beth were just coping with their grief the way kids do, but it didn't help ease any of the tension between Nancy and myself when they'd quarrel. I was hurting, too. I found myself in the company of another woman. We'd shared a few drinks. She was divorced when it wasn't cool to be divorced. I asked her to dance. Back then it was dancing, not all that jitter bugging around. It felt good to feel a woman's softness in my arms again, and the lady was more than willing. I excused myself to the mens room, then found my waitress, paid my bar tab, and left out the back. Back home, as luck would have it, the kids were fighting again, so I threatened them with my belt, and sent them to their rooms. Scared the day lights out of both of them. I'd spanked John a few times, but never used a belt. I've never laid a hand on Beth Ann. I told Nancy we needed to talk, and that it would be good idea to talk downstairs in the rec room so that there was no chance of the kids hearing what I had to say. She knew I was serious. When she heard my confession of what nearly happened, she cried. I cried. She let me hold her, and we cried together. She still didn't stop blaming herself for Jerry's death, but at least she finally realized that I didn't blame her. She let me make love to her again. Don't know what I'd do without Nancy."

Jeff was looking straight at Jack throughout his long story. "Jack, you and Nancy have a special bond. I see it's the same bond my parents have. Somehow I guess the glue that held your generation together didn't get passed down to ours. I love Beth with all my heart, and will love her until the day I die. I don't know what else I could've done. What d'ya say we go downstairs. I'll show you what I've got going, and what my plans are for future expansion." Jeff wasn't going to spill his guts.

Jack wasn't trying to be nosey, but he was disappointed that Jeff wouldn't talk to him. He believed Jeff when he said that he still loved Beth. He knew by watching his daughter that she still loved Jeff. She was silent, also. Jack just wished he understood.

****

On their wonderful honeymoon cruise, Tom bought Beth a brand new exquisite gown for each of the evening meals. He also insured that she had the jewelry to go with each one. She looked like a million dollars on his arm. They danced long into the night, and turned many heads each time they entered a room. Tom's face beamed that his new bride made her debut so well.

Alone in their room, their first night as Mr. and Mrs. Thomas Stephen Ericsen, Beth reached for her night gown when she opened her suitcase. Tom tossed it aside, "You won't be needing that." He aroused feelings in her that made her lose her sense of self. After consummating their marriage, "You like it, don't you Babe?" Tom knew by her moans that she did. He'd kept his promise to God, and God gave him a woman that loved sex. He gave, and gave, and gave to satisfy all of Beth's desires. She was his now. He'd give her the world on a silver platter- as long as she shared his bed.

Chapter 6

Each morning, Jeff got both of the kids up, and fed them breakfast. He'd be on Jason's case to quit fooling around, get dressed, and ready for school. Jason complained that it wasn't fair that Rianne got to stay there all day while he was stuck in a classroom. She would point at him, and make a face and giggle. Jason would tell her to shut up, and Jeff would make peace before driving Jason to school. It was a hassle but, worth every minute of it. On the way to and from school, Jeff would teach them to count, or sing songs in French.

The shop was doing well under Jeff's ownership. Jeff pulled down all the pin-up girly pictures from the walls, the guys didn't seem to mind. Hank was as qualified as anyone in the county on all aspects of auto mechanics, and office procedure. Clark hated paperwork, but was excellent under the hood, or under the chassis of any vehicle. Jeff had a hard time convincing him to stay on after Seth died in the accident at the hunting camp.

With the kids there, especially Marianne, while Jason was in school, he realized he needed help. He tossed around the idea of asking Jodi to take time off from the Alibi Inn, but decided it would make more sense to hire an extra mechanic, and care for Marianne himself. Marianne liked to think that she was helping her Daddy in the office, so he gave her a box of old papers from when Seth owned the place. He shuffled all the papers together in the box and cleared off the left side of his desk. Marianne was on her knees in the chair for hours sorting the papers. Jeff had her stack the pink, yellow, white and blue papers, and then put them in folders. She felt so important. Jeff was busy with a customer when the phone rang. Marianne watched her father writing information on a form like the papers she had been sorting. She knew he was busy. Reaching for the phone she answered, "Madson Moters... Jus' one minute, please... Misser Madson, tel-fone for you."

"Okay, Baby Cakes, Daddy will be with them in a second." Jeff handed the clip board to one of the guys, gave the customer a cup of coffee, and showed her to an area with a couple of chairs, and some magazines. He took the call, and noticed Marianne sitting with her arms crossed. "Are you done sorting Rianne?" he asked after he hung up.

"No, Daddy, we need tuh talk. I am working, and you called me Baby Cakes. I called you Misser Madson. That's not fair."

"You are right, Miss Madison. I will be more careful of what I say while you are on duty. Now, are you going to finish, or should I fire you, and hire a babysitter to watch you while I do your work?"

"I will finish, but watch it from now on, Misser."

Jeff excused himself to go check on the men in the shop. Once he was out of earshot of his little girl, he broke into fits of laughter. She sounded just like her mother. Day after day, he'd shuffle the same box of papers, and give them to her to sort, and put into new folders. He was amazed at how good she was on the phone. Each day they'd eat lunch under the oak tree out front, and take walks in the woods. Jeff told her he wanted to build her a play house near where Jason rode his dirt bike. She took Jeff's hand, and headed for the woods.

"Daddy, look." Marianne pointed to a big tree.

Jeff looked at the tree and told her it was an oak like the one out front, only not as old.

"Will you build me a house in the tree, Daddy?"

"Anything you want Baby Cakes, anything you want. Can I call you that on lunch break, Miss Madison."

"Yes, Daddy! You silly." She held up her arms.

He lifted her, and spun her around in circles until they both got dizzy, and he fell down. They tossed last falls brown crumpled leaves at each other, and Marianne giggled. Hand in hand they walked toward the apartment. He laid down with her until she fell asleep for her nap. He showered, then went back downstairs to get his ledgers, and noticed several girls hanging around Jones as he changed points and plugs. Jeff shrugged as they didn't seem to be slowing him down. He carried the paper work upstairs. The books were caught up, and he had his bank deposit slip made when Marianne came wandering out. "Time to get my brother, Daddy. Come on let's go."

"Yes, boss! Did you use the bathroom yet, young lady? I can't take you into men's restrooms."

"Why?"

"Rianne, we've been through this before. You're a little girl, not a man."

"Jason isn't a man. He goes."

"Jason is a boy. He will be a man."

"Not fair."

"Come on, Marianne, just get in there and pee, okay? We know it's clean here. Do you want to get bugs?"

"What kinda bugs? I like bugs."

"MARIANNE! Go!"

"Sorry Daddy. I go pee now."

"Two smart mouths. I can't believe I fathered two smart mouthed kids," he muttered to himself.

"Wow, Madison! Is that really your dad's car? That is just too cool that your dad has a car like that, and he's an old man. Who's the kid in the car with him?"

Jason beamed, "Yeah, that's my dad. He didn't want any of those old man station wagon cars. We picked it out together a couple uh years ago. The kid is my baby sister. She's three. She's a pain in the neck. See ya tomorrow."

"Your dad let YOU help pick out his car? Wow!"

Jason was becoming a legend in his own time with his classmates. He waved like he was a big shot as Jeff cautiously left the school yard.

"Hey, Dad. I've got something important to discuss with you later, like after the baby goes to bed."

"Jason, me NOT a baby! I gots a job while you're in school." Once again, she stuck her tongue out at her brother.

"Rianne! Daddy wishes you wouldn't do that. It looks rude, and secretaries don't stick their tongues out at potential customers. Jason will have this car someday. What will it look like if he takes the Camaro someplace else because Marianne the Office Manager sticks her tongue out at him?"

Marianne looked like she was deep in thought. Jason smirked. His dad corrected Marianne. Tom thought everything she did, and said was cute no matter how disgusting it was. Jeff pulled into the bank, and made his deposit just before closing. It was still very early so he decided to take the kids to the Alibi Inn for some Bad Dogs for their dinner. The waitresses were all familiar with Jason, but many of them had never met Jeff's daughter. They all commented on what a little cutie she was, Jason just rolled his eyes. When he got home he asked to ride his bike for a while before dark, and promised he'd do his homework later with no argument. Jeff agreed with the understanding that if he broke his word, that would be the last time he'd play before homework. Jason always knew when his dad meant business. As soon as the street lights came on, Jason put away his bike, and headed up the stairs. He pulled out his math book and sat at the kitchen table. Jeff sat with him, with Marianne on his lap. He helped her write 1-2-3 until Jason was done with math. He had to write a paragraph for English class using punctuation marks. Jeff helped Marianne print the letters R-I-A-N-N-E. She did pretty good, but teaching her French was easier. Jason shot his dad a look, and Jeff knew the boy needed more peace, and quiet to write. He filled the tub with bubble bath and water, then put on his swim trunks.

"Come on Rianne, it's time for your bath."

"I want my swim suit."

"Honey, we've been through this before. You need a bath. Secretaries can't stink. We were in the woods today playing in the leaves, you're dirty. You need to wash yourself."

"You need a bath, too."

"I took my shower while you took your nap. Know what? I think you want to take your bath alone. I'll go put my jammies on, and you can play with Rubby Dubby Dolly alone." Jeff stood up to get out of the tub.

"Okay, I get undressed. Don't you peek, Daddy."

"Okay, Baby Cakes. Tell me when you're ready, and I'll lift you in the tub." Jeff shut his eyes and lifted her in. They blew bubbles all over, and laughed as Marianne soaked clean.

Jeff let out a sigh of relief once Marianne was asleep. He sat on the chair under the buck head. Jason shut his school books, and brought his papers over to his dad to check.

"Good job, Jason. Everything's correct. Now, on the way home you said you had something important to discuss with me. Are you ready now?"

"Yeah, but, can we get something to drink first?"

"Sure, what'll ya have?"

"How about a beer?"

"How about a pop?"

"Sure, just thought I'd test ya."

"You test me, boy. Everyday of your life you've tested me."

Jason took a swallow of his drink, and began to speak, "Dad, I used to think I was the only kid in the world that came from a broken home. None of yours and Mom's friends were divorced. Well, the more I get to know the kids at school, the more I find out that a lot of their parents are split up."

"That's sad, Jase. Marriages shouldn't break up."

"Yeah, well that's just the way the ball bounces ain't it, Dad? Anyway, one of the guys said that when you get to be thirteen, you can go in front of a judge, and tell him which parent you want to live with, and he can let you move if he thinks the parent you want to live with is okay. Dad, when I'm thirteen, can I come live with you?"

"Oh my. Jason, wow, I didn't expect that. Son, I would like that, but I think that we should take things one day at a time until the time comes."

"Does that mean no?"

"No, it means yes. You are my son, and I would love to have you, and your sister with me full time, all the time. But, you are your mother's children too, and we have to try to all get along. When you're thirteen, we'll get together, and the three of us will discuss where the best place for you to live is. In the mean time, I want you to do your best to make your mothers life easy, and try to get along with your baby sister."

Jason smirked, his dad thought she was a baby, too. "Three more years..." Jason's voice trailed off. "Dad, I don't think Tom likes me very much. Like when I do all my homework right, like tonight, then he will complain that my penmanship isn't neat enough. There is always something wrong. I love you, Dad."

"Jason, I'm always proud of what you do. I see you take out your books without being told, and I see your brain working when you are studying. As long as I see that quality in you, you will always make me proud. You mean so much to me, and I love you, too, son."

On Saturday Jeff took the kids to the movies, and to Clown Town. On Sunday they all went to Mass, then to a fine French restaurant after church. They each ordered their meal in French. The kids made a good impression on the staff, and other patrons. Jeff's face shown with pride at their behavior. The weeks flew by, and he drove the kids back to Jack and Nancy's house the second Sunday after dinner. His heart was broken as he kissed both Jason and Marianne good-bye. It seemed the time flew by. Sad and depressed, he drove down the street without looking back. He didn't want to be anywhere near the area when Tom and Beth returned from their honeymoon, to take his children to their new palatial home at the top of the hill.

Jeff was not adjusting well at all.

"Jeff, if you want me to be your sister, just say so and I'm outta here. I'm tired of this. Why do you go through all the motions of wanting to make love, and then nothing? If you no longer find me attractive, say so."

"Jodi, you're as cute as a button. I don't want a sister, I never wanted a sister. A couple of years ago I hurt you, and I'm sorry, but you've hurt me, too. I'm not the vindictive type, don't think I'm doing this on purpose."

"Doing what on purpose? You're not doing anything. At least you're not doing anything you used to do with me. Sure, we meet at the Alibi, we have a few beers, we share a few laughs, we dance, you nuzzle my neck, we do a few bump and grinds, we come back to your place, and you turn on the TV. What am I supposed to think? Is it me? I know one of the rules is 'no pressure', but Jeff I could use a little pressure right here!" Jodi said pointing at herself.

"I'm sorry, Jodi. I'm sorry. Geez… Try to believe me, it's not you, it's me. It's just not, ummm. Look, I understand you have needs, I can't fulfill those needs. If you want to find someone else, go for it."

"No! I would like to have sex with you, again. I just miss what we used to do. You kiss me, and you touch me, then nothing! I'm so sexually frustrated right now I could scream. Are you sure it's not me?"

"I'm sure." Jeff said as he rolled over.

Jodi lay on her side, rubbed his back and cried.

There was no way to explain to Jodi that when he tried to have sex, all he thought of was Beth being intimate with Tom, and it made him sick. When he was celibate while in Thailand, he wouldn't have sex. Now it was different, he couldn't. It had been months. It concerned him, but he didn't care enough to do anything about the problem he was having. Beth was another man's wife, and Jeff didn't know how long it would take to accept that. Nobody else mattered. He didn't have to be bothered with any of the chicks that would hang around the garage, or play the game with anyone at the bar. But, Jodi? He just didn't know what to do about Jodi. He liked her.

Jodi noticed Jeff staring at the posters that Jones had hung on the walls at the bay where he usually worked. She walked up close to Jeff, and slipped her hand in his back pocket. He leaned down, and softly kissed her neck. She nodded toward his office, and started to walk away. He followed her in. She drew the blinds, straddled him on his chair, and kissed him deeply until she could feel his passion start to grow. But, she knew if she tried to have sex with him, he'd fizzle out in a hurry. She slipped off his lap and said, "See ya later, big boy."

True to her word, Jodi returned after she knew the shop was closed. She had a full size grocery bag with her. Jeff was surprised that she was back. She pulled out a couple of sandwiches from the Sub Shop, and a six pack of cold beer. She took a couple of beers, her sandwich, and a men's skin magazine, then sprawled out on the couch. Jeff took his sandwich, a couple of beers, and sat in his chair under the buck head. He watched her with amusement as she read the magazine.

"Jodi, you are one of the most uninhibited chicks I've ever known. I've heard you talk about being naked in bed with a guy, and another woman, but I always figured you were both doin' the guy. I didn't think you were bi."

"Well, sweetie, you're right, I did get in bed with Stan and Jenny. I loved Stan with all my heart. If I had to share him, well, so be it. But, I wasn't into Jenny at all. I would have preferred she wasn't there. This is a new men's magazine that has really good articles in it. This one is called, *'Getting It Up After a Nasty Divorce'*. If Stan and I ever got married, we'd probably just end up getting divorced, cuz Stan just isn't the marrying kind."

Jeff was laughing at her. "Jodi, you are so full of crap, and so damn funny. If you get divorced from Stan, *you* aren't going to have to worry about getting it up! Give me that thing." He grabbed the magazine.

She snatched it back, and ran into his bedroom. She flopped down on his bed and yelled, "You want it big boy, come and get it... the magazine that is!"

Jeff stretched out on the bed next to her. She cuddled up under his arm, and read the article out loud to him, as she tenderly stroked his manhood. Before long they were rolling on the sheets. Jodi was satisfied.

Jeff "Mad Dog" Madison was back in action. But, an exclusive relationship was the last thing on earth he was interested in.

Chapter 7

1973

Jeff liked Karen, especially the way she kept herself perfectly groomed. That was a welcome change from the hippie appearance of most of the women these days. One of her best assets was that she could hold a decent conversation on many subjects. Once again they met at the Alibi Inn after work. She came in with a few other ladies from the office where she worked. Karen was on a rant about being a woman working in a man's field.

"Interesting, Karen. So do you prefer replacing exhaust systems, or rebuilding engines?" Jeff teased.

"Ha, ha, Jeff, you're just too funny! Let me tell ya, when I get in my car I want it to start when I turn the key. When the gear shift is on 'D', I want to go forward, when it's on 'R', I want to go backwards. It gets a tune up twice a year. My guy at the gas station tells me if it's low on oil, or if it needs to be changed. If it doesn't do anything else, I bring it to you, and you fix it. I buy four new tires a year whether I need them, or not, you know that. The color has to be sharp so I look good in it. In my opinion, that's all I need to know about cars."

"Know what? If you do that much for your car, you're hell of a lot better than most drivers on the road. So, what is it again that you do that's a 'man's field'?" Jeff wondered.

"I work for the telephone company. I started out as a long distance operator. One day I saw an opening on the board in the engineering department for a person with mechanical drawing knowledge. I couldn't take it in high school, but my brother did. I checked out his assignments, and it looked fascinating. So, I did all his homework for him. He aced that class, thanks to me. I applied, and got the job. Smartest move I ever made."

"Okay... with no high school credit for the course, and no experience, how did you get the job?"

"I slept with the boss." Karen answered without batting an eye. "But, believe me, I did the job, and did it with as much skill as anyone else in the department."

Jeff was taken aback. "Sounds like even though we're in different fields, we share the same passion about our work. Are you seeing anyone special since we, um, last saw each other, or are you still sleeping with the boss?"

"Well, yeah I sleep with the boss. You see, now *I'm* the boss. But, if you are asking if I'm available, the answer is yes." Karen said with a smile.

"Would you be interested in seeing that new movie everybody is talking about?"

"Yes, I would. When did you have in mind?"

"How about?" he looked at his watch, "now?"

"Know what Jeff? That would make my day!"

"I like your sense of humor!"

They both enjoyed the movie. Tough guys with big guns always seem to pump a man up more so than a woman. However, Karen was in rare form, poking Jeff in the back with her finger pointed like a gun and telling him to, "Stick it up!" Jeff was sure he was going to get lucky tonight. They both felt the sexual tension between them. The only question seemed to be, "Your place or mine?" It was decided that Jeff's place would be best as he needed to be home in the morning, since Jason was coming over around noon for the weekend. They drove back to the Alibi Inn, so that Karen could pick up her car. She followed Jeff to his apartment. They laughed and repeated lines from the movie as they climbed the stairs.

Karen kicked off her platform shoes, letting out a long sigh of relief as she flopped down on the couch. Jeff sat with her, admiring how attractive she was. He could hardly keep his eyes off her good looking legs. He hoped mini skirts never went out of style. She absent mindedly put her feet up on the coffee table, then quickly pulled them away when she realized what she had done. He laughed, grabbed both of her ankles, and pulled her gently around so that her legs were on the couch. One at a time, he massaged each foot. Jeff could tell by the dreamy look on her face that she was enjoying every minute of it.

"Karen, would you like a glass of wine? I like wine, but I only enjoy drinking it if I'm sharing with someone special."

"Jeff, since we're both adults, let me ask you this, how much wine are we planning on drinking? I have to drive you know. Or, do you want me to spend the night?"

He grinned at her forwardness. "About spending the night, that's entirely up to you. I'm not a man that puts pressure on a woman. In other words, you call the shots. You're fun to be with, I enjoy your company. I have a very good French wine. We can have a glass, or finish the bottle, then open and finish another bottle if you'd like. As I said, I don't drink wine alone. My mother never fails to give me a bottle every time I see her. I have quite a supply of it here. If I get much more, I'm going to have to put in a wine cellar."

"Yes, I'd like a glass of wine, please."

Jeff went into the kitchen.

"You mentioned your son is coming in the morning." Karen wondered.

"Yeah. His name is Jason. He should be here around noon. Sometimes his step father drops him off early. I don't really like to have company here when he arrives, but sometimes it happens. As long as the bedroom door is shut, he knows not to come in. He seems to be okay with my long time, on again, off again girlfriend, but he gets a little pouty when he sees a stranger. He really doesn't want to talk about it either. I know it's getting close to the time we should be having that father son, man to man talk. He's nearly twelve already. Lord knows, I don't want his stepfather telling him the facts of life. Do you have children?"

"No. I've never found Mr. Right, and even if I did, I'm not sure about having kids. I don't know, I like kids, but they just seem so demanding. I have no intention of giving up my career, so I'd have to hire someone else to raise it so I can work. I see women missing work because of babysitter problems. Good reliable child care seems to be the topic of conversation for a lot of working women these days."

"Uh huh, I hear ya. Last year I had both my kids for nearly three weeks. It was easier to hire a mechanic to do my job than to find a decent sitter. So that's exactly what I did, and watched my kids myself." Jeff reached up in the cupboard, took down two wine glasses, and rinsed them off as he spoke. One was etched with the word, *Bride*. He bit his lip, put it back, then got another.

"You have more than one child?"

"Yes, I also have a little girl. I adore her, but she seems to be closer to her stepfather. She can't remember a time when he wasn't in her life, or a time when I was." Uncorking the wine, Jeff sniffed it's bouquet.

"That's too bad, I'm sorry."

Jeff poured two glasses, and took them to the couch where Karen was sitting. He handed her a glass, and tapped it with his, "To a beautiful night with an enchanting woman."

"Thank you." Karen said, then they both raised their glasses to their lips. "Oh, yes. Jeff this is very good wine. Your mother has excellent taste." Karen remarked as she sipped the wine.

Jeff smiled, "You bet she does, Maman is a most beautiful, and gracious lady."

"She also has a very handsome son." Karen set her empty wine glass on the table. She slipped her hand behind Jeff's neck, and leaned in toward him, kissing his mouth. They'd been together before, she knew he could kiss. *Oh, yes,* she thought, *this man can kiss.* She thought it best to ask a question, before getting any more intimate. Straight to the point, she said, "Let me ask you about Jodi. Right now, is she on again, or off again? I don't have any designs on you Jeff. I'm more into my career than I am into relationships. I just don't want any hassles if I decide to stop by at the Alibi again with the girls like I did tonight."

"Jodi and I have an open relationship. We're there for each other, but we've made no commitment. Before you came in I saw her head together with one of her hippie friends, and I knew what that meant. She left without saying good bye. I'm sure she's enjoying herself. Doesn't talking about my so called girlfriend bother you?"

"Not really, we both know why I'm here." She side glanced her wine glass, picked it up, and held it.

Jeff refilled it, and began to massage her neck. He could feel the tension, and stress ease as she drank the wine. He continued to rub her neck and shoulders.

"Oh, yes, Jeff. You know your stuff. If I wanted a man full time, I'd consider you for the position." She winked playfully at him. She leaned in for another kiss, then she stood up and took his hand. "Are we ready?"

"Mais oui, Madamoiselle, a votre service!"

"Parlez-vous Francais?" Karen asked.

"Oui, et vous? Vous parlez Francais aussi?"

"Je parle Francais un pur, tres pur!"

Jeff smiled. He lifted the hand that was holding his, and kissed it. "Tu es tres jolie. Voulez vous coucher avec moi?"

"En Anglais, yes."

Jeff paused to reach inside his nightstand drawer.

"Jeff, um, I'm on the pill… You don't have to use those things if you don't want to."

"Karen, you crack me up. I use 'those things' because I sleep around. I feel it's a health issue."

"You're something else!" Karen whispered.

They enjoyed the pleasure of each others' body.

"Good morning sleepy head!" Karen whispered as Jeff stretched, and looked around.

He smiled. "Who are you calling sleepy head? I don't think we slept all night."

"The night did pass quickly didn't it? So, are you in the mood again big guy?" Karen wondered.

"You could snuggle up to find out." Jeff offered.

"Hmm, you *are* something else." She giggled.

"Bye, Tom. Thanks for bringing me over to my dad's." Jason said sleepily.

"I'm sorry it's so early Jason. I had to come now to get to the airport on time. Can you get in okay?"

"Yeah, I know where Dad keeps the key hidden. I'll be alright."

"Why don't you lay down, and try to get some more sleep. Enjoy your visit, son."

Jason hated it when Tom called him son. "I sure will. Thanks, Tom. Hope your trip goes good. Bye again." He waved, and climbed bleary eyed up the stairs. He was happy to be at his dad's this weekend without his sister. Jason knew his dad loved Marianne, too, but he enjoyed having his dad's undivided attention. He knew he was getting older, and his dad didn't treat him so much like a kid any more. His dad didn't even care if he glanced at the posters Jones had hung up.

Girls sure were pretty when they got grown. All the girls in his class were yucky and stupid. And, Rianne, ugh! She had to be the nosiest four and a half year old in the world. He had to share everything with her, and all she had was a bunch of stupid dolls that she wouldn't let anyone touch. As if he'd even want to. Jason placed the key in the lock. He fumbled with it a few times, probably because he was so tired. He put the key back in it's place, and locked the door again from the inside. Looking around he noticed the bedroom door was open. He figured he'd just go in quietly, set his bags down in there, then catch a nap on the couch. The buck head wasn't as scary as it was when he was little, and besides it was daytime. His dad's room was very dark, but there was enough light for Jason to barely see that his dad was resting on his side, and stirring around a bit. He set down his bags quietly in case his dad was still asleep. Jason was trying to decide if he should tell his dad that he was there, when he heard the sound of a wrapper being torn open. As he turned, he heard a female voice giggle and say, "Hmm, you *are* something else." He saw his father slide on top of the woman who then wrapped both of her legs around his back.

Jeff was leaning on his elbows, as he lustily thrust himself against Karen's body, he heard a gasp coming from someone else in the room. He knew it wasn't Jodi, she'd be screeching. He didn't look, because he knew who it was. "Jason, it's okay. Just go in the other room. I'll be out in a minute."

Jason didn't know if he was in trouble, or exactly what was going on, but he did as he was told, and shut the door behind him.

"Karen, I'm sorry, seems I've lost the mood."

"Jeff, I'm so sorry. I'm not used to kids being around. I forgot to shut the door when I got up during the night. Do you think he's going to be alright?"

"Yeah, he'll be fine. I just don't think he's going to avoid 'the talk' today. Let me get him out of here, so you can get dressed, and leave in privacy. I'm really sorry, Karen."

Jeff pulled on a pair of jeans, and a tee shirt, then walked out of his room. Jason was at the kitchen table. He looked up at his dad with a scared look, like he knew he was in trouble. That hurt Jeff. "Did you eat anything this morning, Jason?"

"No, Dad." He answered meekly.

Jeff grabbed the box of Puffy Sugar Bites, a couple of bowls, and two spoons. "Jason, get the milk. Let's go to the tree house."

"Dad, can we go to your office?"

"Not today. It would be better if we go out to the tree house. Got the milk? Okay, lets go."

"No, let's go sit under the oak tree in front."

"NO! And don't *you* tell me no! I said the tree house. Move it. NOW." Now Jeff was irritated. His voice was firm and brusque.

They walked across the back of the lot, into the woods, across the stream, and climbed into the tree house. They each sat on a bean bag chair. Silently, Jeff poured the cereal, and Jason poured the milk.

"Dad, are you mad at me?"

"Yes, as a matter of fact, I am." Jeff answered sharply. "It's your sassy ass mouth. Jason, you need to learn how to follow orders. You're a big boy now. Once, just once I'd like to tell you to do something, and have you do it, without getting an argument out of you, or a bunch of your lip." As soon as he spoke his mind, Jeff eased up.

"Just once? I only have to not back talk once?" Jason looked at Jeff from the top of his eyes as he smirked.

"That's it young man!" Jeff slammed down his cereal bowl. He took Jason's cereal bowl from him, and slammed it down, also. He grabbed him and wrestled the boy until he got him over his knee, then play paddled him. Once Jason realized his dad was just playing, he faked crying and pain.

"Dad, I'm gonna need some deep psychological counseling after a beating like that. If you give me the money, I'll see that I get the best possible treatment."

"Boy, you already get the best possible treatment." Jeff walloped his rear end one more time in play, but with just a little sting. "I don't know how your mother puts up with you five days a week." He pulled Jason upright and gave him a hug, and a kiss on his forehead.

"She don't see me all that much. I'm in school all day, and when Tom's there, I just hang out in my room as much as I can. Dad, you really mad at me?" Jason picked up his bowl of Puffy Sugar Bites. He pushed them down in the milk, and watched them pop back up before he took each mouthful.

"I'm only mad about your sassy mouth. Jason, when I said the tree house, I meant the tree house. It wasn't bad when you asked about the office, but I reinforced that I meant the tree house. Then you back talked about going to the oak tree. Son, I don't know what your plans for the future are, but if you decide to go in the military, you're going to be in for a rude awakening. I know you love Colonel Pop, but when I was eleven, if I'd pulled a stunt like that, Maman would be getting an ice pack out of the freezer."

"Really, Dad?"

"Really, son. Believe me, he's certainly changed a lot since I was a boy. I'm not fooling with you about getting hit. Nobody likes to get hit. I learned to think, and speak carefully by the time I was a teenager, so I didn't get smacked."

"What was so important about not getting hit when you were a teenager? Does it hurt more as a teenager?"

Jeff smiled at Jason, and lit a cigarette. "You bet it does. By then, you're older, and smarter, and you think every original thought in the world comes out of your head. It hurts your pride to get hit. With the guys, it wasn't so bad, they just figured that you must've really ripped off a good one to piss off your old man that bad, so that kind of made you look cool. Girls weren't as impressed by stuff like that. I liked girls. Son, I liked girls a lot. I was a year older than you are now when I discovered just how much I liked girls. If I had a bruise on me, it was almost like having the plague. As I started to mature, Dad felt I needed 'the talk'. Being Mr. Smart Ass, I ripped off a sarcastic answer. I saw the look, and knew I had seconds to straighten my act up, or risk canceling the date of my young lifetime. I'd met a very special young lady. No way would I have gone out with her with a bruise. She thought I was a baby on our first date as it was. Jason, please try to learn to control your mouth, okay, son?"

"Okay, Dad."

"Why do you stay in your room so much at your mother's? Are you sent there for punishment?"

"Not always. I can't stand to be around when Tom is there so I go to my room so I don't have to watch him play grab ass every time she walks by." Jason quickly clamped his hand over his mouth. He'd never swore in front of an old person.

"Yeah… Okay, enough of that." Jeff fought his temper thinking about that man acting disrespectful in front of his children. "So? Are you ready for 'the talk'?"

"Are you sure you're not mad at me? I don't want to talk about anything else if you're mad at me about…"

"Jason, you did nothing wrong. My friend left the door open. You didn't know she was there. You didn't break any rule. So, have you heard any guy talk, in the locker room, or on the play ground?"

"Yeah, sounded gross to me."

"Typical answer, Jase! How much did you see?" Jeff laughed.

"Enough to get an A+ in biology. Looked pretty gross to me, Dad." Jason wasn't smiling. "Dad, why are you laughing at me?"

"I'm sorry, Jason. I'm not laughing at you, I'm laughing at how perfectly normal you are. Tell me what you've heard, then we'll talk about the facts of life."

Jason told him the locker room talk. Jeff wasn't impressed. He explained how the physical body functions. Then he proceeded to talk about the emotions involved. "Jason, lovemaking was designed by God for marriage between two people, one male, one female. Sometimes, sad to say, marriages don't work out, but our needs are still the same. I've chosen not to get married again. I still love your mother very much. Outside of marriage, there is still pleasure, but it's not the same kind of emotional, and physical fulfillment as being with a person that shares the commitment of love, blessed by God within the bonds of Holy Matrimony."

Jason was silent.

"Son, it doesn't appear that you are interested at this time in getting sexually involved with anyone."

"ME! Dad! Oh, mannn! Now that's what I call gross. Girls are disgusting."

"Jason, just please come to me before you make any decisions, okay? Son, I want you to understand how important birth control is. Every child deserves to be loved and wanted."

Jeff could see he was deep in thought. "Do you have any questions, son?"

He shrugged his shoulders. "Dad, thanks for talking to me like I'm a big teenager, instead of like a kid. If married people do that, does that mean my mom is doing that with Tom?"

Jeff felt the hair on his neck bristle, he reached for another cigarette, and lit it up before speaking. "Jason, what your mother, and her husband do is none of my business, but to answer your question, my guess is, yes."

"That's double gross."

"Well, Jason, don't go passing judgement about things you don't understand until you're a man. Then do so with caution. Always remember that he who sits in judgement is usually guilty of the same thing."

"Dad, do you really think you'll never get married again?"

Jeff let out a long, loud breath of smoke. "I'm not planning on it, Jason. Don't know if this will make any sense to you, but let me try to explain. I feel it's better for me to be alone, and know why I'm alone, than to be with someone, and wonder why I'm alone."

"You're right. I don't understand. Besides, Dad, you're not alone, you're with me."

Jeff thanked God silently for the son he was blessed with.

"Dad, did you ever play any sports? Way back when you were a kid?"

"I tried them all, but didn't enjoy any sports that involved a ball. I made the track team in high school, and was on the wrestling team. I had to give up track before I graduated though."

"How come?"

Jeff held up his cigarette. "Right here, boy. Bad, bad habit. If you have an ounce of brains in that hard head of yours, you won't ever start smoking. Understand?"

"Yeah, Dad. They really stink. I like the smell of the brand that Jodi smokes. If I ever start smoking, I'll ask her where she gets hers, because she rolls her own. They don't come in packs."

"I don't think that's such a good idea, son." Jeff was going to have to see that Jodi quit rolling joints in front of the kids. "I just told you not to smoke. Do I have to take you down again, boy?"

"No, SIR!" Jason emphasized, moving fast, away from his dad and laughing.

Jeff didn't make a move. He eyed Jason with a twinkle in his eye and told him, "Beware, my son, Daddy's gonna getcha, when you least expect it. So what's with all the sports talk?"

"Umm, I kinda got a bad grade in P.E. and Tom was on my case about getting involved in team sports. He was showing me some basketball stuff. He's really good, but I just have too many other things in my head to be thinking about bouncing a ball, and running around at the same time."

Jeff wondered just what it was that occupied his maturing son's mind.

Chapter 8

1974

"Hey, boss, telephone! Jeff, there's a hysterical woman on the phone askin' for you personally." Sam shouted over the din.

"Yeah, well, they all get hysterical at times, maybe she's on the rag. Who is it, Jodi?" He sounded disgusted as he was soaking wet from the rain that had been pouring down in buckets for days it seemed. Nothing was going right lately.

"Says her name's Beth, 'n she's scared."

Jeff came bounding for the telephone, and nearly pushed the new mechanic out of the chair. "My Beth? Is it my Beth?" The new mechanic just shrugged.

"Hello, Madison speaking."

"Jeff I'm in trouble! My car broke down on the way home from the airport. Tom is gone. My parents are gone. I'm alone. The neighborhood is scary. I'm broke down, the car won't start. I'm soaked." Beth ranted.

"Okay, angel eyes. Try to be calm. Are you at a phone booth, or in a store? Do you have the kids with you? Oh, that's right, I forgot. Are there any other women there? Okay, then stay in the store. What's the address? Calm down, ask... Got it. Do you want me to bring the tow truck? Fine, I'd be happy to. It'll take 20 maybe 30 minutes in this rain. Just stay in the store, don't go back to the car. I'll be there soon."

"Sammy, want some OT tonight? My wife is broke down, and I'm going to need some help."

"Sure. Got nothin' better to do." Sam said idly as he lit a cigarette.

"Go get the truck while I run upstairs for a minute."

Jeff wasted no time getting up the stairs. He grabbed a garbage bag, stuffed a few dry towels, a couple extra garbage bags, and a blanket in it. "Jodi, you might as well go home, I won't be back until late. Got a breakdown north of Waynesboro, and it's an emergency."

Jodi wondered if the emergency was blonde, brunette, or redhead. She was catching on to his games. He didn't even pause long enough to kiss her good-bye. She was surprised to see him leave with the new guy in the tow truck, instead of alone in the Camaro. Maybe this time it was a real emergency.

"Don't mean to sound too nosey, boss, but I, uh didn't know ya had a wife." Sam made small talk.

"You know I've got kids, I didn't have 'em alone!" Jeff grinned. "She is my ex-wife, but I'd take her back in a heart beat if I thought she'd come home."

"Can't relate to that, man. I'm a two time loser myself, wouldn't want either one of my old ladies back. Child support is killing me as it is. I got three kids, by two wives. Got myself fixed after the last one. Geez, I haven't seen rain comin' down like this since I was in Florida."

"Yeah, it's coming down in buckets alright. I'd like to get there faster, but I don't want to risk not getting there at all. Beth's alone in a high crime area." He lit up a smoke. "Florida, huh? I was stationed there during the Cuban missile crisis. My son was born there. Happiest days of my life were spent in Florida. Wife and I had a 1957 Chevy. She got it in the divorce. I don't know what she did with it, probably traded it in for something newer. She's a classy lady, and looks terrific in a classic car."

"Not too many guys talk about their wives, ex-wives the way you do, boss. Ya got a couple uh good lookin' kids there. Your little girl is quiet, but your son is a character. He sure knows his way around the shop. It's amazing how good his ear is tuned to an engine for a kid his age."

"Thanks. He started working with me before he was three. Smartest damn kid I ever saw. Paid attention to every word I said, and never once made a mistake handing me a tool. Rianne is the apple of my eye. I wish that it was more fun for her at the shop, but well, she's just not into cars I guess. So, Sam, you a Florida native?"

"No, uh-uh. Been a lotta places. I'm originally from Michigan. Was in South Dakota just before comin' here though."

"What's in South Dakota? You got family there?"

"No, went there to check things out after the siege at Wounded Knee ended. That's been uh... just about a year ago now. I'm not Sioux, I'm Cherokee, but still felt connected through the ah, American Indian Movement."

"What had them all pissed off anyway? I was barely getting over my divorce, don't remember much about current events from that time." Jeff asked

"They were demanding a public inquiry into the ill treatment of the Native Americans by the Federal Government." Sam's eyes remained focused ahead.

"Wasn't Wounded Knee the site of a Sioux massacre by the cavalry back in the late 1800's?" Jeff hoped he had his facts straight.

"Yer right. Surprised ya remember, most folks don't recall much about history... unless it happened to the white man." Sam replied.

"My dad was a Colonel in the Air Force. I think he studied every war ever fought on earth. He went over my history lessons with me, and we would recreate battles with my plastic cowboys and Indians. The Indians rarely won. We can be thankful that at least this time, there wasn't a blood bath."

"Uh huh, so why do ya think it was that the Indians rarely won?"

"Inferior weapons, and no resistance to European diseases. Certainly not due to lack of intelligence. Is that our exit up ahead?" Jeff wondered.

"Believe so." Sam put on the turn signal.

Jeff was relieved to see Beth from afar, standing inside the store. It was a creepy neighborhood. Sam pulled the wrecker up to the vehicle, then started to work. Jeff grabbed the garbage bag, and ran toward the store. It was pouring. Beth was still soaked after the twenty five minute wait, and she was shivering. He took out the towels, and wrapped one around her shoulders, and started towel drying the ends of her hair. He split open the bag, creating a makeshift rain coat for her, and held the other bag in front of her as a shield from the pelting rain. Once he got her situated in the truck, he ran back in the store to purchase three cups of hot coffee. He grabbed the blanket and covered her with it, hoping it would stop her cold shaking. Sam could hardly believe this was the same man that treated the garage girls with no respect, calling them Bimbo, Blondie, Red, or whatever popped into his head to describe who he was talking about. Sam hopped in the drivers seat, and headed back toward Madison Motors.

Once safely on the road, Beth's lip started to quiver. She was still shaking. Jeff put his arm around her, and told her it would be alright. He kissed her forehead. "Everything is under control. So, angel eyes, why were you out on a nasty night like this? And how did you end up in that neighborhood?"

"Tom left on another business trip. He couldn't get a cab to take him to the airport. They were all booked, I guess because of the storm. I offered to take him. On the way home, it felt like there was nothing under the gas pedal. It just kind of died. I managed to get the car as far as where you saw it, then I walked to the store. I was so scared. If anything serious has happened to that car, he will be so mad. I couldn't call Daddy because of him and Mom taking the kids for spring break. The warranty just expired, and it was after hours, so the dealer couldn't have cared less. I didn't bother to call anyone from church, none of those people could help."

"It's going to be fine. Sammy and I will take a look at her in the morning. I'm sure we can have you up and running in no time. Jason called last night. They're having a wonderful time with your folks. Rianne talked to me a little bit, too. He's supposed to be on vacation, and he's still griping about not wanting braces. He's too good looking to not get his teeth fixed, so I'll have to think of something to make him understand. How long is Tom going to be away?"

"Just a week. Do you think the car will be fixed before then?"

"If it isn't, I'd better find a new line of work!" Jeff smiled at her.

Sam pulled the wrecker around back. The guys got the car in one of the bays. "Thanks Sam. Don't forget to put the extra hour and a half on your time sheet."

"Nah, forget it, Mad. I don't mind helpin' out."

"Sorry, that's not the way I do business. If you work you get paid, if you don't you get fired. Most of my employees have been with me since opening. I'm running a custom shop here, not a slip shod operation."

"Thanks, boss. See ya in the mornin'. Good night, ma'am."

"Beth come on upstairs for a little bit. I'd like to get out of my work clothes, shower, and get into something dry. Is that okay? I won't enrapture your body unless you beg." He teased.

"I know better than to beg from you!" She smacked him a good one with the towel she had just folded. His heart skipped a beat. Once upstairs he could see her clothes were still wet. He offered her a flannel shirt to wear, a pair of boxers and some socks. She was so darn cold that she took him up on his offer. She recalled wearing Jeff's shirts when she was pregnant for Jason.

Starving, Beth checked out what was in his cupboards and refrigerator. She smiled at the new updated box of Puffy Sugar Bites on the shelf. *He's still built like a hunk,* she thought, *maybe they really are good for you.* She knocked on the bathroom door. "Jeff?"

"Yes, dear, you can come in and wash my back if you insist, but you'd better not get fresh!"

"Knock it off you big goof! Can I fix you something to eat? I'm half starved. If Bucky had any meat on him, I'd chew it off, and eat it raw right now."

"Sure, angel eyes, fix anything you can find, just don't drink all my beer."

When Jeff got out of the shower, he found that she had whipped up two of the fluffiest cheese and mushroom omelet's he'd ever seen. He took a bite, and shook his head, "It tastes just like what Maman used to make."

"She's the one who taught me." Beth smiled, "Thank you for coming to my rescue tonight. I've never been that scared. Do you remember that huge housekeeping spider in Florida?"

"What made you think of that?"

"Just thinking about being scared, and how you rescued me. It was the size of a wagon wheel."

Jeff laughed, "Yeah, it sure was a big one. I'm glad we got the bug situation under control before the baby came. Can you imagine, if he'd been in his crib-"

"Jeff, NO! Yuk! Stop it!"

He tormented her further by gnarling up his hand, and making it walk towards her like a spider across the table. She squealed when his hand got close, and nearly stabbed him with her fork. He then started singing the *Itsy Bitsy Spider*, and went through all the motions.

"Madison, you are incorrigible!"

"I've been told it's my most endearing quality."

"You've been told right! Speaking of Maman, how is she? Still beautiful, I imagine. And Vince, is he doing okay?"

"Maman and Dad are both fine. I don't know what Dad would do without her. Did you know they tried to have another baby after Jason was born? It seemed so odd at the time, but when you think about it, Maman was only a few years older than what I am now. I think I could be a parent to a newborn again. That is if I hadn't got cut. Dad's sure changed a lot. He's even apologized for roughing me up as a kid. People had odd ideas back then. He said his dad used to knock him around real bad. They'd call it child abuse these days. I've only hit Jason that once, and I'm ashamed of that. I've play paddled him a couple of times though. That mouth of his gets him in more trouble than his behavior any day of the week. Makes me wonder where it comes from."

"Looked in the mirror lately?"

Jeff made spider hand, and laughed when she squealed again. He knew he'd get it for sure if she got her hands on a pillow. "Dad's actually doing great, but he hates the high blood pressure medication he has to be on. Complains that it interferes with his love life. How's Jack and Nancy? It sure was nice of them to offer to take the kids on vacation."

"They're both doing remarkably well. Daddy always asks about you, mostly he asks Jason since he knows Jason comes over here a lot. I know what you mean about that boy's mouth though. He loves to dig in about you whenever Tom is around at my parents. Mom still has several of your pictures in the living room. Jason will point out each one to Marianne, and tell her whether it's our wedding picture, or your military picture, or whatever."

"And you, Beth, how are you? Are you happy?" Jeff watched her closely.

She squirmed a little. "Ummm, what's not to be happy about? When we married, Tom insisted that I quit my key punch job to let a poor person have it. I have an unlimited spending allowance. Tom likes being at home with me, or at church. On Sunday we still go to his folks ranch so we can ride. His parents like me a lot. Occasionally, we go dancing if Marianne is with you."

"Let's change the subject, okay? Would you like a beer?" Jeff knew he walked right into that one, although he really was more concerned about Beth's mental health.

"I thought you said I couldn't drink your beer."

"I said you couldn't drink it all. Do you want one, or not?" He asked impatiently.

"Is it still raining?"

"What does rain have to do with whether you want a beer or not?"

"Well, if it's raining, I don't want to leave for home yet. If it's not… Oh, duh, you'll be driving. I'll have a beer. Thank you."

"Want it in a glass, or is the bottle okay, or do you only drink from Waterford crystal now?"

"Shut up, smart ass!"

"Getting a little disrespectful there aren't you woman?"

Beth went to take a sip off the foam in the glass, then she blew it at him. He smiled fondly thinking of his baby son nursing, and teasing about him getting beer foam on his face. Beth picked up the dishes, and had them washed dried, and put away before Jeff could tell her not to bother. He asked her to make herself comfortable on the couch. He sat in the chair under the buck head. If anything the storm was raging stronger, and the wind had picked up. Before they could start another conversation, the phone rang.

"Hello… Yeah, I'm back… No, you better stay where you are… Because it's not safe… Are you high? Because no one in their right mind would choose to be out on the road on a night like tonight… Ya workin' tomorrow? Yeah, okay. Maybe… I said maybe… I don't make promises if I'm not sure I can keep them. Bye... Well, don't... You know why... Bye... Maybe... Bye."

"I'm sorry, Beth." They talked about the recession, the never ending war in Viet Nam, and what their old friends were up to. The rain continued. "Beth, since you're alone, and the weather's so bad, would you like to spend the night? I'm not being funny, or fresh, you just look so damn sleepy."

She nodded her head. He put fresh sheets on his bed. He called to her when it was ready. She went to the bathroom, and wiped off what was left of her makeup. Then she crawled into his bed. "Jeff, if you want to lay down with me, it's okay, I trust you. Are you still scared of storms?"

"Only when unexpected thunder claps... God, you remember that? I could always be me with you. Beth, I'm not sure I trust me. But, I'd kill myself tomorrow if I passed up an offer like that tonight." Before he finished brushing his teeth, she was sound asleep. Jeff slipped in between the sheets, wearing his underwear, and pajama bottoms. He'd gotten used to them when Marianne would come for the weekend.

Jeff lay there smoking his final cigarette for the night. "Dear God, Thank you for bringing her home. I pray that she is here for keeps. Amen." He prayed softly. He butted out the cigarette, then turned off the light.

In her sleep she rolled over, throwing a leg and an arm over him. Barely audible, Beth mumbled, "I love you, my Fly Boy."

He stroked her hair and said, "I love you, too, angel eyes." He didn't think he would, but he fell fast asleep, and rested like he hadn't rested in years.

Chapter 9

Beth woke up in a strange bed, but knew exactly where she was. She could hear Jeff's voice in the background. He'd just gotten up, and was in the kitchen. She got up, stretched and walked out to join him. He was on the phone with his back to her. She snuck up behind him and slipped her arms around his waist. Instead of startling him as she'd hoped, he slowly turned around, and wrapped an arm around her. He had the phone to his ear.

"Just a minute, okay? 'Good morning angel eyes. I'll be off the phone in just a sec.' Okay, Hank, I'm back. The three year old white Cadillac in bay two is my wife's. When you get in, could you get the new guy to help you check it out. I know there are others scheduled before her, but this is a special circumstance case. Let me know what you think of the new guy. He did a good job last night, handled the wrecker like a pro... I'm not sure where he learned, but I know for sure he was a Tank Commander when we ripped into Cambodia. I think he may have a bit of a smoke problem. Jodi sniffs around him when she thinks I'm not paying enough attention to her... Hank, Jodi is going to do her own thing no matter how much attention she gets... Well, listen, I'll be down a little later than usual. I'm upstairs if you need to consult with me on anything, okay? Later."

Jeff hung up the phone and wrapped his other arm around Beth. He leaned down, and kissed her softly, full on the lips. "Again, good morning angel eyes. Did you sleep well? I didn't with all your snoring. Have you had your sinuses checked?"

"Good morning, Jeff. Are you serious? Oh! You Dog! Madison! Do you really wonder where your kid gets his smart mouth?" Smiling she swatted his rear, then wriggled out of his embrace. "The coffee smells good." She reached up in the cupboard, pulled out two bowls, and the box of Puffy Sugar Bites. Jeff watched her thighs as the flannel shirt rose up as she lifted. Then she went to the refrigerator, and took out the milk. They sat down as if they'd been doing that routine for years. They gazed at each other across the table while they ate. Finally she spoke, "Don't you read the paper in the morning?"

"Nope, I never did. I'd look at you in the morning, and sneak Puffy Sugar Bites into Jason's mouth when your head was turned."

"I knew."

"You did not, we were careful."

"Oh, bologna, you two couldn't keep a secret even if it was a matter of national security. That's why they stuck you on the flight line instead of making you the Wing Commander."

"Oh, Beth, guess I couldn't fool you." He picked up the cereal bowls, rinsed them, set them in the sink, and put away the milk and cereal. He carried over the coffee pot, and refilled their cups.

She knew why she fell in love with this man. She didn't know why she wasn't still with him. He felt her gaze and said, "A penny for your thoughts."

"I'd pay a million, to understand them myself."

"Angel eyes, I really need to get downstairs to check that everyone is in, and assigned a project. Why don't you freshen up then come on down when you're ready? I'll show you what I do to support the kids."

Beth looked under the bathroom sink, and found a blow dryer. *Cool,* she thought. She washed out her underwear, and used the dryer to dry them before getting in the shower. After the soaking she got last night, she didn't think she'd ever want to be wet again. Her clothes were clean. She'd just changed outfits before leaving for the airport. She was glad that Tom was gone. She cared for him, but never felt totally at ease around him. He had an edginess that sometimes frightened her. If he was tired he could be brusque with her, and Jason learned to stay away. Marianne on the other hand probably could have gotten away with murder, no matter what mood he was in.

Beth was fresh and clean, dried and dressed. She decided to give her old friend Trina a call. "Hello, Trina? It's Beth. Are you busy, can you chat a little while?"

"Beth, when did your phone get fixed? I tried to call you all last night. Tom called here looking for you. Your phone was out. I kept trying for him. All I got was a recording, too."

What luck! Beth thought. "I didn't know it was broke. Must be the storm knocked it out. Trina, are you and Phil back together?"

"No, and I don't know how I feel about it. But I'm glad that we didn't split up until after we got to this base, because at least here I'm close to you again. He's such a slob, my work load is cut in half with him gone. I miss his body though. I've dated a couple of others… they don't push the right buttons if ya know what I mean."

"Uh huh. Trina, could I ask you a super big favor?" Beth sounded timid.

"Sure, you've helped me out enough, getting me started on my own again, and sending over Jason's hand me downs for Todd. I really don't know what I would do without you. What can I do?"

"Cover for me, please. Tom is going to be away for a week. My parents have the kids in Florida for spring break. I want to be with someone else. Someone special."

"Beth, you slut! I love it, you can count on me!"

"Okay, here's the number... When Tom calls make up something, let me know, then I'll get back with him. Thanks. You're a doll. Bye."

"Beth, wait! Who's the guy? You hung up!"

Jeff didn't see Beth enter the shop. He had just sent away about a half a dozen young women, and was having a meeting with his employees. She listened to him tell them that what they did on their own time was their business, but eight to five was his time. If their friends wanted to meet them for lunch, that was fine with him as long as they were gone by one. Jeff glanced around, and asked if there were any questions. His eyes stopped on Beth's face. His eyes grew wide, and his mouth dropped. The men all looked back to see what he was looking at. She was gorgeous in her white peasant blouse, and snug fitting bell bottomed jeans. Her hair was shining in the sunlight coming in through the window. "Okay, men, back to work. You're a great crew, the best I've ever had. Let's not let our hormones mess it up."

"I'm sorry Jeff. I didn't know you were having a meeting. I shouldn't have interrupted."

"I'd close the shop, and declare today a paid holiday, if you were home to stay."

Beth blushed. "Can you give me a tour now, or do I have to wait until lunch?"

"I'm the boss, remember? I make the rules, I break the rules."

The shop was very noisy. Jeff put his arm around her shoulder and leaned in close to her ear as he explained what jobs were done in each bay. "This is bay one. We do front end alignments here. Right next to that is where we work on wrecked vehicles, that's called a frame straightener." He pointed to the tire loft, and various different things, she followed with her eyes. "The hoists in the other three bays are for specific jobs. That one is for lubes. Over there in the middle, that's for tune ups and brakes. The far one is for engine overhauls, and replacing transmissions." He opened a door that led to a storage room that held three, but had room for four engines.

Beth was impressed with his shop, and knew that with time, and the rate of success he was achieving, he was sitting on a gold mine. Some how the money didn't seem important, it was the level of satisfaction, and pride he had in his business that made listening to his talk so interesting. She could see why Jason liked to be here.

"Let's go outside." He held the door for her.

It was a beautiful spring day. *Guess we have to expect some April showers. If it wasn't for the rain, she wouldn't be here,* he thought. They walked hand in hand to the back of the lot where Jason liked to ride his bike and pop wheelies. Beth smiled imagining how much fun he must have being out there in so much open space, where he could play without a lecture about messing up a perfectly manicured lawn. Jeff pointed to the hilly area to the east, and said that is where Jason would hill climb with his dirt bike. She asked how many bikes he had. He told her three as if it was no big deal. They walked further into the wooded area until they came upon a stream. There were two large rocks there, Jeff sat on one. "I bring the kids here to fish sometimes. We only catch when Rianne isn't here. She throws rocks in the water, and that scares them off. I'd rather cut my tongue out than scold her, so obviously she doesn't see the joy in fishing since we never catch anything. One of these days motor mouth will say something to her, I'm sure."

Beth stood behind him massaging his shoulders. He stood up, took her hand and they walked on. "This is where Rianne likes to play. I'm sorry about the time she came home all scratched up. She really likes the wild raspberries. Once they're ripe, I always know where to find her. She now knows to wear long sleeves, so her mother doesn't accuse me of throwing her in a room full of wild cats again. I don't let her play back here alone. I've never had any trouble in the area, but you can't be too careful. The property line in the back isn't fenced. She could wander too far, or someone could be lurking. Jodi says I'm over protective. I'm sorry, forget I said that."

They continued around until the shop was in view again. They walked up the long drive until they got to the front part of the lot with their arms around each others waist. They paused and stared at the flat open space. Neither one said a word, but both recalled that was the area where their home would have been built. Jeff led the way toward the old oak tree to show her the kids tire swings. "That one is Jason's. It's getting pretty beat up. He gets it going real fast and slams it into the tree just to see if he can stay on it. He is so funny. Guess it won't be much longer and he won't be interested in a swing any more. That's part of the reason why I haven't replaced it. He spends less time here, and more time out back now. This is Baby Cakes swing. She loves it when I push her. She's big enough to swing herself, but she likes to play the role of daddy's little girl. I don't mind, she's my last child, my baby girl. We eat lunch out here a lot. I've thought about getting a picnic table, but with a blanket, we're closer. Sometimes we all take a nap if the weather is nice. They probably stay up later here than what you let them, with no school on the weekend." They were sitting on the grass. It was dry now. "I feel bad sometimes. You have them all week when there's school, and projects. I have them on the weekend, so I must appear to be fun time Daddy. I wonder if they know that if the situation was reversed, I'd be the one standing over them making sure their assignments were done, and done correctly. That military mentality still comes out in me sometimes. Jason sees it occasionally, if he dawdles too much on a project. Sometimes I can just see the wheels turning in his head though. Beth, why are you crying?"

"I just wish others knew you the way I know you. That's all." She held her arms open, he pulled her close.

"Nobody else can. I won't let them." Jeff leaned over and gently brushed his lips across her cheek and whispered, "Beth... angel eyes, I love you."

"I love you, too, Fly Boy, I just don't know what to do." Burying her face in his chest, she regained control.

"Wow, it's lunch time already. Let me go check on your car. I've got tuna upstairs, I'll make some sandwiches when I'm done, okay?" Jeff's heart was on fire. She told him she loved him. They both stood up, and stretched. "Hey, Beth, race you to the front door, I'll give you a ten second lead... Ready? On your mark, get set, go!" He whacked her on the fanny as she took off. He waited until he counted to ten, then passed her like she was standing still. He held his arms out and caught her as she plowed into him. They both landed in the dirt. They laughed so hard there were tears in both their eyes. The other mechanics wondered who this man was. Hank and Clark knew. They'd seen Jeff with Beth before.

When Jeff got upstairs, Beth already had the sandwiches made and asked if he wanted a cola or beer with his lunch. He told her he'd rather have her, but since he may have to drive to Centerville to pick up some parts, he'd better not start with her, or the beer.

"Jeff, couldn't you have just said cola? Do you have to make a major production over everything?"

"Beth, if you are going to start nagging, you're going to have to marry me. I don't know whether you realize it, but you need a license to nag in this country. I know you have a license, but it's a restricted license. It restricts you from nagging any one but Tom Terrific."

"Jeff stop it! You are so bad. Let's change the subject. If you go to Centerville, can I go with you? I'd like to pick up a few things-" Beth blushed.

Jeff looked at her with wide questioning eyes, "You mean you're coming back?" His body was quivering.

"I'd like to. I'm not sure if we can work it out. We have a few days now, we've never had more than just a few hours without our kids around, or your girlfriend walking in on us."

"Don't blame it on me, angel eyes, you're the one with a husband."

"Shhh, stop, let's not ruin it. Please. I love you, You just told me outside that you love me. If you meant it, don't dig up old bones. I divorced you, I can divorce him. Can I ride to Centerville and come back, or not?"

"I'm sorry, Beth. Remember on our honeymoon when I told you I was a jerk, and sometimes stupid things just roll off my tongue? Well, that was one of those stupid things. I was wrong to mention Tom. If flippant things come rolling out of my mouth, I can bet my last dollar it's going to be wrong. I have to think everything through before I speak."

"I'm sorry, too. This is what I'm talking about when I say 'if it can be worked out'. We are so good, and happy together, then the old skeletons fall out of the closet. You mentioned getting counseling the last time we talked about reconciliation. Are you still interested? It's not just us in this marriage, Jeff. We have a son that is approaching his teen years, and a daughter that adores, I'm sorry, but she adores her stepfather. It's not just you and me, our decisions will affect each one of us."

"Whatever it takes Beth, whatever it takes. Let's go to Centerville."

"Do you think we could take someone else's car? I love my neighbors, but they know the Camaro from you coming to pick up the kids. I'd like to have the divorce go as smoothly as possible. I don't think having Tom find out I'm going back with you would make anything easier."

"Good thinking, I've got a pick up that I've never driven to your house."

They got a much later start than expected, but it worked out for the best. They picked up parts from a couple of different suppliers. When they were done with all their stops, they went to Beth's home that she shared with Tom. "Jeff, aren't you coming in?"

"I don't know, I feel like I'm invading another man's territory."

"Oh, come on, you can see where your kids live."

As they approached the front door Beth didn't notice a large, long, white box on the front porch. She walked right by it, and unlocked the door. Jeff picked it up, carried it inside and set it on the table in the foyer. She quickly went through the mail, dumping most of it in the trash, and carried some of it in her hand as she headed up the stairs. "Well, aren't you coming?"

"What? Are you crazy?"

"No! This is where the kids sleep, you nut!"

He forgot this was Beth he was with. She still had an air of innocence about her. She pointed to the doorway of Jason's room. "Horses? No frigging wonder he seems so uptight when he comes to my house! He's hated horses ever since the first time he rode Josey. The wallpaper must scare the crap out of him. There is nothing in this room that speaks of Jason. There are no cars, or soldiers, or airplanes. He doesn't belong here."

"Don't be ridiculous!" Beth disregarded his comments. "Over here is Marianne's room. Why don't you look around while I get what I need?"

Jeff smiled as he looked at all the porcelain dolls that his mother had sent Marianne since her birth. All were in mint condition, some had never been removed from their box. He was happy to see them, but happier to know that the dolls she loved, and played with were in her toy box at his place. He looked at the huge doll house in the corner, and made a mental note about her canopy bed.

Jeff's jaw tightened as he glanced down the hall, feeling like he'd been kicked in the gut. He got a glimpse of the big brass bed Beth shared with another man. He walked in her bedroom, and watched as she placed clean underwear in her suitcase. Jeff felt malice in his heart that Tom was sleeping with the woman he still considered to be his wife. If not for Tom, Beth would have come back to him soon after she was released from the hospital, he was certain. For nothing other than spite, Jeff sat down on Tom's bed. Looking at her neatly folded panties stirred his desire. He reached for Beth's hand, encouraging her to sit down beside him. He tilted his head, then in slow motion, he moved his mouth toward her, lightly touching his lips to hers. Jeff gently touched her breasts, soon realizing that they were his for the taking. Beth hadn't felt strong hands massaging her fullness, and hot wet lips stimulating her beautiful nipples since Jeff had made love to her. Pressing her voluptuous breasts into his hands, she responded fervently when his mouth all but devoured them. His fingers ran down her zipper, touching her delicately inside her panties. Jeff was on the floor, kneeling as Beth sensually caressed his head, and sighed long and loud as he placed his lips and tongue where his fingertips had been. Every erotic nerve in her body was on fire. She rose to meet Jeff's lips crying out with pleasure when he nearly brought her to orgasm. Standing, and dropping his jeans, he looked down at the woman he adored. When she looked up at him and whispered, "Yes", he didn't ask if she was sure like he did their first time on her parents couch. Jeff kissed her then made love to her with all the passion in his heart.

Beth wrapped herself around him, eagerly taking all of him into her body. She hungrily pushed into him for more each time he thrust until she felt dynamic bursts of passion overtaking her, centering around the man she adored possessing her body.

Spent, and realizing what had happened in her husband's bed, Beth suddenly perceived she was no better than Diane. But, she gazed deeply into the blue eyes of this wonderful man, and felt no sin, guilt, or regret. "I love you Jeffrey, with all my heart, I love you."

"I love you, too, Angel eyes." Jeff felt guilty, only because he was proud that he'd made love to Beth in Tom's bed, rather than just being pleased that he'd made love to Beth. "I'd better go downstairs so you can finish packing."

"Hey Jeff, will you open that box?" Beth hollered down the stairs.

"Beth, they're flowers. Yellow roses from your husband. Lots of them." Again, he felt resentment.

"Jeff, I'm sorry." *Dammit! I should've known.* "Did you read the card?" She asked coming downstairs.

"No."

"Let's talk in the truck." Beth took the card, and slipped it in the pocket of her jeans, and scooped up the box of flowers.

Jeff carried her overnight case and garment bag, and put them behind her seat. She placed the box of flowers in the back of the truck. "Jeff, I need to do one more thing before we leave, I almost forgot." He watched her walk along the side of the house until she was out of his sight. After a few minutes, he was getting nervous, and was about ready to go looking for her when she popped back into view. She had a big grin on her face.

"What did you do? You look like the cat that swallowed the canary." His voice was monotone.

"Trina said the phone was out. I just made sure that it stays out! Jeff, on the edge of town there's a little nursing home. Could we stop there for just a minute? I want to drop off something."

"Sure." Jeff made no attempt at conversation.

Beth let out a long, deep breath. "Tom was very angry when he left. He was mad at me for not having his brand new pants washed, pressed and packed. He says they put chemicals on them. Part of the reason he couldn't get a cab was because he was waiting for me to finish with those damn pants. I volunteered to take him to the airport as a peace offering."

"Amazing... all his fucking money and he won't hire help for his wife. Besides being chief cook and bottle washer, you do laundry, ironing, and taxi his ass to the airport, too. You do all that for flowers?"

Beth shot him a strange look. "The nastier his sarcasm, the bigger bouquet he sends."

"Interesting... must be nice to own a slave. Does he flog you, and the children, too?"

"Jeff, he's never hit me, or the kids. If he did, I'd leave without looking back. When things don't go his way, he can be verbally abusive. Jase gets the worst of it. It wouldn't be that way if he didn't have such a smart mouth on him, but I'm powerless to stop Jason when he starts sassing Tom. The last thing he would need is me coming down on him, too. And, about your question about household help... *I* refuse, listen closely, REFUSE to have hired help in my house. Look what happened the only time I hired someone to come in my house."

Jeff knew she was referring to Tamiko, and felt like he'd been kicked in the groin.

Beth began to speak, "Let's see what the card says. *Beth, Thank you for doing your job, so I can do mine. If I look good, you look good. Keep trying Babe, maybe you'll get it together one of these days. If not, hire a maid. Love, Tom*"

Still silent, Jeff pulled into the nursing home parking lot. He took Beth into his arms, "I don't know what to say...". He kissed her cheek then came around to open her door. She took the flowers out of the back of the truck, saying she'd be right back. She carried them into the nursing home. Beth knew they had bud vases, lots of bud vases. She asked them to put a rose in each one for the seniors, and pass them around. Usually she did this herself, but she didn't want to keep Jeff waiting.

"Jeff, forgive me. I'm sorry it took so long…"

"Beth you weren't gone five minutes. I didn't even finish my cigarette. Will you quit apologizing every time you turn around? I'm not him, okay?"

"Okay, sor-." She smiled and relaxed.

"I don't feel like a heavy meal tonight, how about you? It was a goof off day for me. Feel kinda bad about it too, after chewing out the guys for their girlfriends hanging around, I spent the day playing with my wife."

"I don't have a taste for anything special. Do you like subs? There's a place called Sub-Zero about two blocks from here. I thought you said you were boss? If you can't handle the crew, maybe I can. I've still got that lady lion tamer teddy with the feather whip that you bought me, ya know."

"You don't!"

"I do!"

"You don't wear it for him, do you?"

"Oh, Jeff, no. No, I don't. It's in a trunk over in mom and dad's attic. I have it locked in case the kids go up there to play. Jeff, I've only played like that with you."

He felt a lump in his throat. Even if he couldn't build her a palace, he knew there was a part of her that Tom hadn't touched. How he loved this woman. He turned into the Sub-Zero. They each ate a sub, and a bag of chips, and drank soda. They liked it. They headed back to the shop. Jeff handed her the key to go upstairs while he unloaded the truck. He came up about twenty minutes later. It was only since last night, but he felt like they had spent a lifetime together this day. He knew it wasn't just the sex. He loved her. He was nervous asking, but figured she was there by her own choice, "Beth, I'd like to take my shower now. Would you care to join me?"

"I bet I can get naked before you can!"

"Ha! I doubt it with that harness you wear!"

"Oh, ha yourself, Fly Boy. I burned it!" Beth laughed, and flashed her bare bosom at him.

They got in the shower together. They got sudsy, and lathered, and tickled, and scrubbed. The giggling was almost out of control when Jeff glanced down, and muttered, "Oh, no."

"What?" Beth questioned looking down also. There was red in the tub meaning only one thing. She rinsed and dried, and remembered seeing a box of feminine products under the sink where she found the dryer. Mother nature struck again.

"Beth, I don't mind… I know you're clean…"

"Jeff, I do. I'm sorry. It's my hang up."

"I respect you, and your feelings. I love you, whether we make love, or not. Don't ever think it's just lust I feel for you. You own my soul."

"Jeff, I can pleasure you whether we make love, or not. I remember the last time I was here. I've not had any more experience, but I ummm, loved kissing you there."

She lay in his arms staring into his eyes. He stared back at her in amazement at how much of this woman was still his alone. She kissed his eyes, his nose, his cheeks, his lips, his chin, his ear lobes, his neck, his throat. Her tongue, and her lips traveled down. She didn't stop until she knew that he had reached the final culminating, highest point of physical fulfillment.

Jeff cradled his darling in his arms after telling her how dear and special his Angel eyes was to his heart. He kissed her forehead and stroked her hair. He knew he was going to get it, but he couldn't help himself. "Beth, if you would have done that in the grocery store, we might never have had kids ya know." Oh, boy was he right. She clobbered him with both pillows, giving him the old one-two slam-blam. She loved him and he knew it, and vice versa. She felt so good in his arms.

"Dear God Bless my children, and their beautiful mother. Thank you Lord Jesus, for tonight." He prayed.

Beth said, "Amen."

Chapter 10

Together Jeff and Beth finished the Puffy Sugar Bites for breakfast. Jeff told her he had to show up for work today. He didn't want to risk her putting on that lion tamer teddy, complete with the feather whip, to chase him down to the garage so he could earn a living. Beth asked where his laundry room was, he told her it was downstairs. She was tidying up Versailles, stripping the bed, and washing the breakfast dishes, when the phone rang, without thinking she cheerfully answered, "Hello!"

"Hello... Beth? Is that you?"

"Daddy! Oh, my God!"

"Hold on... No, Jason, it's not your mother, I made a mistake. Here, go get some ice cream, or coffee, or something for Nana and Rianne. I'll meet you at the Café in a minute." Jack pressed cash in Jason's hand.

"Sorry for lying, Beth, what the hell is going on?"

"Daddy, oh, Daddy don't be mad. But, my car broke down. Tom was gone. There was no one to help me. I was stranded in a bad neighborhood, and Jeff came out in a raging storm, and oh, Daddy, I stayed overnight with him... I love him so much."

"Oh, I see. Beth, well, honey, we love Jeff, too. Follow your heart, but don't lose your head. You're still another man's wife. Whatever you decide, I'll stand by your decision. If you don't mind, I don't think it would be a good idea for me to tell your mother about this. Jason wants to talk to his dad."

"He's at work downstairs. Thank you, Daddy. More than not telling Mom, please don't tell Tom. Jeff and I, well, we haven't... decided yet. But, I love him, and I want to be with him. We're trying to work things out. Jeff makes me feel good about being me."

"Beth Ann, you're an adult. He was your husband, and I know that you loved each other very much. He is your children's father, and you'll always have ties to him through them. I know your feelings are deeper than just the kids though. I'd better get over there before- too late here he comes. I'll tell him the truth, his dad has gone to work already. Bye, honey."

"I love you, Daddy. Bye"

Beth walked downstairs carrying a laundry basket full of towels, bedding and clothing. She looked adorable with her hair tied back, and wearing a Madison Motors tee shirt. *Another pair of perfectly fitting jeans on her tight ass,* Jeff thought. He grinned as one of the guys asked if she was the laundry mistress, or the upstairs maid. He knew Beth could take care of herself in response to playful jesting. True to form, she didn't let him down. She set down the basket and said, "Alright men, listen up! I'm the new management around here. I demand, and I get respect. Insubordination will be no longer tolerated as it was under the old sissy pants management. A pansy ass chewing is a thing of the past. Public humiliation is the new form of punishment for minor infractions of the rules. The rules change often, and without notice. Major infractions require stiff penalties payable with your own life blood, or that of your children. So... Watch, and beware!" She was funny, and added an air of class to the place. After starting up both washing machines, she walked into Jeff's office, and found him buried in a sea of paperwork. "Can I help?"

"Are you serious?"

"Sure, why not? My office skills aren't that rusty. It's not been that long since I finished business school."

"Okay, sort this stack of bills by due date. This pile of paper by date of services rendered, and put these inventory receipts in alphabetical order. But, before you get started, service my lips."

Beth walked around the desk, sat on his lap and kissed him deeply. There was much hooting and hollering from the garage. Beth walked to the door and yelled, "Okay, show's over. Back to work, or I'll bust your wages, AFTER I bust your chops!" She shut the door then pulled all the blinds.

"What did you do that for?"

"Just to keep them guessing."

"You little wench."

"Guess what?"

"What?"

"I still have the little French Maid outfit that you bought me with the black fish net stockings and the little white apron and cap." She sat back on his lap, and kissed him all over his face.

"Beth… angel eyes, do you get some sick pleasure out of torturing me?"

"Did you say sick? Lil Jeffy gots a temperature? Nursie still has that outfit, too." She swirled her tongue in his mouth. Oh, how she loved this man.

Most of the laundry was done, folded, and put away before lunch. Jeff's work clothes would have been done, except Beth decided to run them through the wash cycle twice before putting them in the dryer. Jeff didn't know if she was a workaholic, or if she really did care that much about how he looked.

Jeff stared at her tackling the stack of paper work he had given her, thinking about what a great team they made. He wondered if everything that happened, that shouldn't have happened, wouldn't have happened, if he would have stayed in the military. He wondered what his rank would be by now, and if they would have had more babies. She looked up at him. Catching his gaze she puckered her lips, blew him a kiss, and went back to working on the papers. The phone rang, "Madison Motors." Hearing a click, Jeff hung up the phone. "Must've been a wrong number." He wasn't quite so sure.

It was lunchtime. Upstairs they made sandwiches, and packed the picnic basket. They walked toward the mighty oak tree. Jeff spread a blanket, they ate and talked about the shop. Beth picked up a little Gearhead speech listening to Jeff on the phone, and hearing his interaction with the guys. She wondered, "Don't you work on cars anymore? All I've seen you do is office work."

"I'd rather work on cars than anything. Good office help in a place like this is difficult to find. Women come in talking serious business in their interview, then next thing I know they're out on the floor playing pocket pool with the guys."

"Jeff, don't be a dog!"

"I'm sorry, angel eyes, it just pisses me off. One secretary I had in here… I walked in my office, and there she was doin' it on my desk with Jones, a guy I recently let go. She just grinned at me and said, 'take a number and wait, sir, I'll be at your service in a moment.' I about blew a gasket. I told her to gather up her shit, and leave now. I paid her for the full week, and the next as severance pay, thought that was fair, considering. Before she walked out she turned and said to me, 'a secretary is a permanent fixture once she's been screwed on the desk'. She swore vengeance. She almost had an eerie witch like quality about her. Scary bitch."

"I think you told me about her before. That is creepy though. Think she's the one that just called?"

"Hmmm, maybe. Hey Beth, let's see if I can show you how Jason crashes the swing into the oak tree."

"Jason! Oh, I forgot to tell you! He called, well, Daddy called. It was so weird. Jase heard Dad say my name, so Dad told Jason he made a mistake, and gave him money to go get ice cream. We had a good talk. I told him I'm in love with you. He seemed pleased, and said he'd stand by me no matter what. I thought he'd go off on a morals issue with me. But, it sounded like he wants us to get back together. If I could've seen his eyes, I would've known for sure, but it sure sounded like he wants me to go back with you."

"I knew I liked your dad from the very beginning. Now that I have a little girl of my own, I appreciate how he was so protective of you. He asked me what my intentions were the Thanksgiving we met. He wasn't dumb. He probably knew I'd try to nail his daughter after I saw your garters hanging out while we played pool."

"Oh, you are a dog! How do you remember that?"

"I remember the green mini skirt you had on, too. I liked the stockings, and garters you chicks used to wear better than panty hose. I suppose they look alright, but there was something arousing about seeing where those stockings ended, and imagining what was beginning."

"Jeff, weren't you going to crash into the tree, or something? You really are incorrigible!"

Jeff stood on Jason's swing and spun it around the way the boy did and crashed. "Hey this is fun! C'mon, Beth."

She climbed on it, too, but they went off balance and they tumbled to the ground. Lying on the blanket they kissed long, warm and deep. Lunch was over, it was time to go back to work.

Beth went upstairs and put the sheets back on the bed. She thought it was odd that one wall had a curtain all the way across it and yet she couldn't remember seeing a window on that side of the apartment from outside. She studied the track. It appeared that it was like the curtains around beds in hospital rooms. That somewhat freaked her out, but she kept her head together. She peeked behind the curtain, and saw little doors that opened to the area under the eaves of the roof. She wanted to look inside, but decided it was none of her business. There really wasn't much left in the apartment to eat. She wondered what they would do for dinner. The phone rang. This time, she nervously answered it, and heard a familiar voice. "Hey, Beth! Guess what? I know where you are!"

"Oh, really? And where would that be Trina?"

"You're balling the old, old man again, aren't you? I know you are so fess up!"

"Shut up! How did you find out where I am?"

"I called the number you gave me, after so many rings, it made a clicking noise, and it rang again. I heard a voice from the past say 'Madison Motors'. I hung up so I could laugh my ass off! This is just too cool. I'll never forget the look on your face when you first laid eyes on him. I told Phil I bet he'd have you in the sack by the third date. Was I right?"

"Trina, you're such a sleuth! Guess it depends on when you start counting our dates. On a darker subject... Has Tom called back?"

"Nope. But, I'm ready for him when he does. You know what Beth? I still love Phil, he's my first and only. We're still married. I don't like living with him because he's such a slob, and has no respect for 'woman's work', but he knows me better than anyone. I think I'm going to invite him for a sleepover. That way he can swill in his mess at his place, and pleasure me at mine. Do you think it will have a negative influence on Todd?"

"That's a tough one to call Trina. When he was eight, Jason saw Jeff and I together after we separated, it kind of blew him away."

"What?!? You've been doing your ex *and* Tom this many years? Woman! You must have an appetite!!!"

"No, Trina, that was before I married Tom. Jeff and I weren't divorced yet." Beth grinned at that one.

"I'm happy you're back with Jeff, you two belong together. I think separate houses would work for us."

Beth smiled as she thought of her Jeff. "I guess you're right on both statements. Where's Todd? With Phil for spring break?"

"Yeah, hey, I'm gonna let you go, and call them to invite them for dinner. That way I can see how Todd reacts to us being in the same room together. I don't want a divorce, I just don't want his mess. Bye, Beth."

"Bye, Trina." Beth smiled. She looked at the clock. *Where did the time go?* It was ten to five. Jeff would be off work in a few minutes. She decided to go down stairs. She heard men's voices.

"I *know* it's none of my business, Jeff. I'm concerned about you, and the shop. Don't forget, I've worked with you since this place was Seth's. It's just that she's done this before. She came back, let you play with her ass, then she married her rich husband, and moved into his castle on the hill. You were a drunken mess for months." Hank's voice held a tone of warning.

"Hank, I know. I've thought of that, too. But, what you don't know is the depth that I love that woman. You've seen us around here. No lie, this was my life until I got messed over in Okinawa. We played like this every single day of our married life until the incident. Before that we had one disagreement in our seven years of marriage. That was because of some stupid remark I made on our honeymoon that was rude, cruel, and totally uncalled for. I wish I could just turn back the hands of time and change the past. I can't, so I live and breathe hoping this time she'll stay with me."

"What's her new meal ticket have that you don't?"

"From what I can see, my wife, my kids, and anything else a few million dollars can buy."

"Well, her car is ready. Runs like a charm. I signed off on it, I don't know how you want it billed, so you can handle that. Please don't misunderstand, I like the lady, we all do. We're all routing for you, Jeff. Whatever happens, we all wish you the best. And, if she dumps your ass again for Mr. Big Bucks, well, we'll keep the place going for you until you sober up. I wish that I could be more optimistic. Good night. See ya tomorrow."

Beth hid around the corner and cried.

Jeff left the office to go up stairs and spotted Beth. He took one look at her, and knew she'd overheard. He hugged her and swayed with her in his arms. "Beth, Beth, Beth nothing or nobody matters to me besides you, and our kids. And, when you decide to come home to stay, well, come upstairs. Let me show you something. She held his hand as they walked up the stairs together.

Jeff glanced around the apartment. "Oh, Beth Versailles looks wonderful. But, wait until you see this." He led her into the bedroom, and motioned for her to take a seat. He moved back the curtain, and opened one of the doors. He slid out a box, and removed a set of house plans. "I remembered everything you wanted in a house when we almost got back together three years ago. I did some extensive custom work on a race car for the owner of Home Design Services, he drew up these plans for me in trade. We both thought we got the better end of the deal."

They went over every detail of the drawings from the front door to the back, upstairs and down. Outside, they walked around the property determining what the view from each window would be. They went back inside and sat on the couch looking at the drawings again. "Jeff, you've taken my dream house, and put it on paper. I can see it in my mind already. I love you, and I want you to know that I'd be happy living here in Versailles with you for the rest of my life. I guess it must look like I'm with Tom for his money. But, it's not the money, and it's not the social position."

"It's the sex?" He braced himself for her answer.

"He doesn't rock my cradle the way you do. But, he is… good." She darted her eyes away from Jeff. "I'm so sorry for saying that."

"No, I shouldn't have asked if I couldn't take the answer like a man. You talk about not being able to compete… Geez."

"Jeff, I want to be with you. You. Do you understand? I like being with you, and talking with you. You listen to me as if what I think is important, and what I do matters. My kids are your kids, and you don't find fault with my precious son." Beth was shaking, and Jeff began to worry about her stability. Out of the blue, she asked, "Do your parents hate me?"

"The word hate is a little strong. I haven't told them anything, when I do, they'll understand. And, if they don't, too bad. The Bible says 'a man shall leave his father and his mother and cleave unto his wife'. That's Genesis, Chapter 2 verse 24."

Beth's jaw dropped when he quoted the Bible without looking it up. "Jeff, you're the most fascinating man I've ever known. I must've been insane to let you go. No wonder I ended up in the loony bin."

"Well, it was only temporary insanity, and don't worry about it, I'm coo coo nuts over you!" With that Jeff started to tickle Beth. She squirmed all over the couch trying to get away, laughing until her sides hurt.

"Do you know what I'd like?" He asked.

"I'm scared to ask."

"I'd like a Bad Dog from the Alibi Inn."

"Jason talks about that place all the time. I've been wondering what they're like."

"Beth, um, I don't want you to get mad. I only bring the kids there in the day time, and only on Sunday. It's a different atmosphere at night. I'm going to change my clothes, wanna watch?"

"You bet I do, Fly Boy."

111

"Hey Jeff, what is that for?" Beth asked pointing to the curtain and the ceiling track.

He grinned. "It's for my Baby Cakes. Watch this dresser." He rolled it around. It wasn't a dresser. It had a bed inside. He placed a bright green spread over it, then he tossed around a pile of stuffed animals. He pulled the tropical print drapes around, and invited her in for a peek.

"Oh, my! It looks like a jungle in here!"

Jeff beamed. "She picked everything out herself. I'm glad she has some taste. I wouldn't have said no, even if she had wanted more pink frills and ruffles." He pulled the curtain away from the wall, and opened up the other doors showing Beth where Marianne's play clothes and shoes were, and her baskets of toys, dolls, and books.

"Over here is where Jason keeps his things." He was opening up the door on the opposite side of the room. Jason had clothes, books, and his bucket of cars. Jeff's eyes looked far away. "Beth, he's going to be twelve in a few months. Soon, he's not going to want these things. Gosh, they grow up so fast."

"For sure. So do you sleep in here with them?"

"No. Both kids were scared of Bucky. It worked out better to put them in here. I sleep on the hide a bed in the living room on the weekend. I don't want any crap about my little girl sleeping in the same room as me. I don't know about when Jason starts puberty…"

"Jeff, maybe our house will be built by then."

"Are you ready to go?" Jeff smiled.

"Give me a few minutes in the bathroom to freshen up, okay?"

"I wouldn't even attempt to stop you."

"Wise guy."

Chapter 11

Hand in hand they walked into the Alibi Inn. It was obvious within a minute that Jeff was well known in the place. The bartender yelled, "Hey! Mad Dog's back!"

"Hey Doug! How's it going?" Jeff led Beth over to the bar.

"Cool. The usual? And, how about your lady friend?" Doug smiled, his eyes nearly fell out of his head.

Jeff shook his head no, as he slipped his arm around Beth's shoulder, and introduced her as his old lady. Beth smiled as she elbowed Jeff, so he figured he'd better correct himself. "Doug, this is my ex-wife, Beth. She's the mother of my two children. Beth, this is Doug."

"Pleased to meet you, Ma'am. I can see why when he's with you, we never see him around this place."

"Thank you, Doug. It's a pleasure meeting you, too. Any friend of Jeff's is a friend of mine."

"Doug, send over a couple glasses of ice tea."

They found a booth, and sat down. Beth didn't think it was so bad, but she did agree with Jeff, it wasn't a good atmosphere for kids after dinner hour.

"Hi, Jeff, what can I get for you tonight? Coffee, tea, or me? What's goin' on, church in the morning?" She set both glasses of ice tea in front of Beth without acknowledging her presence.

"No, Moonbeam… Moonbeam? Weren't you Flower Pedal last week?"

"Ha, ha! They said you were too drunk to notice. Guess I won the bet this time. So seriously, what it'll be tonight? The usual? Double scotch on the rocks, with beer chasers?"

"Tea, I ordered ice tea."

"New York ice tea?"

Jeff was getting annoyed, "No! I've said it three times now, ice tea. That's tea with ice, a spritz of lemon and sugar. And if it's not too much trouble, I'd like a Bad Dog special, no onions, and extra cheese. What would you like Angel eyes?" Jeff asked Beth.

"I'll have the same, but put double onions on my Bad Dog, please." Beth smiled sweetly at the waitress, and then glared at Jeff, shaking her head in disbelief.

Jeff grinned at her, "What? Beth maybe this was a mistake bringing you here. Look, I had one beer the first night you stayed over, and haven't had anything since. You haven't seen me go through any alcohol withdrawals have you? I'm drinking tea tonight, it's probably the joke of the tavern. It's okay with me, let them laugh. I'm sitting with the most beautiful woman in the world. The men are envious, and the women are jealous because they don't measure up. Come on, Angel eyes, smile at me. Come on… they'll think we're married if you don't!"

Beth broke into a wide grin. "Madison, just wait til I get you home!"

"Shall I cancel our order?" He smiled back.

"Know what? If it wasn't for 'the curse' I'd say yes." She blew him a kiss, and looked coyly at him.

"You're breaking my heart." He smiled shaking his head.

Nobody could hear what they were saying over the loud music, but the pleasant smiles, silly grins and lingering gazes produced a lot of gossip among the Alibi Inn waitresses.

The new waitress was taking particular notice. She'd sworn vengeance on Mr. Madison, and she aimed to get it.

Beth was embarrassed that she'd ordered extra onions on her dog, and ended up scraping most of them off. "I'm sorry, I was just being rude." She giggled, when he smirked at her. She bit into the Bad Dog, and her eyes rolled. "Oh, my gosh, they're as good as Marianne said."

"Rianne? I knew Jason loved them since he was about seven, but my little girl likes them, too? Cool."

"Yes, she does. She just isn't as vocal as her brother. I miss the kids, Jeff. I've never been away from them for this many days, since my honeymoon. It's nice having the freedom, but I miss their hugs."

"Tell me about it. Would you like to dance?" Jeff bristled thinking of the fiasco prior to her "honeymoon."

Beth looked dreamily into his eyes. She couldn't remember the last time they danced… Yes, she did, it was in their home in Okinawa, before she got pregnant for Marianne. "Jeff, I would love to dance with you, next slow one, okay?"

He reached across the table, picked up both her hands, leaned in, and kissed them. Neither of them noticed that all the while, they were being observed by many, actually by all that knew him. There was much buzzing going on about the beautiful lady Jeff Madison was with. The talk was how he never took his eyes off of her. They were used to seeing him attract women in the bar. Many of them had gone home with him a time, or two, or more. Most often he'd be dancing with one, and winking at another across the room. But, he actually walked in hand in hand with this one, and never left her presence. The new gal felt the mystery woman might just hold the key to satisfying her wrath. She would have to talk to Doug later. They'd all seen Jeff introduce her to him. Everybody told Doug everything.

Finally, the band stopped playing rock 'n roll, and performed a ballad from the past. Jeff nodded toward the dance floor, and Beth smiled into his deep blue eyes. He walked behind her with his hands on her hips. When they reached the floor, Beth turned and slipped her arms around Jeff's neck. His arms were around her waist as his hands stroked her back. Both with their eyes shut, they swayed as one to the music. For all they knew they were the only two people on the dance floor, and maybe the only two people in the whole world. When the dance was over, Beth whispered in his ear, "Let's go home."

Jeff paid the tab and they left. They held hands. Beth just stared at his profile as he drove. He was still gorgeous, and her heart pounded thinking of lovemaking with him. She felt betrayed by her own body, but just being near him was a comfort. Jeff was so easy going and loveable. Beth wondered if anyone in the world disliked this man. She started to feel odd, "Jeff do you feel okay?"

"Sure sweetheart, don't you?" He glanced over at her. She looked panic stricken. Sweat was rolling down her face. "Beth, what's the matter?"

"I think I'm gonna throw up!"

Jeff slammed on the brakes. She opened the door just in time. He had a feeling of déjà vu. "Beth, what the hell brought that on? Geez… Are you pregnant?"

"NO, I'm not pregnant you ass! I'm on my period remember!"

Jeff felt like a jerk, then thought out loud, "I'm wondering if someone slipped something in your drink. If the food was bad, we'd both be sick." He kept thinking about the new waitress that brought over their last glasses of iced tea. She looked familiar, but he couldn't quite place her. He was glad Beth only took a swallow of the tea before they left, or this could be real serious. "Do you feel any better?"

Before she could answer, she got sick again. "My head's spinning bad, I feel jittery, the pain in my stomach is severe. Ohhh nooo!" She vomited again.

"Beth, I saw Jodi on a bad acid trip once. I want you to tell me if you think you see anything strange, or out of the norm, okay?"

"Who would do this to me?"

"Probably someone who wants to hurt me."

"Who would want to hurt you?"

"That's it! It was her!"

"Who, or what the hell are you talking about?"

"Remember the secretary I told you about? She's bleached and permed her hair, but I know it's her. She swore she'd get even with me for firing her. I bet she intended the tea for me. Do you think it's okay for me to start the car again?

"I think I'll be okay, now. I've barfed my guts out three times now. There isn't much else in there left to puke. That was a pretty gross thing to say, I'm sorry."

"Hey, I'm a grown up. I've seen it before."

"I don't want to hear about your drinking stories."

"I'm insulted." He wasn't smiling.

"Serious?"

"Yes, I'm serious." He still wasn't smiling.

"I apologize. Then, what are you talking about?"

"The time Jason double dog dared Rocky to eat a worm-"

"STOP!" Beth yelled clamping her hand over her mouth again.

He stopped. She barfed. Jeff kept quiet the rest of the way home. Jeff needed to have a talk with both Doug, and the manager, Mack. That chick was unstable and dangerous, to put it mildly. He'd have to go through his personnel records to look up her name, so he could prove it was her.

Beth had fallen asleep after the last stop. He whispered her name softly a few times to awaken her. "Oh, I feel better now. Glad that I didn't finish that tea, or I would've ended up in the hospital. How would I explain that one to Tom? This was no fun at all."

After they entered the apartment, and Beth had washed and rinsed her mouth, she asked, "Honey, do you have any music?"

Jeff selected several albums that he liked. He told her to take her pick then he went into the bathroom. She was flipping through them when the phone rang.

Beth's face was stone cold when he returned to the living room. "Beth, are you okay? You look like you're going to get sick again."

"Jeff, you just had a phone call. It was a woman. She tried to tell me she was Jodi. I told her I knew Jodi's voice, so I knew she was lying. She said and I quote, 'No matter. If you value your life, you'll stay away from him', then she hung up the phone."

"Are you scared?"

"Not unless she has a weapon. I had an older brother, remember? She comes near me, I'll kick her ass."

"You're tougher than many give you credit for being. With that threat, and the fact that you got that sick on one swallow of tea, it's my guess it's the waitress. Do you want me to call the police?"

"Oh hell no!" Beth looked as surprised as Jeff at how quickly she responded to that idea. "Tom gets pissed that I'm friends with Trina because she's separated. I'd hate to think of what would happen if he learned… Let's just scrap that cops idea." Beth's heart skipped a beat as she spotted an album they'd danced to years ago. It had French Café music, and it was her favorite. She looked up into Jeff's blue eyes and said breathlessly, "This one."

Jeff put the album on the stereo he'd sent home from Thailand. She was still feeling weak, so Jeff helped his beloved Beth into bed. He pledged his love to her until the day he died, and again thanked God for her, and his children. Beth told Jeff she loved him. She thanked God for him, and their children, and they both said, "Amen."

Beth used the electric can opener on a new canister of coffee, and got the pot brewing. As she stood staring into the refrigerator she stated, "Honey, we're out of everything. Can we go to the grocery store later?"

"Sure, Angel eyes, but we can 'do it' here at home now. We're almost remarr…"

Beth looked up to see why he stopped talking mid sentence. She felt so bad to see Jodi standing there with tears rolling down her cheeks. She wished she had on a robe instead of just Jeff's tee shirt, and panties. "Jodi, I'm so sorry, I didn't hear you come in. Please excuse me." Beth hurriedly walked past her, into Jeff's bedroom. Her heart was actually hurting for Jodi.

"Couldn't you at least have had the decency to call me, and tell me to stay away? I know I'll never replace your goddess, but I'm still a human being with feelings, even if you're not." Jodi turned around, and walked out.

Jeff sat at the breakfast table with a cup of coffee, and a piece of toast. He had his elbow on the table, and his chin in his hand. Beth came out of the bedroom, fully dressed, poured herself coffee, and warmed Jeff's cup.

"Thank you, Angel eyes," he spoke softly. "I am such an ass. I didn't mean to forget her. Beth, when I'm with you, the world stands still. I don't know how I held a job when we were married."

"I'm sorry, too. She must care for you very much. But, as for your job, you went to work out of fear. Fear for your life. You knew I'd love you to death if you stayed home day in and day out."

"Hmmm… That's cool with me. I've already promised to love you to the day I die. What a way to go!" He reached for her hand as she walked back to the table.

"Stop it," she giggled as he pulled her on his lap, and he kissed and nuzzled her neck. Beth kept giggling and squirming.

"Stop it? Who are you? I've never heard my Beth say stop it" in my life!" Before they knew it, the kitchen chair tipped over, and they both fell to the floor with three loud clunks.

The men downstairs glanced at the garage ceiling as they heard the loud, heavy thumps from above. Hank looked at Clark, Clark looked at Hank they just smirked, and shook their heads. The Ex-Madison's were going at it again, or so they thought.

"Jeff, please no. You know I don't fool around, this time of the month."

"Beth, how long is this going to go on? You've been here a month already. I want you, Angel eyes."

"A month! If it's been a month already where are the kids? Didn't we have children once upon a time?"

"Yeah, we did. Let's make some more," he grabbed, and tickled, and nipped as Beth tried unsuccessfully to wriggle away.

Beth reached for a pillow to smack him, and the box of records went sailing downward with a thud. Before she felt she had sufficiently pelted him enough times, the phone rang. As Jeff reached for the receiver, the phone hit the floor making the bell reverberate. "Hello!" Jeff answered.

"Jeff? Clark. Is everything okay up there? At first we thought, well then with the third clunk, and thrashing noises, we wondered... Well, never mind. You sound okay. See ya when you come to work. You are coming in, right? Just wondered if you needed any help."

"You wish! Bye"

"Who wishes what?"

"The guys wish they had the day off to fool around like their boss." He returned to tickle torturing Beth.

"Come on Jeff, knock it off now. You're not going to change my mind, and I'm starting to hurt. I haven't had any relief, you know."

"You're right, and I'm sorry. I'd be willing to do the deed, but I promised to respect your wishes." He paused, "I'm sad, our time is running out."

"Our time has just begun. That is, unless you've withdrawn your offer."

Jeff looked stricken. "Beth all I live for is the kids coming to visit me on the weekends, and the hope that you will come back to me." He kissed her as if he worshiped her, and perhaps he did. Jeff went to work and Beth went to the bathroom.

As she took her shower, she realized her monthly was over. There was no longer any question that Beth wanted to divorce Tom to be with her first love. Just being near him made her heart sing. But, thinking of Tom, she decided to call Trina.

"Hello, Beth! I was just picking up the phone to call you! I just hung up with Tom. He's irritated about the phone not being fixed yet. I told him it didn't matter because you were staying here with me. He asked if he could talk to you. As luck would have it, I'd just turned on the shower, and I know that he could hear it running. I told him I'd have you call him back as soon as you were out. How's it going over there? Getting laid?"

"Every chance I get." Beth lied. "I'm so glad I did this. I didn't realize how hollow my life has been since Jeff and I split up. I want to be with him all the time. So what number did Tom leave for me to reach him? Okay, got it. Did he say it was alright to call him any time? Crap… no matter what time I call, he'll be pissed. Thanks Trina. Talk to ya later. Bye"

Chapter 12

Beth took a deep breath and dialed the number, "Thomas Ericsen's room please."

"Hello, Ericsen speaking." A strictly business voice answered the phone.

"Hi Tom, Trina said you called while I was in the shower. How are you?"

"Beth, why can't you just stay at home like a good wife? What do you think it looks like for you to be staying at a divorcee's apartment while I'm out of town? Don't you have any respect for yourself? Obviously you have none for me."

"Tom, you didn't even say hello to me. I was scared to stay alone. I was afraid in the storm. You know how they frighten me. I didn't even have the use of a phone in case of an emergency, and my kids are out of town. I was scared to be by myself."

"I, I, I, me, me, me. Same old, same old. You act like I have you housed in the ghetto instead of in the most prestigious neighborhood in Centerville. You could be living up over a garage someplace, you know. Well, enough of that nonsense, the job here is almost wrapped up. I'll be home tomorrow evening at 7:00. Don't pick me up at the airport. I want you waiting for me in the bedroom. I'll light the candle. Love ya, kiss, kiss. Bye."

"Bye, Tom."

I hope it's good bye, she thought.

Jeff looked at Beth's face when she entered the office, and was on his feet immediately. He held out his arms as he walked toward her, "What's wrong?" He wondered if she got hurt when they fell off the chair. He asked Hank to listen for the phone as he took Beth's hand and they walked out the door.

"Let's go to a special place, Beth. I can't believe I forgot to show it to you the other day. That shoulder massage you gave while sitting on the rock distracted me."

They saw a big tree just past the stream. Jeff scooped her up in his arms and carried her across. His arms felt so good. He was so strong when he carried her over the threshold at each hotel they stayed at on their honeymoon, and when they moved into base housing. He felt like a man to her now, but she still adored him as much as when he was her lean twenty year old Fly Boy. She clung tightly to his neck, and didn't let go when he set her down on the other side. She kissed him long and deep, and he knew she loved him with all her heart.

"Come on," he whispered. Taking her hand again, he led her around to the back side of the tree. "Go ahead up!" He said pointing to a ladder.

"Jason never told me you built him a tree house."

"I didn't, I built it for Rianne. She's such a little rascal. I had all the material, and was going to have Hank and Clark help me build her a play house. Then she started in about wanting it in a tree. I can't say no to that kid. I'll build a little walking bridge over the stream when she gets a little bigger. So, what's going on? Something's wrong, I can read you like a book. Out with it."

She gave him a weak smile. "I, ummm, I just talked to Tom."

He let out a deep sigh. "He didn't figure out where you are did he?"

"No, but he expects me to be home when he gets there. He's taking a cab, and instructed me to be waiting... ready... when he comes in. I had planned on picking him up at the airport, and asking for a divorce on the way back. He'll be annoyed when I greet him at the door instead of in our bedroom."

"You're scared aren't you?"

"Yes."

"Why?"

"I don't know."

Beth looked around inside the tree house and silently admired how nice it was. She scooted the bean bag chair she'd flopped in closer to the one Jeff was in, and pulled him over, on top of herself. "No matter what happens, I want you to know, this is where I want to be."

Jeff felt insecure. He rolled back on his side, and pulled her close to him. "I love you, Angel eyes." They snuggled for a while, touched and kissed. She wanted him, and he knew it. She didn't say no, or don't, or stop. They completed their love making in the treehouse with the spring breeze gently cooling their naked skin. Neither expected or planned on it happening, but the spontaneity kindled their deepest passions.

Back in the office, Jeff was showing Beth the books. He was telling her that if she was interested, she could work in the office while the kids were in school. She told him it sounded like a grand idea to her since she missed using the skills she learned in business college, and she knew how much he preferred to work on the vehicles people brought in for service. She wondered if there would be a check in it for her, or if being in his presence was to be payment enough. He teased back that something could be worked out in trade. He reached for the phone.

"Madison Motors."

"Madison, I've got a warning for you. I know who 'she' is and where 'she' lives. I know 'she's' been shacking up with you for a week now. Personally, I couldn't care less, but I despise you so much that I want to see you suffer. Give her up, and everything will be fine. Ignore my demands, you'll have social services climbing all over your ass. There are child endangerment regulations that you can't pass. They'll learn of your excessive drinking, and the endless stream of women flowing through your revolving door. You'll lose all visiting privileges when they find out you screw around with your kids in the house. I can make it so you won't even have supervised visits with Marianne because she sleeps in your bedroom. Jason will hate you when he learns that you fuck his mother every chance you can get rid of him, and your whore of the moment. The best choice is, give up Beth Ericsen. That's right, I know her name, too. Don't forget, she's a rich man's wife. You've got twenty four hours to say good-bye. Good-bye."

Jeff hung up the phone, and was silent. Beth asked what the problem was. He told her it was a pushy salesman, so he hung up without saying a word after listening long enough. He asked Beth to handle the office. He transferred the phone lines to the floor, so she didn't have to be bothered with them. Sticking his head under the hood of a '66 goat, he got lost in tuning it's 389. This definitely was his favorite type of work.

Beth asked Jeff if he'd like a pizza for supper. When he said it was fine, she placed an order, then went upstairs. She could still hear the distinct roar of a muscle car engine. She knew he'd be dirty tonight. The pizza hadn't arrived yet, when he walked in the door. He was every bit as greasy as she expected him to be. She handed him a cold one, and he looked at her like he did when she was his new bride. It gave her butterflies.

"Hi, honey, I'm home," he kissed her on the cheek, and went into the shower. She joined him and they were as lusty as when they were teenagers. Even so, his heart was breaking, and he couldn't tell her why. Maybe it was just a hoax. Beth was the kids mother, and if she was there, and they showed social services the plans for the new house... He was very sure no matter what, it was going to be okay. There wasn't any sense in worrying Beth about a foolish nonsense call. But, still he worried.

They enjoyed the pizza, as they watched TV. News was sick. They were both ticked that the Viet Nam war was still unresolved, yet the blah blah blah about the White House Tapes dominated the news. Beth couldn't get over how upset Jeff was over the break in, and cover up. He was very angry that the Democratic headquarters had been burglarized, and he went off like a wild man about the wire tapping. "I don't give a flying fuck one way or the other about the Republicans, or the Democrats, it's simply unethical irregardless of who did it," he ranted. "It's prying into their right to privacy that's totally pissing me off." He declared as he grabbed a beer, chugged it down in one gulp, then crushed the can in his hand.

Beth hadn't seen him that agitated over current events since the problems in Montgomery, while they were still in Florida. During the commercial break, he was staring at Beth's face. She smiled and said, "Jeff, I know you weren't Army, but I'd like the right to pry into your privates." She still hadn't lost her ability to make him laugh when events out of his control got the best of him. He turned off the TV, and spent the rest of the evening holding, and kissing, loving and enjoying his wife's touch.

Beth baby oiled her hands, and massaged his body. Again, they melted into each other. It seemed she couldn't get enough of his lovemaking. Maybe tomorrow night when she came back, after she asked Tom for a divorce, they would never again have to think of saying good-bye. They fell asleep in a warm embrace after praying that God Bless them, and their children.

Beth got up realizing they never did make it to the grocery store the previous day. All there was to eat was the left over pizza. She found a baking sheet, and put the slices on it while the oven was preheating. She poured Jeff a cup of coffee as he had done for her on previous mornings. He looked so sad. She slipped her arms around his waist before he sat down, and nipped, and pulled the hair on his chest with her lips.

After they ate, he reached for the phone, "Hank, I won't be down at all today. I need to spend time with my wife. Thank you, I will. Later."

Beth asked if she could look at Jason and Marianne's things again. She missed her kids. They both went in the bedroom, and started going through the baskets. She laughed at the Rubby Dubby Scrubby doll's hair since it was almost rubbed off.

Jeff told her how Marianne kept begging him to play dollies with her one Sunday when Jason and Rocky were out back on the dirt bikes. "We ended up both putting on our swim suits, and filling the tub with as much water as it would hold with the two of us in there. We must've used a whole bottle of bubble bath, when she sat down the bubbles were up to her eyes. We blew them all over the bathroom. It took two days to get all the soap bubbles off of everything. She is so beautiful, smart and talented. And Jason, it's hard to believe how much I love that boy. I wish we could have more kids."

"I'm sure you would! You didn't have to walk around like an egret that swallowed a bowling ball. You're lucky you got the two you've got. You're right, if I knew then what I know now." Beth opened her lips.

Oh, yes, yes, yes, he thought, if we both knew then what we know now. His heart was full of love as he kept stroking her head, and her soft shining red hair.

The afternoon hours ticked on by. Beth and Jeff knew the time was near. He offered to go with her to face Tom, but she thought it best to go alone. If Tom wouldn't let her take a car, she would call Jeff for a ride. It looked like it was going to work out.

She got home safely, and walked around back. She remembered exactly which wire she had loosened, and tightened it back up. She checked the mail, throwing out the junk, and was on her way upstairs to put the rest of it on Tom's desk. She startled when the phone rang so quickly.

"Mrs. Ericsen?"

"Speaking."

"If it isn't 'thee' Mrs. Thomas Stephen Ericsen, Beth Ann Campbell Madison Ericsen. Well, well, well. So, you didn't listen to my warning. I told you to stay away from him, or else. Do you know what they call women that do what you just did? I mean really call them? I don't mean the usual bitch, slut, whore names, I mean what the officials call your type? Do you think that Tom will still keep you around if he learns you spent most of the past week fucking your ex-husband? Oh, don't panic, this isn't black mail. I'm not interested in your money. I'm only interested in making Jeffrey Vincent Madison's life as miserable as I possibly can. And how do I propose to do that? Simple. I go for the Achilles' heel every time. At first I thought his weakness for women would be his demise. Then I happened upon you. What a stroke of luck! When trying to kill you didn't work, I learned even more. Having you live, but not live with him would turn him into a habitually intoxicated, inebriated, drunken, low life, scum bag. By watching that happen, I can enjoy my handiwork for years to come. As for you, and what you really should be called, let me ask you this, when did you last speak to your children? Do they know who you slept with last night? How did you pay for your car repairs? Well, listen up Mrs. Ericsen, in addition to being a fine church going member of polite Centerville society, you are also an *unfit mother*. I've got enough verifiable facts in my notebook to make those kids wards of the state. You can kiss your fancy ass life as you know it good-bye."

"Who are you? What is it that you want, if you don't want money?" Beth was terrified at the thought of losing her children.

"Doesn't matter who I am. Give up Madison, and you keep your kids. Go back with him, the kids are gone. Simple as that. I informed him yesterday. Good-bye."

Beth immediately dialed Madison Motors.

Jeff's stomach hurt bad, he knew it was his nerves. He'd had one beer last night with Beth. He'd gone days without a drop, and didn't get the shakes, or foul tempered one time. He knew drinking wasn't the problem. He startled when the phone rang.

"Jeff, did you get a phone call from a woman yesterday about our kids?"

"Yes, I thought it was a hoax."

"I don't think so. This is what she said…" Beth repeated the conversation word for word. Jeff was silent. "Well? What do you think? I'm very concerned. I don't care about a scandal for me, I'm over my bitch, slut, whore persecution complex. But, I don't want to lose my children, or have a public exposition that could scar them for life. If I lose them, I'll crack up, and end up back in the hospital. I'll never get better if they take my babies away from me. Never. Jeff, I'm sooo scared."

"Beth please, relax. We have to think about this logically. Well, we could send the kids to France to live with my parents until this passes over."

"NO!!!!! I'll *die* without my babies." Beth was hysterical. "You're not taking my babies away from me!"

Jeff got a grip and firmed up. "Beth! Stop it! I'm not taking your babies. It was just a thought so that social services don't stick their nosey asses in our business. We can't risk losing our kids. What good would our life be together if we lose Jason and Rianne? I still think it's the former secretary that's behind this. On the outside chance that she could get the kids taken away from us, it would be better if you stay with Tom to throw off suspicion. If you go to your parents, and she finds out, and she will since she knows you were a Campbell, she'll put two and two together. She'll know we're still planning a reconciliation. Let's back off for now. I'll talk with a lawyer to find out what, if anything can be done. This may take awhile though. I know the difference between an alleged incident, and an actual occurrence. You are always in my heart. I love you, and I always will."

"Jeff, you mean everything to me. You are the love of my life. I want to be with you. I wish there was some other way. Please help me think of something. I don't want to send my kids away, but I'd do anything else I could to be back with you. I'm a good mother. My kids love me. I love them. I take good care of them. I don't want to go back to the hospital. This is tearing me up. I want my husband, my Jeff back, and my children with me. Oh, Tom is right! Everything that comes out of my mouth is I, I, I, me, me, me! I've gotta go. Bye."

Jeff put his head down on his desk, and cried.

Beth knew Tom did his best for her, and her children. Feeling hopeless, she did the only thing she could do now. She showered, put on black patent leather four inch spike healed pumps, and waited naked on the red satin sheets for Tom to come in, and light the candle. She knew what he liked, she knew what he expected, she knew the routine.

Tom gave her a box with an expensive trinket inside. "Babe, I'm sorry for scolding you on the phone. The client was being a pain in the neck and your call, well, it just came at a bad time. Please forgive me." He began to touch her very sensually. She missed Jeff so much. Beth recalled Jeff's lovemaking just days before on that very bed. Tom didn't have Jeff's gentle, loving touch, but he did arouse her, making her moan. Pushing lustily toward him, her body fervently responded to the erotic pleasure he was giving her. After losing all sense of self to hedonism, she lay breathless, her heart pounding wildly.

Knowing he had once again satisfied her, he smirked as he stated, "I know how to take care of *my* wife. I bet you couldn't wait for me to come home, to slip you that. Hmmm, Babe?"

"Yes, yes Tom, you're sooo good." She knew what he liked to hear, and she knew she didn't have to lie to say it. Beth hated that she enjoyed the power he had over her body. When Jeff made love to her, she felt like a loved woman. But, once Tom touched her, he had an animal magnetism that could trigger a burn within her that made her lust for his body like a wanton woman. Jeff satisfied her, but Tom… She would shamelessly beg for him. When she heard the rhythmic sound of his breathing, she knew he was asleep. Her tears began to drop. Silently, she prayed, "Dear God, Thank you for the time I had with my Jeff. Please help us through this mess. Bless him and our children. Amen"

Chapter 13

1975

"I'm sorry, Mr. Madison. With no police report, or any hospital records you have no evidence that an attempted poisoning ever took place. There is nothing we can do about the phone calls you received. Even if they had been recorded, they couldn't be used in a court of law." The attorneys words echoed in Jeff's head. As the time ticked by, hope diminished. Jeff downed a beer.

He had gone through the office files forward and backward, before emptying out the drawer, then he went through them one at a time. He found no personnel file on the secretary he suspected of blackmailing him and Beth. She must have removed her records before he'd fired her. He drank another beer, but it wasn't strong enough.

Jeff hadn't been back to the Alibi Inn since his meeting with the manager. Neither Mack, nor Doug would believe that DeeDee, the new waitress was capable of harming anyone. He had been a regular for years, and was probably their best customer, yet they doubted his word. He resented that. Jodi wouldn't speak to him as she was still ticked off for being dumped once again for the woman she referred to as "the goddess". It had been months since the threats. He was still being faithful to Beth, so it was best he stay away. He could drink at home and not worry about being on the road drunk. He understood Beth had to do, what she had to do. No matter what she did, she could never catch up to what he'd done. When the mess was cleared up, she would come back. He took another drink and began to fantasize. They would begin again, and start construction on their new home. Jason would be with him all the time. Marianne would be home before she made her First Communion. He had a tear in his eye as he pictured his little girl walking up the aisle in her white dress and veil, with her little praying hands folded, and her rosary beads wrapped around her fingers. Jason may even decide to take instruction, once he was away from Tom, and if Beth agreed. Jeff leaned back in his chair, chugged another beer, rubbed his eyes and continued to think. He reached in the small refrigerator, and pulled out two more beers. He had knocked back both of them before the crew had punched out, after saying goodnight.

Hank and Clark exchanged looks, then entered the office. "Jeff, what do ya say we get you upstairs?" Hank suggested. "It's not good for business when customers, see you passed out at your desk from the night before with an empty bottle of scotch clutched in your hand, and beer bottles strewn about first thing in the morning."

Jeff nodded, and each of the guys took an arm as they walked him up the stairs. They figured tomorrow was going to be another repeat of today, yesterday, last week, last month… The only time Jeff was coherent was when the kids were around. The boss worked double time then, trying his best to keep himself together, and spend quality time with his kids. As soon as they were gone, he was juiced up again.

Yet another night Jeff sat upstairs alone. He poured himself a shot, and chased it with a couple of beers. Jeff was in that twilight place in his mind where he still had memories, but wasn't fully alert. He slouched down on the couch, as he took another swallow of beer, then took a long drag off his cigarette. The silence was broken as a car came over the hill, the squeal of the brakes, and sound of the tires burning caused Jeff to sit bolt upright. He listened to the vehicle regain control, then screech around the curve. He let out a loud stress releasing breath. The noise brought him back to the accident in his youth, the one that stole his best friends life, the one that left Bev in a wheelchair and mentally disabled, the one that nearly got him sent up for contributing to the delinquency of a minor. What the hell was her name? Jeff could not remember. He couldn't remember back then, let alone fifteen years later. He stopped drinking, and went to bed. "Dear God, Every night I ask for my wife to come home. Lord please hear my prayer. Bless Beth, Jason, Marianne, my parents, my grandmother, and my in-laws. Amen."

"Bonjour."

"Bonjour, Maman! Comment va tu?"

"Mon petit bijou! Tres bien. Vous aussi?"

"Oui, Maman. Jason et Marianne est tres bien aussi. Et Grande-mère?"

"Comme ci comme ça."

"Je regret. Maman, je desire a parle avec mon père. Je t'aime beaucoup."

"Certainement, je t'aime beaucoup, aussi, mon petit garçon, au revoir… Vincent, c'est Jeffrey."

"Hi, Dad. How's it going? …Are you doing okay? …Are you taking your medicine? …Oh, quit your complaining, I'm not getting any either. Dad I have to ask you a tough question, I hate to open up old wounds, but, well, let me give you some background first."

Jeff lit a cigarette and began, "Last spring, Beth and I got back together. She was going to file for divorce from Tom. We were going to have a court house wedding to make it legal.

She and the kids were going to live here in the apartment until our new house was built... Well, it just didn't work out. It's deep. Got time to listen?"

"All I have is time Jeff. I'm intrigued. Shoot." Vince answered.

"Then I got a call from a woman making threats ordering me to break it off with Beth, or else risk getting the kids taken away from us. She listed charges of child endangerment, and morals issues involving Marianne, because she doesn't have a room of her own here. I didn't pay much attention, as I figured with Beth living here too, the children would never be unsupervised around the garage, and if need be she and Marianne could share a room, I could put Jason on the portable bed, and I could sleep on the couch. Beth doesn't have any hang ups about doin' it in the day time, so I figured what the hell, I'd come up for a battery recharge at noon... Dad, I'm not bragging... I am not... How can I be bragging, she isn't living here... Now you are being ridiculous! Have you paid any attention to anything I've been telling you besides that? Okay, so I pretty much brushed the call off as a hoax. The next day, Beth went back to the palace to wait for Tom to come back... He was away... On a business trip... No, Dad she doesn't sachet her ass over here every time he leaves, but I'd be a happy man if she did. No, I take that back, I really don't want to share, I want my wife back. Can I finish? Before he arrived she got a worse threatening phone call than I did. At first Beth thought the woman wanted to blackmail her for cash since she knew so much about who she is, where she lives, her parents, her overseer... Yeah, Tom. She asked when Beth last spoke with the kids, insinuating that she hadn't, and she was right. If they knew where she'd slept the past week, how she paid for her car repairs... Dad! I don't believe in divorce, as far as I'm concerned, she's still *my* wife... You sound like you agree with the-... Okay, apology accepted. Well Dad, she claimed she had enough information to accuse Beth of being an unfit mother. Her only demand was that we stay away from each other."

"Wow, Jeffrey, I didn't expect that ending. I've been disappointed in Beth because of the way she hurt you. But, that aside, she is an excellent mother. Thought for sure you were going to say that Tom found out, and was behind making the calls. Did you think about that?"

"Actually, no. It's a good point, but I'm sure I know who it is, kind of… A couple of years ago, I decided to hire a secretary to do the office work, and handle the telephones so I could spend more time in the shop, and on the '69 Camaro. Jason and I had so much fun test driving cars before we finally decided on that one. I want to keep it, got a gut feeling it's going to be a classic someday. There were women in and out of that office faster than the revolving door in my bedroom… Dad, it's a joke… No, I'm not bragging… Will you listen to me? Finally this one chick comes in with a resume that boasted business school. She had excellent personal references, and had worked in some impressive offices. She interviewed well, and said she liked to be around muscle cars. Everything checked out, and she came highly recommended. She was the first one that didn't neglect the office by spending more time in the shop trying to put her hands in my pockets… Just listen, okay?… I wasn't paying any attention this one day, so I didn't notice the blinds were pulled. I just walked into my own office, and found her sitting on the edge of my desk, spread eagle with her chicken legs wrapped around Jones' back. He's standing there, pants around his ankles, pounding her pistons, you know. I'm standing there looking at the ugliest, hairiest ass I've ever seen, and I lived in a military barracks for nearly two years before I married Beth. I fired them both, him much later on, her on the spot, I wrote her a check for two weeks severance pay, and told her to get the hell out. She swore vengeance."

"That hardly seems like enough to piss her off that bad, especially since you paid her severance. That wasn't required under the circumstances. Do you have any more on her than that?"

"You betcha. Last spring, I took Beth to the Alibi Inn for some of their Bad Dogs. I introduced Beth to Doug as my old lady. After getting the elbow, I clarified that she was my ex-wife, and my kids mother. I didn't want anything to drink, so we both had ice tea. I could see a thousand eyes on me because I'd never brought a date there before… Sorry, I don't consider Jodi a date… Hey, Beth walks in the door, Jodi and the others walk out… Well that's just too damn bad… It's just the way it is. Dad, I'm getting pissed… After we ate, we went out on the dance floor. Now I'm bragging, my wife wanted me and she wanted me bad. She wanted to go 'home'. On the way out the door, she took a swallow of the fresh ice tea brought over by the new waitress. On the drive back, she got sick, vomiting no less than three times, then she fell asleep. She was not feeling the greatest, but she felt well enough to- well, I'd better not brag. Since I wasn't sick, and we ate the same thing, process of elimination told us something had been slipped into her drink. Thank God she didn't finish it. Then on the other hand, a few swallows more, and she would have had to go to the hospital. We might have had grounds for an arrest if we had, but that would have opened up another can of worms when Tom found out she was with me. Any questions?"

"Well, I'm really confused, first you tell me about a woman blackmailing you, then you tell me about a secretary balling a shop hand, then you finish with a waitress. Just what does one story have to do with the other, and what question do you have for me that would open up an old wound?"

"Well, Dad, as it turns out I didn't recognize the waitress right away, because she got contact lenses, bleached her hair blonde, and got one of those new afro perms that the white chicks think we guys like. She was the secretary that once had a black bouffant hairdo, and dark horn rimmed glasses.

Now here is where it gets touchy. Last night, I was jolted by the sound of tires screeching and I had a flashback. The secretary/waitress is also the girl that was in the car with me in the accident when Chas died. She's the one whose parents filed the charges against me. Back then she had mousey brown hair, pink glasses, and braces on her teeth. It's her, no doubt in my mind. Dad, do you remember their name?"

"Jeff, you really didn't have sex with her, did you?" Vince sounded flabbergasted.

"Dad, I've been telling you that for fifteen years! I first met her that very morning when we skipped school. Chas made arrangements with Bev to meet him behind the Swing Bowl. Bev said yes, if she could bring a girlfriend. Then they wondered why I was half crazed when Phil had Trina fix me up with Beth. Do you remember her name?"

"Let me think… Her father was a Senior Master Sergeant going for Chief… Boyd? Boynton, was his name. Seems to me that his first name was Don… No! Dean, Dean Boynton. I don't remember the girl's name, son, sorry."

"Deana! That's it! Thank you, Sir, ummm Dad. At least I have a starting point now. Dad, please don't skip your medicine. I'm not ready to be an orphan yet. Kisses to Maman. Bye."

Jeff's head still felt heavy from the previous evenings drinking, but at least he started this morning with a cup of coffee instead of a beer. That was one of the best phone calls he'd made in a good long time. He was actually awake, and alert, and smiling when Hank, Clark, and Sam came in. They briefed him on what had been going on in the shop over the past few days. Some of it clicked some of it didn't. They were surprised, today wasn't going to be like yesterday.

"Hello, Hot Pants?"
"Yes? Hey! Is this you, Mad Dog?"
"None other, Trina! How the hell are you?"

"Happy in the sack, how about you?"

"Okay. Does that mean you and Phil are back together? Or is there a new roll in the hay?"

"I'm happy, that can only mean my Phil is back!"

"Congratulations. That gives me hope. Shall I send over another box of defective…"

"Jeff, you ass, shut up! No wonder Beth calls you a pig!"

"She does, huh? Well, maybe I'll have to give her a free demo on makin' bacon. Say, Trina, can you get a message to Beth for me without her warden finding out?"

"You couldn't mean Tom by any chance could you? Yeah, I can handle that. I'd cover for her again in a heartbeat if it meant her having another weekend away from that sorry bastard."

"Trina! That surprises me to hear you say that."

"Why? He'd be a nice guy if he'd come down off his high horse. Guess he can't help himself. From what I hear he's hung like a… around horses all of his life. Raised on a ranch, his folks had horses and ummm. So, uh, Jeff, shall I have her call you, or what would you like me to do. Really, anything. I don't like that man, and I know her well enough to see that she'd rather be with you. He gives her anything and everything, but it's only to make himself look good. I thought you two were getting back together last spring? Can you talk about it?"

"I really can't right now, Trina. It's twisted and I don't know if it can be straightened out. That's why I'd like to talk to my wife."

"Oh, Jeff, you really love her, don't you? You don't even know how much she needs you to love her. I'd take Phil back as a slob rather than put up with Tom on a good day. What shall I have her do?"

"I'd really like to see her again. I don't want to worry about the telephone. Old memories of the party line days I guess."

"Don't worry about a thing. I've got plenty of time to dream up a totally wild and devious plan. Phil hired a housekeeper to come in twice a week to give me a hand around here for taking him back. He'd rather pay than change his slovenly ways, I guess. In your own way, you're both PIGS!!! Love you, Mad. Bye."

"Bye, Hot Pants."

It was one of those mornings for Beth. She tried her best to stay calm, and stick to her routine. Tom was finally out the door after the long winded lecture he'd given Jason about his model car glue stinking up the whole house. And, how Jason needed to be just a tad more grateful that he was one of the kids that had parents that cared enough about his teeth to get them fixed. Marianne was still whining and carrying on about having to be at her dad's last weekend, and how boring it was just watching him and Jason blab about horse power when she wanted to be "riding a real horse with my new daddy". Tom had complained that his eggs were just slightly more than over easy, the toast wasn't quite golden enough, the bacon was too crisp, and the coffee was too strong... Oh, well at least he was going to be gone until tomorrow. Jason was spending the night at his buddy Nathan's, and Marianne had a pajama party to attend. *Hopefully, the topic of conversation at those things is still dolls and hair bows,* Beth thought, as she remembered her teen years. Once the kids were off to school, she continued to work out her frustration, by cleaning up the breakfast dishes. She then went upstairs, made beds, and scoured the bathrooms.

Before she could get in the shower the doorbell rang. She ran back down the stairs, and opened the door to a smiling delivery man with a familiar long white box.

"These are for you, Mrs. Ericsen. Your husband sure knows how to treat a lady! The only other women that get flowers as much as you, usually earn them with a black eye, or a bruise!"

140

Beth knew she was running late, but she needed her shower. Finally, she grabbed a cook book. She put the box of yellow roses in the backseat, and headed over to see what Trina was so hopped up about. Giving Trina a cooking lesson was their code for 'got a secret, wanna share, let's cook'. Tom had eased up on their continuing friendship since Phil moved back into the family home.

Trina met Beth at her car door, and was practically yanking her out of the seat, she was so excited. "Leave the stupid book in the car. Oh, goodie he sent flowers! That will save me a phone call."

Beth couldn't wait to find out just what Trina was so worked up about, and was giggling right along with her as they ran up the stairs. "Wow, Trina, the house looks beautiful."

"Thanks, it's not too bad keeping up with the daily stuff now that I have help with the heavy cleaning. Mrs. Baker comes in Monday through Friday, and can't believe what the place looks like again by Monday. You know Phil, he never wants me to lift a finger unless it's on him when he's home."

"Okay, Trina enough small talk, what's going on? You'll never convince me that you got me over here on the pretence of a cooking lesson just to show me your spotless house! What? What? What? Are you pregnant?"

"Arrrgh! Nooooo! Well, not yet anyway… maybe again… someday. We'll see. No! This is about you! And Jeff!"

"JEFF! Oh, my God. What? Just look at me shake! Did he call? Why did he call you instead of telling Jason to have me contact him? Is he okay? He's not getting married is he? IS HE?"

"Well, Beth, if you would shut up I could tell you. Evidently what he has to say is so private that he doesn't want to use the telephone. I'm surprised he trusted me with giving you a message again, but well face it, I'm his only safe link to you. Beth, I doubt he's getting married, I could hear in his voice how much he loves you."

"Good point, but let's not forget, I love him, but I'm still married to Tom. So what's the message?" Beth asked trying to recapture her happy mood.

"Beth he needs to see you. He didn't say why, but any time, any way, any day he want's to talk to you, face to face. I told him I'd think of a way, and did I think of a beaut!" Trina showed Beth the contents of a brief case she had packed, then unfolded her plot.

Beth was back in hysterics laughing at the depth of Trina's mischievous scheme, right down to the most minute detail. They went over the timing while whipping up a couple of quiches. They laughed about old times in Florida, and talked about their kids. Beth put the briefcase, a quiche, and the flowers from Tom in Trina's Skylark. They were giggling like school girls as Beth drove away waving good-bye.

"Good morning, Mrs. Ericsen. You'll never know how much the flowers you bring cheer up the lives of the elderly in this place. People get so busy with their lives that the families of some of these old folks only visit once a month. Flowers are such a kind gesture. After you're gone, they still have the yellow rose as a reminder that some one cared enough to spend a little time with them. The modern day meaning for yellow roses is 'friendship'."

"It certainly is a blessing for me to see smiles on their lonely faces. My husband is a very generous man." Beth smiled as she filled the bud vases with water, placed a rose in each one, then put them on a rolling cart with her purse and brief case. She thought about their meaning in days gone by, yellow roses meant 'decrease of love', or 'try to care'. Either way, it wasn't a comfort. She took the time to share pleasantries with each person, and gave each one a little peck on the cheek. The odd part was, even though she started doing this because she hated throwing the flowers away, she actually was starting to like visiting with the seniors.

It was nearly shift change when Beth had finished her visiting. She returned the cart, then took the brief case, and her purse into the ladies room.

"Hello, oh my, there's been a shift change! My name is Mrs. Phillips. I was just looking over your lovely facility. My mother is nearing 72 now, and we must be prepared... Thank you. Will keep in touch. Bye now."

"Thank you. We try." The girl at the desk smiled and nodded. A lot of people came in and out like that. She smiled sweetly again, and went back to her magazine.

Chapter 14

The guys lost track of how many days in a row Jeff had showed up on time, sober, and happy at the shop. Things were back to normal again. Once the filing was caught up, Jeff was back where he liked it best, under a hood, in it to his elbows, tuning an engine. The rumble seemed to make his heart beat a little faster. He thanked each of the guys, once again, for keeping it together for him while he was "out of it".

Nobody recognized the burnt orange colored car that drove into the yard. They were baffled when a dowdy middle aged woman marched in demanding to speak to the management about the shoddy work someone had done on her vehicle. The three men looked at each other and shrugged. None of them had ever seen that car before.

"Perhaps another shop did the work, Ma'am?" Hank insinuated she was at the wrong shop.

"You're trying to tell me I don't know where I took my own car? By the looks of the beer bottles in the trash around here, it appears that not one of you is sober enough to know what you've done. Is there a manager on sight? I demand satisfaction!"

"Yes, Ma'am. Through that door over there. He may be washing up, but he'll be with you in a minute. Go ahead on in." Sam, Hank, and Clark just shook their heads, as she stomped into the office.

"Glad the boss is sober having to deal with that bitch." Sam remarked with a devious grin.

"You got that right." Clark answered him.

Jeff had heard every word of the irate woman's tirade. Calmly he stood filing the previous days work orders. He lit a cigarette, took a drag, and then he turned his undivided attention to the lady.

"Yes, Ma'am?"

She started right in like she had with the crew, dissatisfaction, poor performance, second rate parts, she went on and on complaining. Jeff made mental note of each of the men's vehicles as they left the yard. His jaw grew tight. When he was alone with the woman, he looked her straight in the eye. He stated firmly, "No one in history has ever complained about poor performance in my place, and no woman ever leaves until they're satisfied." He crushed out his cigarette. "Lady, I'll show you which one of us has second rate parts!"

He walked around from behind his desk, and sauntered toward the chubby middle aged woman until he'd backed her into a corner. He placed one hand around the back of her head so she couldn't turn it one way, or the other. Quickly, his other hand reached up, and removed the fake teeth out of her mouth, before he kissed her with all of his heart and his soul.

"Beth, WHERE on this earth did you get those teeth?" he was laughing convulsively.

"When did you know?"

"The minute I saw you, but those teeth! Can I have them? I gotta use them to show Jason how much he needs his braces. Put on a little weight there haven't ya, butter ball?" He pinched her padded bottom.

"The minute you saw me!?! Sure you can have the teeth, but really how could you tell? I've never been fat, or grey, or worn glasses."

"Beth, Beth, Beth... You look exactly how I imagined you'd age when I used to stare at your face while you slept, way back when you were the size of a whale in '62, after I knocked you up. Once I got past the glasses, I knew it was you! But those teeth! Really they were the dead giveaway... You know everybody says Jason looks like me, but him without the braces, and you with those teeth, he's your son!" Jeff was laughing again.

"Jeff, I never wore braces, I didn't need braces."

"I did, and I needed them bad. He's got your face, but he's got my eyes, hair, and teeth. Want to come upstairs and eat some dinner with me? I've got some news." He tossed his coveralls in the laundry.

"That's what I'm here for."

"Food?"

"No, you goof!" She slipped her hand in his back pocket as they started up the stairs. Did she ever have butterflies! She wondered if they traveled in flocks or herds... They were no sooner in the door, and she was all over him. Her lips and her mouth were on his as she friskily clawed at his clothes with her hands.

"Beth, can I at least say 'I love you', before you ravish me? How long do you have?" Jeff couldn't get over her aggressiveness. "Can I shower first?"

"I only have a few hours, please Jeff, I don't want to waste a precious moment." She was down to her underwear, and reaching back to unhook. One look at her breasts, and he was hers. Collapsed and spent, on the couch, she held his face in her hands, and kissed him tenderly. "Jeffrey Madison, you are the love of my life. Ready for your shower now?"

"A shower sounds wonderful, but I'm half starved to death. Let's see what I can whip up."

"Wish I had my riding habit teddy, with the satin ribbon crop. I'd whip you up one side, and down the other. Tell you what, my love, in the car there's something for you. It's in a casserole dish wrapped in some towels. You go get it, and I'll run us a bath…"

Jeff looked adoringly at his wife for making him a quiche. His Beth made it special for him. He was moved to emotion, and he loved her with all of his heart for the care she put into pleasing him. "Beth, I just don't know how to put into words how much you mean to me. I swear, I'll love you until the day I die." He reached across the table, picked up her hand and kissed it.

They luxuriously played in the bath lit by candle light, until the warm water cooled. Their eyes were locked on each other as they washed, and closed as their lips touched. Dripping wet, still embracing, they fell into bed.

His heart was full. He felt her familiar tremble as his finger tips ran along the soft curves of her body. He touched her special places, and thrilled at hearing her delightful noises that he remembered so well.

Her heart was free to enjoy the arousing bliss his strong, but gentle hands gave her. She enjoyed hearing his breathing intensify, and quivered while touching him fervently as his desire passionately grew.

They came together as they had so many times before. They rocked on and on. Stretched out across the big bed in a loving embrace, they wondered why they ever had to leave the comfort of each others arms. They shared love, and they shared tears, and they shared more love.

"Beth, I needed to know that you still wanted to come home. I found out who the secretary/waitress is. There is nothing we can do legally, but now that I know who she is, maybe I can find out why she is so hateful. Maybe I can reason with her. Her name is, or was Deana Boynton. She goes by

DeeDee now. She was the girl that was with me in the car accident when Chas died. I went to the Alibi Inn to talk to Mack about the night you got poisoned. He didn't want to believe me… she's screwing him. We guys get kind of nuts when we get a sniff sometimes. I talked to Doug a bit. Seems she pumped him for all the information she could get. He thinks she's harmless, thinks she was just trying to get to know the regulars. She asked Jodi a million questions, too, and since she was still mad at me for not telling her about us, she spilled her guts. She's since realized it was a mistake talking to her, but it's too late now."

"So, are you seeing Jodi again?"

"No, Beth. I haven't been with a woman since we were together last spring. I've drunk myself silly, but I have been faithful to you."

Beth cried and cried. Jeff tried to console her, but she covered her face with her hands, hung her head, and sobbed. "What have I done? What have I done?"

"Beth… Angel eyes, I understand. He's your husband. You can't not… I don't like to think about it, so I don't. I live for the day you're back with me, so we can finish raising our kids, and get on with our life. Angel eyes, I want to grow old with you. I want to go from rockin' to the rocker with my Beth. As ridiculous as you looked this afternoon in that grey wig and glasses, and those frumpy clothes, you still turned me on. From the minute you walked into the shop, all I wanted to do was get rid of those teeth, I couldn't wait to kiss you… and to feel you up to find out how much of that was real fat. Hey, Beth, do you think you could put the teeth back in and, well, kinda work your way down?"

Whack! The pillow swung. "Not this time, Mad Dog! I want you, I want your tender touch, I want your hard body. Kiss me, now, Fly Boy." The Ex-Madison's didn't waste one precious moment.

Beth, dressed in her wig and glasses, left Versailles and headed back to Trina's. As she turned the corner, she pulled off the glasses and the wig. She stuffed them in the glove box when she parked the car, she swapped the keys in the secret hiding place, and drove off in her Cadillac. She waited for Jeff's next message.

As the months kept passing, and no progress was being made toward reconciliation, Jeff's drinking again began to increase. The crew was at a loss for what to do except what they had always done in the past. It was getting more difficult. Jeffrey Madison was known throughout the area as "the best" when it came to auto mechanics. They were proud to be a part of his business life. They knew they were no part of his private life, but something had to be done.

Hank, Clark and Sam headed for the Alibi Inn, and asked for Jodi's booth. It was a long shot, but what the hell, she knew him better than anyone except for his demigoddess, the former Mrs. Madison. There was no communication allowed with that woman once she drove off the property. Jodi was their best chance to reach him before he totally lost it all.

"Well, far out! If it isn't the back bone of Madison Motors all at once sitting right here at my booth! It's so good to see you guys! How have you all been? Hey, let me take your order, then we can chat."

Jodi brought them their beers and scooted off without any chat. The guys didn't know what to make of that. So, they decided to try to hatch plan B. A few minutes later Jodi emerged in a ribbon skirt, and peasant blouse.

"Hey, fella's, sorry about that. Shift change, and Mack's broad won't tolerate an extra minute on the clock. I had to punch out. Now here's the real kicker... We aren't allowed to stay after we are off the clock in the same clothes we wore while working. I don't know how she comes up with this crap. She's driving this place into the ground and Mack's got his head so far up her… Oops, I better be quiet." Her eyes darted around. "Well, you're all lookin' good! How 'bout I slink in here next to you, Sammy?"

"Only if ya sit real close, sugar britches."

Hank began, "Jodi, it's Jeff, he's-"

"He's in here three times a week sniffing around DeeDee Dixon. I haven't seen him on any other chick's scent like that, with the exception of his beloved goddess, the mother of his progeny, his baby cakes, and the golden boy. He doesn't seem to get the hint, DeeDee isn't interested in him as a lover. She's got a bigger fish to fry with Mack in the sack. He's ruining his reputation around here as the bars number one stud muffin, the way he keeps striking out. Since it was over six months that he didn't even cross the doorway around here, the young stuff don't even know who the hell he is. I'm usually out of here before he shows up. I'm on day shift now. I've been going to school nights. So what's up with you guys?"

Sam had been rubbing her neck, shoulder, and upper arm with his finger tips while she talked. He then began consoling her with his sympathy for how poorly she had been treated, but thought she might be a little too harsh. Everyone knew Beth was always going to be in Jeff's heart. No doubt the boss was whipped, if he couldn't see that Jodi was the better pick. Sam side glanced Hank to pick up the ball, and run from there. Sam kept up the sensuous touching.

"Jodi, if we don't do something, Jeff is going to lose the shop. He's drunk five days out of seven, but he's totally devoted to his kids the two days he's sober. It's not for him we're asking you this favor. It's for us. I've known him the longest. I've got a good wife, twin girls, soon to be teenagers, but I still have a mortgage. Clark's oldest son wants to go in the military, but the youngest wants to go to the police academy, it's not free. His wife works part time at Clown Town, and wants to go back to school when the kids are on their own. Sammy was married to two piranhas, by the time he's done paying child support, he's lucky to make rent, and his Hog payment. Jodi, we need our jobs…" Hank pleaded.

"So what do you want me to do? Take up a collection, or go to church and light a candle? Really, I don't know what you expect of me. He cast me aside, and I'm on my own, too. Does any one ever think to ask about Jodi? Happy, smiley, hippy chick, Jodi? What do any of you know about me, besides I was Jeff Madison's main throw for five years, and I'm the mother of a fatherless son… I hear no comment's. None of you knows, or cares a damn thing about me! Do I cease to exist without Jeff?"

"Jodi, you're right. We've been unfair to you. None of us know a thing about you, or if Rocky even knows who is father is."

"Do you think I don't know who Rocky's father is? Well, I do! Rocky's father knows he has a son, and he loves him as much as any of you love your kids. Stan came home from Nam with a drug problem, and he's doing time because of it. I love him, I will always love him, but I doubt we could ever have a life together. Jeff fulfilled my needs, and I cared for him a lot. I knew he didn't love me, nor me him. I just thought I deserved better than to walk in and find him playing house with the little woman. Silly me." Jodi ranted sarcastically.

Clark responded, "Jodi, we're sorry, truly sorry, but let me explain. We work for Jeff, he signs our pay checks. How would it look if we as married men, except Sam, tried to get to know the bosses chick? Come on. I don't think I've ever treated you with disrespect, but if I have, I apologize. So, now you hate him, and don't care that the best engine mechanic in the county is going down in a heap fast?"

"I didn't say I hated him. I just don't understand what it is that you want from me."

"We were thinking of having a small thirteenth birthday party for Jason. Have it be a surprise for the kid, and his dad. Maybe if we can keep Jeff sober long enough, he can see that he does have a support group that cares for him, and he'll snap out of it. He was doing great, then he completely fell off the wagon. Never seen him this low. Would you call the ex-Mrs. to see if she'll give you a few of the kid's friends names, and phone numbers? And without a doubt, you and Rocky are to be there, that is if you care to be…"

Jodi thought it over carefully. She liked the guys, and understood how they felt. She'd known Jason since he was six, or seven years old. She agreed to make the call for them. Jodi took a long deep breath, and let it out before dialing the phone.

"Hello."

"Hello. Is Mrs. Ericsen there please?"

"Yes, she is."

Clunk.

Ring.

"Hello?"

"Hello. Is Mrs. Ericsen there please?"

"Yes, she is."

Clunk.

Ring.

"Hello?"

"Jason Madison! Don't you dare hang up on me again, or I'll…"

"You'll what, Jodi? Tell my mom you fed me Puffy Sugar Bites, Bad Dogs, and let me sip your beer? I didn't do anything wrong, you asked if she was here, I told you she was. You never said you wanted to talk to her! Hold on a minute while I go get her." Jason was laughing.

"You hang up the phone as soon as she picks up, you got that mister wise guy?"

"Yep, hold on… MOMMMMEEEEE, IT'S ONE OF THE TRAMPS MY DADDY SLEEPS WITH. PICK UP THE PHONE! I miss you Jodi. How's Rocky?"

"I don't know why, but I miss you, too, you stinker. Rocky's fine, and he misses you, too."

"Hello?" Beth answered wondering who it was.

"Hello, Beth, this is Jodi... Jason! Hang up the phone, and before you start with that mouth, I know I'm not your mother, just do it because I said so, or I'll spit on your Bad Dog next time your father brings you in. Hang it up, please!"

Clunk.

"Beth, I'm sorry to bother you-"

Click...

"JASON Charles Madison! I *am* your mother. Hang it up if you know what's good for you, buster! Tom is coming home tonight."

Clunk.

"Beth, Jeff's crew wanted me to ask you for a couple of Jason's buddies names and numbers. They'd like to have a little surprise birthday party for him. This one is a milestone. The stinker is soon to be a teenager, look out world!"

"Yeah, tell me about it! He can be a hand full, but he's still my baby boy. How's your son? Will he be there?"

"Rocky is fine. I'm hoping he can meet his dad again soon. I haven't mentioned Jason's party to him yet. If he hears about it, I know he will start pestering me, and he won't let up until I cave in, and say yes."

"Is there a reason why you don't want him to go to my son's party?"

"I haven't seen Jason's dad since, well, since the last time I saw you."

"I'm so sorry about that. Jeff really should have told you that I was staying there- Oh, my gosh, what did I just say! Tom... doesn't know. He never even found out... about... the car breaking down... Please, Jodi, I'm at your mercy..." Beth was gasping.

"Shhh, Beth, calm down. Did anyone hear you say that?"

"Oh, I don't know... Marianne is outside riding her bike, and I don't know where Jason is..."

"Don't worry if he heard you, you'd know it by now. Tom isn't home you said, so your secret is safe. I'm not your rival... I'm not in love with Jeff. I care about him, but we were never exclusive, no strings, no pressure, no commitment. He's not cruel, but sometimes he's thoughtless..." Jodi lit a cigarette, and went on. "About Rocky at the party, Jeff doesn't like Rocky around without me there. Rocky is a bit on the hyper side to put it mildly. I think it's a food allergy, but I can't get him to give up Popsicle's. I'll have to think about it."

"I understand. Let me give you the phone numbers for Todd's, and Nathan's parents. Would you like me to give them a call first to let them know you will be getting in touch with them?"

"Good idea."

"And Jodi, thanks, for everything."

Chapter 15

It may have been because Sam was also divorced that Jeff seemed to relate better to him in certain life situations. Sam volunteered to go in early, to head Jeff off at the pass so to speak, before he had a beer for breakfast.

Jeff groaned as he heard the unrelentless pounding on the door. He finally dragged himself out of bed to see who was there before 7:00 a.m. He shot Sam the 'there better be a good reason for this' glare.

"What? Mad, yer not ready yet? Thought ya said we're headin' out early today to preview the cars for next weeks auction. Geez, I could uh smoked three more joints last night, and banged another chick if I'd uh known you were gonna be a screw off today." Sam looked put out.

"I don't remember making any plans about going to any auction today."

"No shit? Look at this place. Did ya have the Olympic drinkin' team up here last night? If my parents would uh known you were gonna be born, they could uh invested in hops, 'n I'd be easy ridin' in Hog heaven today. Here, man, I brought ya a cup of coffee."

"Nah, I'll just have a beer."

"Nah, I'll just have a beer…" Sam mocked. "Hey boss, why don't ya turn over a new leaf…"

"Sam… Don't mess in my personal life."

"Hey, man cool yer jets! I meant leaf…" Sam grinned, and pulled out a nickle bag from the inside of his boot. "Don't tell me you never tried it… I know better. You were in Nam. Drink the coffee while I roll one."

Sam smirked knowing there were no plans to go view cars for the auction, but hey, there could have been. Sam took a deep drag while Jeff lit a cigarette. He blew on the lit end to burn off the paper, then he handed it to Jeff. He took a long, deep drag, and held it in his lungs. He passed it back to Sam who took a hit, then he handed it back to Jeff. Sam excused himself to the bathroom, figuring Jeff would have it half gone by the time he returned. He was right, he suggested Jeff put on a tee shirt so they could get over to Auction Auto. He took another toke before pinching it out, then hid the roach on the inside of his hat band.

The ride over was a hoot. Sam stopped at Dippy Donuts for more coffee, and some doughnuts. It was a hot, muggy day, and the ceiling fans were gently spinning. Jeff remarked that the timing of the music was perfect for the rotation of the blades. Sam told him there was no music playing, and to shut the hell up. He opted that take out would be best. They did have a good day hanging out doing guy things. They made it to Auction Auto, and thought it would be a great idea to come back for the auction next week. There were some good parts vehicles, and a few cars that both guys believed would be collectibles someday. Jeff was almost straightened out by noon. They stopped by the Alibi Inn for food. Sam marched right over to Jodi's booth, and slid in. Jeff saw DeeDee, and nearly freaked. Sam told him to cool it, she was the managers girlfriend. Jeff figured Mack had to be pretty hard up to lower himself to banging that broad. Just as planned, Jodi brought over two colas, but Jeff insisted he didn't want his. He wanted a beer in an unopened bottle. Sam suggested if he wanted something in an unopened container it should be a soda though... it might not be a good idea to mix weed with beer. Jodi rolled her eyes at that one, but Sam winked at her, and she got the drift. She brought their Dogs, and another unopened can of cola for Jeff. He didn't miss Sam watching Jodi's back side, as she walked toward another booth.

"She is cute." Jeff commented.

"That she is Dog. She has a heart of gold, too. I'd like to slither right up next to that heart, 'n take a bite. She's been hurt enough. I'm as much of uh snake as you are, but, I don't wanna mess with that one. I dig unsatisfied in the sack, married women. They're more than willing to put out, and some other sucker supports their ass." Sam took a drag off his cigarette.

"What d'ya mean, snake?" Jeff asked bluntly.

"It uh, don't bother me if they're married... It bothers you."

"The only married woman I mess with is my wife."

"She ain't your wife no more Mad, ya know. It's over, ya know... Like the War. Over."

"Don't rub it in. Jason's coming tomorrow, I want to be sober."

"That's why you're with me today. So, what's wrong with Jodi?"

"Not a damn thing." Jeff answered honestly.

"The way you live ain't normal, Mad. Your biggest problem is, you need to get laid, ya know. Think about it. If you don't change your mind, I might change mine. Might be awhile before her kid's old man is back. She might not be as hard up as the married broads, but she's not lookin' for a commitment, or any emotional involvement either." Sam butted out his cigarette, and immediately lit up another.

Hank had pizzas delivered, and had all kinds of munchies set up on the table, and a variety of soda on the counter tops. Trina brought both Todd, and Nathan from church, over to the garage before Sam and Jeff returned from their day journey through man land. Clark made the arrangements to pick up Jason from Beth and Tom's place. He told Jason that Jeff and Sam were still at the auction lot, so his dad couldn't pick him up. Jodi and Rocky brought a personalized cake. Sam and Jeff returned before Jason and Clark arrived. Making an excuse that he'd left his Zig Zag papers on the table, Sam said he wanted to come up to get them, so he wasn't late for his date by having to stop to buy more. Jeff was shocked to see Hank, Jodi, and the three boys sitting in his apartment.

"Jeff, we wanted to do somethin' for Jason. He's a teenager now. This is when God gets even for all the shit you pulled on your folks" Sam grinned.

"Jason isn't coming until tomorrow at noon."

"Wrong again! He and Clark should be driving up at any moment- and here they are!" Hank said, watching the driveway from the window.

The guys had chipped in to buy a top of the line slot car race set for Jason, and he was as happy as a thirteen year old boy could get. They ate pizza, and drank soda pop. Jason rolled his eye balls as Jodi insisted that they sing *Happy Birthday to You*, and that he blow out his candles. The coolest was that the boys had brought their sleeping bags, and they were going to spend the night in the tree house. Jeff was impressed at the length his friends had gone through to pull off a surprise like this for his son. The three older boys were settled in the tree house, with plenty of chips, dip, other munchies, and a cooler full of sodas that Jodi had packed for them. Assured that they were safe and settled, the adults went back upstairs.

Before it was dark, the three men left. Jodi and Rocky lingered behind. Jodi's eyes welled up with tears, and her throat was tight. But, neither a tear rolled down her cheek, nor a sob came from her throat, as she picked up her purse and keys.

"Jodi, Rocky is so much younger than the other boys. If you'd like to stay, he'd probably get a kick out of being with the big guys. He can use Rianne's sleeping bag. I, ummm, I'd enjoy your company."

Joyously, Rocky was on his way to the tree house. Jodi was stunned at Jeff's words. Her tears began to flow.

"Jodi, no promises, okay? No strings, no pressure, no commitment." He kissed the top of her head, and rubbed her back.

Jodi nodded her head yes, as her arms slipped around his waist.

Nathan had taken Rocky to the downstairs bathroom in Jeff's office. Jason and Todd filled the odd shaped balloons that Todd had found while snooping through Jeff's night stand with water from the hose. The boys hurriedly ran back up into the tree house. Nathan challenged Rocky to a foot race to the tree. Nathan was as fast as the wind, and made it up the ladder into the treehouse as Rocky was still coming across the wooden bridge. Armed with two water balloons apiece, they each pelted the nine year old one at a time until their weapons were gone. Rocky was soaked, but he would have died before letting the big boys see him cry, so he took it like a man. The older guys were rolling with laughter. Rocky pulled a half pack of Lucky's out of his knapsack, then asked if any of them had a match. "Oh, never mind." He'd pulled a lighter from his pocket. The big boy's eyes popped when they saw Rocky light up, and inhale before he offered the rest of them a smoke. Not to be out done by the baby, they each took a cigarette. Jason noticed they were the same brand his dad smoked. He wondered if he looked as cool as Jeff did smoking. They told ghost stories. Rocky crawled inside the sleeping bag, and fell asleep. They smoked the rest of the pack, and wondered how a kid of that age bought cigarettes.

Nathan fell asleep next, and kept groaning whenever Todd and Jason burst into fits of laughter watching Rocky squirm as they tickled him with pieces of popcorn dangling from strings. They decided to let the two party poopers sleep. Silently, they snuck out of the tree house. Up the long driveway they walked, and didn't stop until they got into town. Once they were out of the yard, Todd began to grumble. He was visibly agitated, and Jason was becoming annoyed with his behavior. Finally Todd let loose with a string of profanities about that little kid Rocky having cigarettes.

"Well, as long as that's all that's bugging ya… I thought that I'd done something to piss you off. You're making my birthday a bummer. Get your act together, or let's go back." Jason stated bluntly, sounding like Jeff.

"Got any money on ya?"

"I got about three dollars and some change. Why?"

"There's a Dippy Donut's around the corner, just a block off Main Street. I think we can get some there."

"Doughnuts?"

"No. Ya jerk! Cigarettes! We need exact change for the machine though, to not attract any extra attention. That is if ya wanna spend some of that birthday money you got. Did you think I looked like my dad when I smoked? You sure looked like Jeff. If you'd looked any more like him, people would start calling you Mr. Madison every time you smoked."

Jason reached in his pocket. Besides his dollars, he had a couple of quarters, two dimes and a nickle. He held it in his hand as Todd reached into his pocket, and pulled out his change. Todd told Jason to go in, start ordering a dozen doughnuts, mixed variety, and keep changing his mind, until he got inside. Jason kept flip flopping his order as he did with Jodi sometimes, and was amused at how the girl behind the counter was getting as flustered as Jodi would. Just as Todd walked in looking as puffed up as the Chief of Supply, Jason had finally decided, and had ordered two hot chocolates. As the boys were leaving Dippy Donut's, two policemen walked in. Todd looked at them, and smiled politely, "Good evening, officers! Quiet night on the beat, I hope?"

"So far, so good, son. It's early though. Hope you left a couple of doughnuts for us! Be careful on your way home, boys."

"We will. Thank you, sir."

"Todd! You are such a dope! Why did you talk to those cops when you got cigarettes on you? Are you a total idiot?"

"Jason, you look 'em straight in the eye, and talk to them like they're military officers... they all wear uniforms. They all fall for the same line of bull, 'Good Morning, sir. Good Evening, sir. Yes, sir. No, sir. There's no excuse, sir. Thank you, sir. No, thank you, sir. Will that be all, sir?' Trust me on this one, Jason. Gimme a cocoa. You got any matches?"

"Yeah, I stole some from Rocky's knapsack before we left."

"Dang! I even hate to use them just cuz they're his. Why do we hafta depend on that baby for everything? It's as disgusting as having to rely on your sister!"

"Well, Rianne comes in handy sometimes when it comes to getting stuff out of Tom. She's got him wrapped around her little finger so all I gotta do is convince her that what I want, or need is gonna benefit her, too. Then it's a done deal." Jason had it down to a science.

"Still in all, I'm glad my parents weren't stupid enough to have another kid. I like being the only one. It was really cool when they were split up for awhile. Dad took me to far out places just to piss mom off, and she used his credit card to get me a Space Landing Station for my Galaxy Travel Collection. Played 'em both 'til they got back together. Damn! Wish we had a lighter."

"Look, do ya want the damn matches or not? So what if they're Rocky's? We got 'em now. It's not like he can use 'em, we smoked all his cigarettes. I paid for half the pack, I want my half. They'd better be Lucky's."

"Yeah, they're Lucky's. Figured we'd better get the same kind your old man smokes. If we get caught, we can just lie, and say we bought them for him. I'm a Camel man myself."

"I believe it. You got the breath, and the fleas."

"Shut up!"

"You shut up."

"I said shut up first, so you shut up."

The boys walked to the Depot, and watched the trains pull in and out. They talked about what they thought it would be like to be a hobo, seeing the country that way. Todd said he preferred being in the military. It would be boring living in one place all the time. He liked it that every few years they moved some place new. Jason told him he kind of remembered living in Florida, and felt good about that. Something about Okinawa rubbed him the wrong way, but he was glad that they moved back stateside. He didn't like that his parents split up. And, he thought his step father was a jerk, but he liked his money. They threw the empty doughnut bag, and their cocoa cups away. They each smoked another cigarette, and headed out. Not really knowing where they were going, they took a short cut back to Main Street, and unwittingly walked straight across the red light district. Although the boys wide eyes took in all the action, they wandered through virtually unnoticed, as the police were busy picking up drunks, and busting johns.

Feeling it was way too early to go back to the tree house, they headed straight over to the elementary school playground to check out the new broad jump pit. As they approached, they saw two people wrestling on a blanket in the sand.

Todd said in a coarse whisper, "Mad, hit the dirt!"

Both boys dropped, and crawled commando style to investigate. Inching closer they noticed it was a teenage boy and girl. They watched silently as the couple got up, and dragged the blanket into the woods totally unaware that they were being observed. The boys continued their recon mission following about thirty feet in the rears. Cloaked in darkness, stealthily like cats, they approached the broad jump. They hit pay dirt. The boys discovered the holy grail of treasures. Left behind were six unopened long neck brown bottles, which they immediately confiscated as spoils of war. Pleased with their loot, they retreated to their private fortress deep in the woods where they had found the remains of an old 1800's farm house. Todd retrieved his Swiss Army knife from his pocket, and used the bottle opener. After he popped two bottles, he handed one to Jason.

Jason knocked back a few swigs then stated, "A cigarette always goes good with a cold beer. Let's have a smoke." He reached in his shirt pocket, and found they only had two cigarettes left. He gave Todd one. He lit his own cigarette, and blew out the match before he realized it was the last one. Todd was ticked. Jason told him to cool his jets. He snatched the cigarette out of Todd's hand, and put it in his mouth. Jason lit it off of his own cigarette. Todd stared in wonderment at the skill, and ease that Jason accomplished that feat. He knew it must be really something to be thirteen. They sat on what was left of the old fire place hearth, and talked of things that only young boys on their own in the woods can understand. After they finished the remainder of their beer, they were ready to head back to the auto shop. Before they were completely out of the woods, they both heard the unmistakable noise of rustling brush, breaking twigs, and a female voice repeatedly hollering "Ohhh". Once again, like soldiers trained to operate inside enemy territory, they moved clandestinely through the woods until they rediscovered the couple that had just left the broad jump.

"Madison! Search and rescue!"

"Phillips! Shut up!"

"Insubordination! You shut up! He's attacking that girl, we gotta save her!"

"No, you shut up. Idiot! They aren't fighting! Let's get the hell out of here, before they catch us watching them like we're a couple uh kids, and we get the crap beat out of us." Knowing what he'd just seen, Jason felt a twitch in his jeans. He began to grasp what his dad meant when he talked to him about sex a few years ago after Jason caught him naked with that woman.

Jason nearly dragged Todd out of the woods with his hand clasped over his mouth. Jason started ragging on him on the walk back. "Geez Todd, I thought you knew something. Didn't your dad talk to you yet? Mine talked to me when I was eleven. That's a whole year younger than you are now. I'd tell you, but hey, it ain't my job. You better stick with working in Supply, boy. Issuing condoms, cigarettes, and beer are your strong suits. Stay away from Vehicle Maintenance. You don't even know headlights from a tail pipe- and at your age! Geez! Even Rocky would uh known he was rockin' her chassis. And Nathan would, too, and all he does is go to church."

They walked quietly toward home for awhile. Finally Todd broke the silence, "Jase, what's a condom?"

"Are you kidding me?"

"Okay Mr. Know It All, if you don't wanna tell me, fine. I'll ask Mom at church in front of everybody. ...And, I'll tell her you told me to ask."

"The water balloons you found in my dad's drawer... they weren't water balloons, okay? They were condoms. Men use them for birth control. They're probably why you're an only child. Look Todd, it ain't my place to talk to you about this stuff. Get your dad aside when your mom's not around. Ask him something important that will make him think you are really mature, and looking for his advice. Just like the cops, they really eat that crap up. Then kind of turn the conversation into something like, how come you're an only child. If that doesn't lead into him telling ya, he's gotta be pretty dense. You might have to just tell him you been thinkin' about getting married, or somethin'. Make sure you stress the 'or somethin'. That'll really get his attention, guaranteed. The key point is, your mom can't be around. Women get all bent out of shape about that kinda stuff."

"You were eleven, huh? Are you sure my dad knows? Like I'm twelve almost thirteen in six months, so if he hasn't told me, maybe he just doesn't know."

Jason looked at him, and shook his head. "Todd, when people look at you, who do they say you look like? Your mom, or your dad?"

"Everybody says I look like my dad."

"Well, think about it stupid, you know that women have babies, right? You do know that much don't you?"

"Yeah. They get fat, go to the hospital, and come back with a kid."

"Well, if father's didn't have something to do with it, none of us would look like our fathers, right?"

"Makes sense."

"Todd, ya look like your father, trust me on this. He knows."

Soon they reached the long driveway. Todd was in awe at the knowledge his older friend had. They were almost past the garage when they heard, "Jason Madison and Todd Phillips, get over here!"

Both boys startled hearing Jeff's voice bellow in the night, and they froze in their tracks. Slowly they turned to see Jason's dad standing in the doorway of the garage office with his arms folded. "I'm not fooling around. I said, get over here. NOW."

The boys walked back toward the building, and Jason sassed, "So, what do you want?" acting like a big shot in front of his friend.

"Nothing." Jeff smirked to himself. "Hey, guys ease up. Just wondered, whatcha been up to?"

"Well, we been hangin' out."

"That doesn't sound too interesting. Hangin' out doing what? Come a little closer so I can hear you better. Don't want to wake up the neighborhood."

"Well, Dad, it's like this… Rocky, bein' a baby and all, we knew he needed his rest. We didn't want to disturb him. And, we still wanted to have fun."

"Gee, son, that was mighty thoughtful of you. What about Nathan? Isn't he the same age as you? Didn't he want to have fun, too?"

"Oh, yeah, Dad, but that Nathan is such a nice guy. He figured since it was my birthday, he'd just stay back with Rocky to make sure the little guy was safe."

"Hmmm, ya just don't find friends like that everyday. So why did you leave the property? This is a big place. You couldn't find anything to do here?"

"Great place ya got here, Dad. We just didn't want to risk waking up the kid with any noise, or maybe interrupting you and Jodi…"

"Uh, huh. You are a thoughtful young man. So tell me, where'd ya go?" He continued to badger the boys.

"Into town. So what?"

"Into town? In the middle of the night you walked into town? Well, how about if you enjoy walking that much, I don't pick you up any more? You can just walk here after school on Friday."

"Dad! No, it takes too long. If I walked it would just take away from our special father son time. Neither of us would like that, right?"

"Oh, right again, Jason. Good thought. I just wasn't thinking about the wasted time. So what did you do in town?"

"We went to Dippy Donuts, and visited with a couple uh cops. Todd here struck up a conversation with them, and we hung out with them for a while."

"Very impressive. Did they share their beer and cigarettes with you?"

"Cigarettes? Beer?"

"Son, you boys reek of smoke, and beer. Care to explain?"

"Pollution. Fossil fuels, noxious gases, it's getting to be a real big problem, Dad. I'm thinking of joining one of those environmental groups to help save the planet."

"Jason, you'll be lucky to save your own ass, if you don't smarten up. Both of you, upstairs, in the house, NOW."

"But, Dad! Please, it's my birthday. I've never done anything wrong before. Please let us finish the night in the tree house. Please?"

Jeff looked at his son and realized, the boy hadn't done anything wrong before, and he was no where near as frisky as he had been at the same age. He placed his arm around Jason's shoulder. "Okay, since this is a first offence, you can go back up with your friends. Todd, you go on ahead. I have a few more things I want to ask Jason about before he joins the rest of you."

Todd walked away thinking how cool Jeff was, and how neat it was that he still needed to ask Jason advice on stuff. Jeff waited until Todd was out of sight, then he gripped the back of Jason's neck, and shoved him inside the garage. He turned his boy so his back was against the wall, and leaned heavily on his shoulder. With a furrowed brow, Jeff got in Jason's face, glaring at him. "Don't you *ever* forget I *let* you talk like Mr. Big Shot out there in front of your friend. *Don't* you ever talk to me like that again. I let you get by with it because it's your birthday. For two cents right now I could take you down, and teach you a lesson that you'd never forget. Pull a stunt like this again, and trust me, as God is my witness, old Pop Madison will have nothing on me for the beating you will get." Jeff held his glare. "Jason, I love you more than I love my own life. When we had our 'talk', I only explained the normal side of life. There is a whole nother world out there that you don't even have a clue exists. What you did tonight, was not only foolish, it was ignorant. If you want a hint, just imagine one of the social outcasts that you must have seen. Suppose one pervert decided he liked your pretty face, and your tight young ass. Both of you boys could have been taken to places unknown, and abused in unimaginable ways. The sad part is, sometimes the derelicts aren't satisfied with just the sexual gratification, they often end up killing their victims so they don't talk. You're thirteen now, son. Grow up."

"Sorry, Dad."

"Sorry, Dad, my ass. I get tired of hearing how sorry you are. Jason, think. Use your head, boy."

"But nuthin' happened. No big deal."

Jeff turned Jason around, and cracked his bottom several times. "Happy Birthday, and be grateful that's all you're getting." Jeff released him from his grip to go back to the tree house. His heart was pounding as he thanked God that the boys were home safe and sound, and only a little drunk.

Todd was already passed out by the time Jason reached the tree house. He was humiliated that he got his first real spanking on his thirteenth birthday. Jason understood what his dad had told him, and did appreciate that he wasn't spanked in front of his friend.

Jason must have had one full hour of sleep when he was hit square in the head with a 'water balloon' being shot by Rocky. Before he fully realized what was happening, he was hit again by Nathan. The two boys repeatedly attacked the hung over party animals with the stock Rocky had secretly stolen from his mothers purse over the years since he was a little kid. He never knew what those things were for. Thanks to the big boys, now he knew. Nathan hit the hardest as he was super ticked about being left behind with the little punk kid, while Jason and Todd had the real fun. Helpless, unarmed, and unable to retaliate, they both took it until the ammunition ran dry. Soaking wet, they dragged out of the tree house, and crawled up the stairs into the apartment where they crashed on the floor. All in all, it was a night worth remembering.

Jeff grinned at the pathetic duo passed out, and suffering with their youthful hangovers. *Boys will be boys,* he thought, and thanked God again that they came home unscathed.

Chapter 16

1976

Jeff felt a little guilty that he had given in to his desires and slept with Jodi while the boys camped out in the treehouse. It had been so long since he'd enjoyed the pleasure, and Jodi was someone whom her could trust. His relationship with Beth was reduced to fleeting glimpses when he would pick up the kids on the weekend, as Tom wasn't traveling as often. His relationship with Jodi was the same as in the past. She did her own thing, and he did his. Girls would still come by the shop looking to play with him, or Sam, either one of them, it didn't matter. As it had been since his teenage years, attracting willing female companionship took little, or no effort. Caring took a lot, and was basically non existent. If one was new to the Alibi Inn, it didn't take long to learn of Jeff's reputation. He was a confirmed 'bachelor', with an ex-wife, who loved his kids, and as long as no one tried to get inside his personal life, he was a perfect gentleman. He enjoyed sex, he was willing to please on the sheets, he didn't kiss and tell, and he remained friends after the fling.

Refusing to call her DeeDee, Jeff tried reasoning with Deana when he confronted her about threatening to turn him in to the child welfare department. She seemed to derive some sick pleasure from rejecting his methods, whether he used logic or counter threats, she was steadfast. The woman was vile.

Jeff sat at the bar, and watched as Doug drew him a draft. He was polite, but their good buddy status was a thing of the past. Doug made small talk, and felt bad that Jeff never got over him telling DeeDee who Beth was. Since that time, he had grown less fond of her also, but couldn't understand Jeff's continuing grudge. He also couldn't understand why he kept pursuing conversation with her when he'd obviously leave disgruntled, and she'd always have the same haughty smirk on her face.

Mack had been enchanted with Deana since he'd called her into his office to question her about Jeff's accusation of an alleged poisoning incident. She'd sat on the edge of his desk facing him with her knees slightly parted as he asked her version about what had happened. It didn't take long for him to be sucked into her tale of woe. She told him that Jeff had pursued her constantly through his senior year of high school. She and her best friend had skipped school one day so her friend Bev could meet her boyfriend, Chas. It just so happened Jeff was Chas' best friend, and was with him that day. Jeff had insisted to Chas that Bev bring her along so he could be with her. They were out cruising around, and Jeff was getting fresh with her in the back seat. She told Mack that there was a serious accident, Chas died, and Bev was permanently disabled. "I was in the hospital for months with severe injuries, but I recovered fully, and with much physical therapy, I'm better than ever. Jeff had no physical injuries, but I think in a lot of ways, he came out the worst. He's never gotten over my rejection of him. He joined the military to get away from the constant possibility of running into me in the small town where our father's were stationed. I really don't know what his attraction was to little me. He was one of the hottest boys in school and could have any girl he wanted...

Maybe that was it... He couldn't have me... He wasn't my type..." She had kicked off her shoes, and placed a foot on each of Mack's knees. "He talks to me a lot when he comes in, but I'm sure he has accepted that I still don't want him... I know he's a regular, and I am always polite to him, but I'm still not interested in his type... It's hard to forgive him for accusing me of this terrible crime. You do believe me, Mack? Is it alright that I call you Mack?" She had slid off the desk and was straddling him in his big chair. He stared into her hypnotic gaze, and was bewitched.

Mack lost all sense of reasoning. Shock waves stormed the Alibi Inn as rumors were confirmed that Mack had filed for divorce from his wife of nine years. He didn't request visitation rights to see the kids, he just wanted out.

Deana Jean Boynton Jacobiac Smith Dixon was already thrice divorced, with no children. She couldn't be bothered with brats. She didn't want to ruin her figure by cranking out rug rats that would just mess up the house, and spill crap on the carpeting. If she felt motherly, she'd add to her family of cats.

Mack and Deana were married in a small civil ceremony, and went to Niagara Falls for their honeymoon. He left a lot to be desired as a lover, but that wasn't a problem... She'd learned in her last marriage that getting out of the house for an early evening tryst was as simple as mailing herself an invitation to a Plasticware Party, and picking up a new bowl at Discount Mart on the way home. If it worked on her ex husbands, it would work on Mack, too. Oh, yes, Deana knew the ropes, and wasn't about to be hung by one. She made changes in Alibi policies that didn't make the waitresses happy, but she didn't care. It wasn't the changes that mattered, it was the fact that she had the power to make the changes. Changing the policies became as entertaining as taunting Jeff Madison. She had back stabbed Jodi in the past, but had method to her madness in her quest to befriend her again.

"Hello, Jeff. How's my high school sweetheart?" Deana twisted so that her entire breast was visible to Jeff.

"Are you sure you didn't sustain a head injury in the accident, Deana?" Jeff sarcastically quipped back.

"No head injury for me, but I think it made you cross eyed. You seem to not be able to look me in the eyes. They're up here, not on my tits. Do you remember groping them, while this perfectly manicured hand right here was polishing your gun?"

"Deana, you are vulgar."

"Yeah, and if it wasn't for that dumb fuck Chas having that accident, I would've screwed what little brains you had out, and you know it."

"Bev seemed so nice. I never could figure how a sweet girl like her could be friends with a loose piece of dog crap like you."

Daggers shot out of her eyes. Jeff knew he'd finally hit a nerve. He decided to drop it until another night. He knew he always had to have a plan, and always needed to think his words through carefully before letting them spill off of his tongue. He just had to rethink which remark triggered the reaction. "See ya, Deana Boink'em!" He smirked as he left the Alibi Inn. It was a small remark, but it spoke volumes to Jeff.

Jeff was doing great in the shop. He would have a few beers with the guys after the day was done. He'd see Jodi on weeknights, occasionally she'd stay over. If she didn't come by and if he was in the mood, he'd mess around with a garage girl. Or, he'd invite one of the ladies he'd meet at the Alibi Inn to his place, unless she invited him to hers. If he wasn't in the mood, he didn't mind being alone. He'd been watching the new miniseries *Roots: The Saga of an American Family*. The idea of a TV show combining fact with fiction was unique. He enjoyed the blend of actual history, and the personal touch of the family member's experiences. The program made the injustices become very real, as he recalled the turbulent times in the 60's when the Civil Rights Movement was picking up momentum.

Jeff would have the kids on the weekends, and depending on the weather, he'd either play outside with them, or they'd go to a movie. Life was fun with Daddy.

It wasn't as much fun for Marianne; she was coming over less often. He continued to spend much time with Jason, teaching him all about the Camaro. Jason started driving it around the lot when it was just the two of them there, so his interest in keeping it running in top notch condition peaked. Since the arrival of Deana at the Alibi Inn, Jeff hadn't taken Jason there for a Bad Dog out of fear that the woman might harm his son. Jason complained. Jeff hated to lie, but oh well. He'd hand him the car keys, and after he drove around the lot for a few hours, they'd go someplace else for dinner. Jeff wondered why, since Jason was thirteen, he hadn't asked again about coming to live with him. What he didn't know was Jason had figured out that by staying with his mother, he had the best of both worlds. His mom got nearly everything he wanted from Tom for him. If he didn't get what he wanted from them, he'd put Marianne up to asking for it after convincing her that it was totally necessary that they have whatever it was. She was a push over for her idolized big brother, plus she had Tom wrapped around her little finger.

Jeff enjoyed hearing about Jason meeting his grandparents while in France, at Tom's expense, during spring break. He was excited for Jason as he beamed telling him all about his adventures in Paris with the school group. He was glad that Jason seemed to only have normal boyhood pranks to share. And share them he did, his tales went on and on and on. Jeff smiled. *Maybe his life will turn out better than mine,* he thought, remembering in detail how lusty he was at Jason's age…

By thirteen years old Jeff knew very well the pleasure of soft, stroking feminine hands bringing him fulfillment. Being good looking, and knowing it, only added to his charisma. Speaking English in seductive tones intrigued the young French girls, and speaking fluent French seemed to excite the teenaged American girls living on Base. Young Jeff never lacked for girlfriends.

Lieutenant Colonel Madison and his family were sent to northern Italy TDY Enroute. Jeff was looking forward to visiting the land. He didn't speak the native language, but he loved the sound of it's musical tones. After getting settled, he wandered alone through the market place. He smelled the aroma of fresh baked bread, and followed his nose until he stood in front of a lovely, voluptuous, older teenage Italian girl.

"Buongiorno!" She smiled noticing his beautiful blue eyes.

"Bonjour!" He responded in French.

Jeff watched her hands kneading the bread dough, and she watched him watching her hands. She smiled at him with her sweet, full lips. She leaned over slightly, exposing her cleavage, as she pulled a piece of dough from the soft, thick mass. She began squeezing and rolling it. He gazed up into her northern Italian blue eyes, and felt a thunderbolt as her meaning became very clear. She spoke no English, or French. He spoke no Italian. She pointed at the clocks small hand, and pointed at the number six. Then she pointed at the big hand, and the number three. She smiled and asked, "Avete capito? Capite?" Oh, yes, the frisky fourteen year old understood. She pointed to the bench out front, nodded yes, and he eagerly nodded yes back. Never touching him with her flour covered hands, she leaned over the table, and placed her lips on his with gentle pressure, yet seductively, with no tongue. "Arrivederci," she whispered, smiling as she pointed to the door, and waved good-bye.

Jeff walked calmly through the market place like he was Mr. Cool until he knew he was out of view of the bakery. He then took off running like a streak of lightening toward the Base. Bursting through the door he was hollering for Maman wondering, "What time is dinner?" He ran to the bath, and filled the tub. He was bathed, dressed in his Sunday clothes, and had his hair perfectly Brill creamed, as he sat down to eat.

Michelle had observed her petit bijou's behavior, and watched him as he nervously played with his food, and kept checking his watch. Knowing full well that her son spoke perfect French, she decided to not pull any punches. She said to her husband in English, "Vincent, Jeffrey needs the man to man talk. He has the behavior of an adolescent in love."

Jeff kept fidgeting as Vince talked to him about blah blah blah. "Look, I'm fourteen, I've had broads grabbin' for the gun since I was thirteen. I know it's not just to pee, okay?" He caught the look, and knew he'd better straighten up fast, or risk going out with a fat lip. "Dad, thank you, sir, for the useful advice."

Maman handed Jeff the bouquet of fresh cut flowers she purchased that morning for their dining table. She looked carefully at her darling son, and was relieved to see no bruises. She hoped he'd finally learned to listen, obey, and think before he opened his mouth to his father. She gave him a hug, and he kissed her cheek before bounding out the door.

It was ten after six. Jeff sat nervously on the wooden bench staring at the flowers. DiFiori's Pasticceria was closed. Looking at his watch, he thought maybe the older girl was making fun of him by only feigning interest, and making a date with him. He watched the second hand tick as the big hand moved closer to the three.

"Ciao!"

He startled, and leaped to his feet smiling. He was embarrassed when he heard her amused laugh. Smiling happily, he handed her the fresh bouquet of flowers.

"Grazie," she replied. She pointed at herself, "Caterina DiFiori," she looked questioningly at him.

"Jeffrey Madison."

Caterina opened a small white bag, took out a delicious fresh cannoli, handed it to Jeff, and enjoyed one herself. Smiling and giggling, she playfully teased, and kissed the powdered sugar off of his lips.

He grinned at her as he took the bag, reached in, and got more sugar. He patted it on her lips with his fingertips, and kissed her back softly.

"Giocondo giovanetto! Vive bene, di risata molto." Smiling, she linked her arm through his as they walked through the market place. They stopped to look at baskets, marble figurines, and ceramic religious statues. She led him up a path, away from the noise, and stopped outside a small, neat, stucco covered building. She nodded for him to open the door for her. They stepped inside. There was a small wooden table with two chairs, and a divan against one wall. There were gardening tools hanging on another wall, and lots of empty pots stacked up on shelves above a potter's bench. Caterina placed the flowers in one of the water cans, and set them on the table. She looked at him, and smiled at his thoughtfulness. She motioned for him to have a seat on the 'divano'.

He imitated her word, "Grazie," and sat down.

Caterina sat down by his side. She noticed again that his eyes were as blue as hers. He looked from her eyes to her lips, and back to her eyes. She nodded her head yes, and their lips met. Again, no tongue, but she rolled her mouth over his in a way that rumbled his being. For several long minutes she kissed him in that manner, and then she stopped to look at him. She took his hands in hers, and placed them on her breasts. Jeff moaned deeply as he reveled in feeling freely what he'd only dreamed about, and had more than once, been slapped for trying to touch. Considering where girls touched him, he couldn't figure that out, but right now he wasn't going to try. She kissed him with more fervor as his young hands touched, and learned. Finally, he felt her hand on himself. He pressed into her erotic stroking as they continued to kiss. He discovered more about breasts as she allowed him to unbutton her blouse.

Uninhibitedly, she unbuttoned, then unzipped his dress pants. She reached inside his underwear, and caressed him eagerly and firmly. He was happy and content, until she stopped everything, and looked at him again. He didn't understand exactly what she said, but it didn't take a genius to figure out that he'd at least been called a baby. He cast his eyes down. Caterina had thought he was self centered, but then realized he was much younger than she'd guessed. He was merely inexperienced. She smiled sweetly. She took his chin in her fingers, and raised his face to look at him. His eyes stayed downcast.

"Jeffrey, bene," she whispered, "Voler bene a." He raised his eyes to look at her. She spoke one of the few English phrases she knew, "It's okay." She looked kindly at his boyish face. Gently she kissed his lips, until he kissed her back. She placed her hand on him again, then she reclined coaxing him to lie down along side of her. Jeff learned that not only did he enjoy the feel of her breasts in his hands, he learned he had the ability to thrill her with his touch when she placed his hand down there. He was starting to catch on to the grown-up rules of give and take, in the game called love. Although he didn't think so, she was young, too.

Caterina had an older lover that treated her like a lady. While he was away, she yearned for loving. This young boy was very, very handsome, and well built, and she wanted to make love. He obviously had good breeding, fine manners, and he could kiss with passion. With proper indoctrination, he could be as skilled a lover as her Salvatore…

However, it wouldn't happen this night she decided. She continued to love play with him until he did what he was accustomed to doing. They cuddled, and kissed a little longer, before sitting up. They adjusted their clothing, and she took her flowers. Stopping to smile and kiss along the way, they walked back toward the market place arm in arm.

"Domani." Caterina pointed at the bench, then pointed to the six, and the three on his watch. "Jeffrey, vive bene, spesso l'amore." Kissing him seductively she whispered, "Domani."

Right on time, not even close to breaking curfew, Jeff walked into his house. He was happy to see his dad alone, looking over papers, as he sat in his chair. He could hear his mother in the bath.

"Dad? Sir… Are you busy?"

"No, Jeffrey." Vince answered looking up. "Sit down, son."

"Dad, do you think we could have that talk again?" Jeff listened closely as Vince spoke.

Promptly at six ten the next day, Jeff was sitting on the bench outside the Pasticceria. He wanted to go earlier, but decided that being too early may make him appear childishly over eager. Caterina appeared at six fifteen, and smiled sweetly as her eyes met Jeff's. She glanced at his hands, and looked disappointed.

He stood and said, "Ciao," he took her arm, linked it through his, and started to walk. He stopped at a flower cart, and selected some tiny blue flowers. He held them close to her face and said, "Bella di azzurro fiori. Bella Signorina Caterina DiFiori." He paid the florist, kissed her cheek, and placed them in her hand. She was touched by his gesture, and flattered by his romantic words. He motioned with his arm for her to lead the way. She stopped at the sidewalk Negozio di Caffè, where they each ordered a cappuccino, and biscotti. They sat in the balmy early evening air, smiling at each other as they watched little children feeding the pigeons. When they were finished it was dusk. Caterina looked deep into Jeff's eyes, as they held hands. She glanced at the path leading through the garden. He wanted to scream "YES!" and run, but instead, he pressed her hand to his lips, and kissed. Again, with arms linked, they walked up the path, and stood outside the casetta di giardiniere where they had nearly made love. He opened the door, then carried her inside. He kissed her long and passionately before he put her down. It was much later than it was when they arrived the previous night. Caterina lit several candles that he didn't remember being there the night before. There was a bottle of spumante on the table, and two stemmed glasses. She handed Jeff the bottle. He'd never opened a bottle of wine before, but had seen it done at many a hail and farewell parties in his young lifetime. He opened it as if he'd been doing this all his life. He poured a small amount in his glass, sniffed, then tasted it. Jeff smiled at Caterina, and filled both their glasses slightly more than half full. "À votre santé! À la votre!" He toasted.

"Alla salute! Cin! Cin!"   She tapped her glass lightly to his.

Jeff was fascinated by her awesome presence. Caterina was captivated by his virile good looks. They drank their wine, and then drank another. Caterina blew out all but one candle. She slipped out of her white cotton dress. His eyes traveled up and down the length of her, admiring every curve of the first nude woman he'd ever seen. Standing unashamed before him, Caterina slowly unbuttoned Jeff's shirt, and removed it from his shoulders. Their lips met, and he once again felt excitement in her sensuous kissing. With her bare bosom crushed into his chest, he felt his heart pound as her hands kneaded the muscles on his bare back, and traveled down to the fleshiness on his buttocks. Her hands moved around, unfastened his pants, and they dropped to the floor. She stretched the elastic of his boxers. He stepped out of them as she led him to the divan. Much the same as the night before, but with more confidence, he kissed, and touched her with unhindered freedom. She languidly guided his hands to touch places he hadn't yet explored. When she knew he was ready, she nudged his shoulder with her fingertips until he was on his back. Caterina slid on top of him. She moved in gentle swells and undulations as she took his body into her own. Jeff was overwhelmed with the eroticism of being sexually united with a woman. Hearing her sigh as his hands reached for, and caressed her breasts seemed to release more passion within him. She moved up and down his length enjoying his youthful exuberance. His heart was pounding, and his breathing was heavy, feeling that he was ready to let go… He suddenly feared he'd done something seriously wrong when she lifted herself off of him. She rolled to her back, and pulled him on top of her. Instinctively he entered her and found himself moving within her body. Nothing he'd ever done in a back seat compared with the heat he felt lying between her legs, moving at the speed of a jack rabbit. He moaned each time as he felt wave after wave release from his body into hers. Jeff laid there like a ton of bricks for a few minutes before she started to squirm, and giggle. Soon they were cuddled face to face on their sides. He gazed at her with awe, and began to speak the words, "Me amore tu."

Caterina sweetly placed her finger on his lips, shaking her head, she softly whispered, "Shhh… No, no Jeffrey, no. Cotta adolescenziale." It took a few minutes, but he soon understood, puppy love. She smiled at him, thrilled as she kissed his lips, that Jeff was soon ready again. This time, Jeff learned the joy of taking the time to satisfy a woman. Caterina made delightful trills as his hands firmly grasped her bottom, and strongly held her to himself as he repeatedly thrust deep until her trills turned into moans of passion. Caterina enjoyed the pleasure, it had been such a long time since she'd been with her lover. *Oh, yes,* she thought, *when this boy is thirty four... like Salvatore... hmmm...*

Jeff entered the living room. Vince looked crossly at his son. "Jeffrey, do you know how to tell time?"

"Yes, Sir."

"Look at your watch. Did you make curfew?"

"No, Sir."

"What is your excuse?"

"There is no excuse, Sir... ummm, Dad?"

"Son?"

"Dad, do you remember our talk last night?"

"Yes, I remember, Jeffrey."

"Dad, for what you told me, thanks. Also, Dad, you said when I was older, that we would continue with our man to man talk."

"Yes, son. I did say that." Vince knew exactly where this conversation was going.

"Tonight I'm older, Dad."

"Dad, Dad, Dad? Earth calling Daddy..." Jason was waving his hand in front of his dad's face laughing.

"Yeah, Jase?" Jeff kind of shook his head, and snapped back into the present.

"Do you think next spring break you could go on the school trip with us? They always need more parents for chaperones, and you're about the neatest parent there is. I think next year the trip is to Italy. It's going to be an art and culture tour. Wanna go?"

"Sunny Italy. Yeah, Jason, that may be a wonderful father son trip. Let's get some books, study the customs, and the language, and make the most of it. Do you think we will have any free time to explore the northern area near the Alps?"

"Dunno, Dad. Weren't you there when you were a kid?"

"Uh huh. Nothing but pleasant memories of Italy. Your Colonel Pop and I made a giant step forward in our relationship in Italy. I'm glad that you and I never had the same issues to deal with. Jason?"

"Yeah, Dad?"

"Son, do you ever think about girls?"

"Dad, girls seem to be a pain in the neck. Mom is uptight most of the time trying to please Tom. Rianne gets on my nerves with her constant blabbing, and the way she plays suck up to Tom. Jodi's alright, but she's a space cadet. The girls at the garage are stupid. I used to think they were stupid because of the way they laughed about serious stuff like water hoses and drive shafts. Now I think they are stupid because they still think I don't know that they aren't talking about water hoses and drive shafts. My opinion is most of them have loose chassis. There's not a crankshaft in the world that would fit the size of their V design… irregardless of how many cylinders they got pushing down their pistons."

Jeff himself had no idea his soon to be fourteen year old had such a broad understanding of the double meaning of Gearhead. He snarfed his beer, and smiled widely at his son.

Jason smirked the way he always did when he pulled one over on his dad.

"So, what did you think about Maman, your Grande-mère? She's a girl, too."

"Incredible, Dad. I just love her. She kept running her hands through my hair, saying 'mon petit bijou' and laughing and crying at the same time."

"Hey! That was her pet name for me!" Jeff faked jealousy. "Her sweet loving nature has kept me going throughout the years. Do you ever think about girls your own age?"

"Mais, oui, mon père. Elle m'appelle Colette et elle est tres jolie. Avoir l'objet de son désir a portée de main, le bouche est sucré du vin. Elle parle, 'Jason, je t'aime beaucoup, je voudrais bien se préparer à donner un baiser. Je me réjouis. Tu te réjouis. Nous nous réjouissons! Oh, là là'."

"Jason, you are so full of crap! If you weren't the fruit of my loins, I'd send you to Military School just to get rid of you. So you kissed her, huh?"

"Uh huh. C'est la vie! Can we talk about something else?"

"Sure, I just wanted you to know you can talk to me about anything, then you dump on me, every time you dump on me. Merci beaucoup."

"Tres bien, PaPa. Can I drive some more when we get home?" No way was Jason telling his dad that Colette touched his privates, and he liked it.

"Do you think you can see to drive through all that hair?" Jeff really hated the length of Jason's hair.

"Dad. It's the style."

Chapter 17

Jodi was chatting with Deana, about her problems with Rocky. Deana suggested that instead of having him going home to an unsupervised apartment, it would be fine if the boy came to the Alibi Inn. He could do his homework in the break area, there was always someone around to help keep an eye on him. A ten year old was too old for a babysitter, and it would give Jodi a bit more time to spend with him. With Jodi on day shift it would only be for an hour or so Monday through Friday. Mack was okay with the idea. Jodi thanked her, but didn't totally trust the woman. When it came to offering favors, there was always something in it for DeeDee.

"Well, if it isn't the stud dud from Northern High." Deana hissed as Jeff walked by, and sat at the bar. As usual he watched Doug intently as he drew his draft.

"Need to ball? Give Deana a call, she's the gal that Boinks'em all." Jeff taunted, again noting her reaction. It was blank. So, his hunch was correct, Bev was the sore spot that riled Deana so much the other week. "Hey Doug draw me another, I want to go grab a booth." He knew Deana would be by to torment his life before long. He felt he was ready for her.

"So, sissy boy, does rattling off nursery rhymes from school days make you feel like a man?" Once again she wore clothing that revealed her wares.

"Who just brought up high school, Deana? Was it Doug, or was it me? Gee, I think it was… YOU! Since you brought up the subject, do you keep in touch with your dear friend Bev? After my Dad got his full bird, we left the north woods, and I lost contact. But, you two were so close… How is the dear girl? Have there been any changes in her condition with all the new medical technology, and neurological advances that have been made since 1960? And, speaking of nursery rhymes, how would your miscarriage's daddy have liked that jingle being recited to it's mother every time you walked the streets to earn a buck?"

"You SCUM!"

"Me? If I'm scum, what the hell are you? Who's bright idea was it to blame me for your screw up? I could have gone to prison for your lie."

"I never claimed you were the father. My parents just assumed it was yours since my blouse was off, and my bra was unhooked at the scene of the accident."

"It took more than that for you to get knocked up. Why didn't you tell them the truth?"

"Everybody in school knew you and Chas were systematically combing the halls looking for virgins. You were the cutest boy in school. You never would've given me a second look had goody two shoes Bev not dragged me along with her to meet you guys that day. So what the hell did I care if they wanted to blame you? Someone needed to pay for the way my crap life turned out. Speaking of finding virgins, did you ever find one, or were you always number two on the list? Guess your hot looks, and blue eyes couldn't overcome the allure of the number one stud man, Chas Edmund, and his infamous 'Black Dragon', the 1959 Chevy Belle Air, with blood red interior. Chas was always the primary ride."

Jeff still smirked to himself. She was on the defensive now. He never felt competition with Chas since often times they'd flip a coin to see which one of them would pursue which girl. The only one Chas cared about was Bev, and Jeff always respected her. "Answer my question, Deana, how is Bev? Don't you keep up with your dearest friend? What did you refer to her as, 'goody two shoes'? That doesn't sound like anything a best friend would say. My best friend Chas wouldn't have talked about me that way. Chas was a good loyal friend."

"Loyal friend my ass. Chas was a worse piece of dung than you. Chas Edmund deserved to die. Had I been able to go to his funeral, I would have spit in his casket."

"If you weren't so vicious in your depraved, wickedness, and if I weren't a gentleman, I'd slap the shit out of you for defiling his memory."

"Defiling his memory? HA! That's a joke! That's so funny, I forgot to laugh. While the suave, debonair Jeffrey Madison was sweet talking all the girls Chas had already screwed, he was out breaking in new ones by the droves. How did it feel to be 'second in rank' Madison? Was your position lower because his daddy's bird flew over your daddy's oak leaves? Whatever... the mighty oak casts a long shadow, too, my unrequited love. Chas was a lewd, coarse, depraved rapist."

"Pretty rough words coming from a pig like you." Jeff snapped. "It's been said you can't rape a whore."

"Oh, really? Were you with him every minute? Do you remember the summer you went to France? Do you think Chas put his life on hold because his little side kick, tag along, leftover catcher was away with the high and mighty Vincent Madison, maker and breaker of mens' careers? Hell, no my little fly boy joy toy! Chas kicked it into high gear. He didn't want to leave a girl untouched in the village for fear you might find a virgin. Guess what Jeff? Chas was the father of my 'miscarriage' as you called it. While he kept Bev pure as the driven snow, he fucked me. I didn't want him, I wanted you. He kept asking me out. I kept telling him no. He called me and said you were back. If I wanted to go out with you, he'd come pick me up. He showed up without you, or Bev. He immediately left the base, headed north, and turned down a hunting trail out in the middle of no where. He ripped into me like I was a cream filled cookie. I told him I was a virgin, he told me 'good I like to make 'em bleed'. I told him I knew karate, then he gave me a chop, and forced himself into me. If that wasn't horror enough, he told me I had to do it with whomever he sent over, or I'd get more of the same whether I wanted it, or not. So, when your dear old Lieutenant Colonel fucking Dad started to put the squeeze on my father about dropping the lawsuit, he conveniently found all of Chas' buddies that could, and would admit that they'd had me. My dad unexplainably didn't make Chief. He laid in wait until I healed, and finished physical therapy. Then he beat me with an old razor strop until I couldn't stand up. When I healed from that, he did it again, and so on until I married the first guy I could get, just to get the hell away from him."

"Deana, why the hell are you blaming me for all this? Maybe some of your story as it pertains to me is true. I was always hot for chicks. That didn't mean I would never look at you. I didn't have any classes with you. Until the day of the accident, I didn't know that you even existed. What did, or do you expect from me? I still swear I was innocent of everything except skipping school. Yes, I was feeling you up, but as I recall it, you removed your blouse. That looked a little needy on your part, to me."

"Chas told me I *had* to fuck you if you wanted me. I would have fucked you just because I wanted to, because I had a giant crush on you. Instead of making me out to be a total tramp, you know you could have just married me... it would've taken care of all my problems. Once things settled down, I would've given you a divorce."

"WHAT??? Now I know you are totally out of your mind. Deana, you may not believe this, but I'm a religious man. I don't believe in divorce. No way in hell would I be tied to a low life whore like yourself for the rest of my life for love or money. Furthermore, I hope you don't think I believe that fairy tale about Chas. You are as sick as they get. It doesn't surprise me that you could come up with a story as sick and twisted as that- after all you've had sixteen years to dream it up."

"Well, Mad, if that's what you choose to believe, oh well, just stay away from your old lady. She's an unfit mother, and nothing more than a high class whore. You got a lotta nerve bad mouthing me since you fucked another man's wife."

Once again, Jeff left the Alibi Inn disgruntled, and Deana had a smirk on her face.

Jeff had Trina tell Beth to telephone when she could safely talk to him.

"Jeff I've been living a lie ever since we tried to get back together. Tom wants a baby. I can't hold off producing a child for him much longer. I'm running out of excuses."

"Beth... Deana won't back off. She is totally convinced that everything that has gone wrong in her life is my fault. I don't know how much of the story she told me last night is true, and how much she wishes was true."

"What is that supposed to mean?" Beth asked.

"She tried to tell me that the baby she lost at the time of the accident was Chas' baby, and if I would have married her all of her problems would have been solved."

"WHAT? If the kid was Chas' why would she expect you to marry her? Is she a total fruitcake, or are you conveniently leaving out a lusty part of that story?"

"Just what do you mean by that?" Jeff demanded.

"Well, darling, let's get real... you weren't exactly fumbling around looking for body parts at age nineteen when you first made love to me. Quite obviously, you'd done the deed before." Beth snapped sarcastically.

"I resent that remark, Beth."

"Jeff, something just doesn't add up. And, sorry to say, given your track record with women, it does cast a shadow of doubt."

"Okay, so unlike yourself, the pure and holy virgin, I wasn't celibate before we got married. That doesn't mean there wasn't a girl in reaching distance that I didn't seduce. You accused me of banging Tamiko, and I did not. Also, I guarantee you this, I did NOT have sex with Deana Boynton. First my dad, now you are insisting that I did. It *never* happened. You talk like I'm a total dog. It's getting old, Beth. It's the same old argument over and over."

"Well, fine! I'll just shut up then. What time are you going to pick up the kids tomorrow?"

"Same time as usual, 5:30."

"Good, and good-bye. Have a great life." She slammed down the receiver.

Jeff reached for his bottle of scotch, and headed up the stairs. It was going to be one of those long meaningless nights. Wondering what went wrong, he knew it was over, again.

Beth was livid. Dinner was in the oven, and she was literally slamming the dishes on the table when Tom came in, and set down his briefcase.

"Hi, Babe. Were the dishes naughty today?" He grinned.

She shot him a look, then saw the humor in what he'd said, and started to laugh.

Tom had seen both kids outside playing. He walked over to Beth, and placed his hands around her waist. He inched them down as he kissed her hello. He rarely showed any affection outside of their bedroom. She savored the moment. "What time is dinner?" he asked between kisses.

"About 45 minutes from now." She said as her temper cooled.

He playfully smacked her bottom, and told her he wouldn't hurt her too bad for not having his meal on the table when he got home. "What do you say you come upstairs with me, and tell me what had you so riled up while I change my clothes?" He said pulling off his tie.

Life with Tom was comfortable, and could be fun when he was in a good mood. She headed for the stairs. Tom watched her rear end as he followed closely behind. If only she'd lose more weight... He locked the bedroom door, turned on the stereo, and cranked it up a few notches. He then went into the bathroom. Beth heard him turn on the shower full force. "Aren't you coming in?"

"Tom, I can't take a shower now, dinner'll burn."

"I didn't ask you to take a shower. You're clean, I've got a nose. I just want some noise for more privacy. Get in here. Now, what caused the china abuse?" He pulled her into his arms. He nibbled on her ear, and pressed his manhood into her abdomen.

"Well, Jeff called about the kids-"

"Okay, enough said. If you have to move your lips any more, move them right here." He pointed to his mouth. Beth kissed him. "I like the blonde streaks in your hair. Kristina did a great job. Next time have her frost it more. Blonde is beautiful." Tom's hands wandered across her crotch, then back up around her waist. Jogging's paying off Beth, keep it up. You've dropped a few pounds, haven't you? Know what I like best about these new running shorts you've been wearing, Babe?" His thumbs were in the waist band.

"What?" She looked puzzled, wondering what brought on the change of topic from complaining about her weight, to her wardrobe.

"This!" He had the elastic stretched, shorts down, and had her sitting on the vanity of the bathroom sink. Her shorts and panties were off in one fell swoop. He continued to kiss her as his pants dropped to the floor. She was pulling off her matching tank top. "Don't bother Babe, unless you want to play with them." He pressed his manhood into her as she welcomed his attention.

"Ohhh, Tom!" She breathlessly whispered, as his hands drew her to himself.

He stood giving, giving her pleasure... "Talk dirty to me, Beth, it's the only time you can. Talk dirty."

The dirtier she talked the hotter he got. The hotter he got the harder he pounded. The harder he pounded the dirtier she talked until she burst into an orgasmic frenzy.

"Tom, that was sooo good." Beth wasn't lying as she leaned forward with her cheek resting upon his chest.

"Babe, it never ceases to amaze me how such a little thing can make you so happy." He kissed her head, and rubbed her back.

"Tom, it isn't such a little thing." Her arms were hugging his ribs, and her legs were still wrapped around his waist. She was still breathless as he continued to stroke her hair and back. "I'm finally ready, Tom. Let's work on making our baby when he takes the kids tomorrow. Okay? Please? Please, Tom. Let's start tonight. I'll do what you like if you will, okay? Please?" Still exhausted from their pre-dinner tryst, Beth was already looking forward to another rendezvous with the man to whom she finally committed her life by agreeing to have his baby.

Chapter 18

1977

"I just don't understand you, Madison. It seems to me if some hot lipped young punk was lusting after my daughter, I'd be a bit more concerned."

"Tom, I really don't know what you're so upset about. So Rocky kissed Marianne. She's nine, he's eleven. I'm sure we're not going to have to go after him with a shotgun to defend her honor. It took two stitches to put his lip back together after my little girl decked him, so I'm sure he'll think twice before making another move on my Baby Cakes."

"Just don't come around here acting bewildered wondering what went wrong if she ends up pregnant before she's out of High School. What an attitude!" Tom sniped.

"High School? Tom you're starting to really tick me off. She's nine years old. NINE. And like I said, she defended herself just fine. I've talked to Rocky much the same as I talked to Jason when he was eleven. Kids these days are exposed to more than we were with television, and radio, and rock 'n' roll music. Jason kissed a girl in kindergarten when he was six. Beth had a fit, but you know what? We're still not grandparents. Ease up, they are my kids, they are my responsibility, and you needn't concern yourself. Have you asked Beth if she's given Marianne 'the talk' yet?"

"The talk? About sex? Are you kidding me? The child is only nine years old."

"My point exactly."

Jason was already sitting in the Camaro, ready to go as he watched his dad, and Tom having a serious conversation in the driveway. He was sure he knew what it was about, but he didn't care to snoop. He was hoping that once again Marianne would get out of going to their dad's, that way he could con Jeff into picking up one or two of his buddies so they could hang out, and have fun.

Marianne came skipping out with her little Happy Family dolls, and gave Tom a hug, and a kiss as he lifted her in his arms. "Give Buttercup a kiss for me, if you go to Grammy and Poppy's to ride, okay?" Marianne asked as she pressed her cheek to Tom's.

"Well, Marianne, that was only one kiss you gave me, honey. Was it for me, or was that for Buttercup?"

"Daddy, are you being funny?" She put a hand on each of his cheeks, and kissed him six more times. "One for you. One for Grammy, one for Poppy, one for Buttercup, one for Mommy, and one more for you!"

Jeff had turned his back, grit his teeth, and walked toward the Camaro. He couldn't stand to watch.

Tom put Marianne down, waved good-bye to Jason, and walked into the house. Marianne ran to catch up with her father, and grabbed his hand. "Hi, Dad, did you buy me anything?"

"No, Baby Cakes, I didn't. Ummm, I thought we could stop by a store and you could pick out what ever you would like. How does that sound?"

"Great Dad. I get so bored at your house."

With the kids away for the weekend, Tom and Beth did what they had been trying for months, to conceive a child. This particular weekend though, the kids were not at their fathers. Jason had gone on a weekend trip with Nathan and others from the church she and Tom attended. Marianne was with Nancy and Papa Jack.

"Tom, I've been to the doctor. There is nothing wrong with me. You've been to the doctor, there is nothing wrong with you. Let's just have sex? Okay? One of these times we'll hit it right, and I'll get pregnant. I've had children before, and so have you."

Tom was depressed. Beth led him upstairs to the bedroom. Since he had been away he hadn't seen the improvements she had made to the master suite. They now had a double jacuzzi tub in the bath. After a delicious dinner, and relaxing in the new tub, Tom seemed more receptive. He sat naked in the new burgundy velvet chair watching Beth as she sensuously smoothed lotion all over her nude body. She knew he didn't like touching her breasts because of their size. She didn't mind as much since he tied a black silk scarf around her eyes. With her eyes shut and blindfolded she wasn't as self conscious touching herself. There was no way that Tom could ever see that it was Jeff's hands she was imagining on her beautiful voluptuous breasts. She massaged lotion over them and rubbed her palms in circular motions around her taut nipples. Tom loved to watch her pleasure her own body very much. He sometimes touched himself watching her, but tried not to, because he didn't want to risk ejaculating and not making a baby. He didn't know why it took so long to think of the blind fold. She was like a different person when she wore that thing. Blindfolded she never knew when he was going to enter her. She was like nothing he'd ever imagined as she begged him to command her sexually. "Touch yourself, Babe. Only you know how you like it." He encouraged her, taunting her and when she was nearly ready to explode, she'd beg for him. Oh how he loved to hear her beg. Tom wasn't a sadist, but he did get off on her need to be dominated. He grabbed both of her wrists and stretched her arms straight over her head and held them firmly to the bed as he drove her home. All the while she begged using language he loved.

Beth really didn't want another child, but she hungered for attention any way she could get it. For the most part, she tolerated Tom's day to day idiosyncrasies, and disliked the way he treated both of her kids, but he provided well, and that man could, well... fuck.

Tom often wondered about Beth. Even if her body didn't especially turn him on, no man in his right mind would say no to a woman as hot as her. Beth did everything right for a woman in her social position, and she was a good mother to her kids. And, she knew better than to ever say no to sex whenever he wanted it. Still he missed the tender moments with his beloved Renée and wondered how his own son was growing up.

Another weekend was over. Soon they'd learn if this time their attempt at making a baby was successful.

"Madison Motors."

"Hello, Jeff?"

"Speaking."

"Hi, this is Beth."

"I know your voice. Is everything okay?"

"No, not really. Jeff, um, Jason got into some trouble last night on a Church trip. There's going to be a big meeting on Thursday. Oh, this is so embarrassing... He got caught with his pants down on the Church bus."

"Damn. Was he, um... was he with anyone?"

"Yes, he was with a girl. Do you think that you could be there?"

"Beth, I will be there. But, I insist on talking to my son alone first, before we go in to face the pack of wolves. Is this the first meeting? Uh, huh. What is the girls name? She his girlfriend? I see. What time does he get home from school? How about I pick him up at your palace, er, place then?"

Jason knew he was in deep trouble when he saw his dad's red Camaro sitting out front on Thursday. "Hey, Dad." Jason said with his eyes downcast.

"Son, go inside, let your mom know that you're home from school, and you are leaving for a while with me. Tell her I said you'll be back in time to go to the meeting."

Jason did as he was told. He came right out, and got into the car. He let out a deep sigh, and was very visibly upset. Jeff drove to the park in silence, and parked the Camaro away from the other vehicles. He reached in the back, and pulled a couple of root beers from the cooler. He opened them both, then handed one to Jason. "Want to talk, Jason?"

"Thanks. Dad… Everything just kinda went nuts, and I'm not really sure what happened. I don't know what's right, or wrong about anything any more. Now everybody's mad at me." His head still hung in shame.

Jeff gave him an odd look. "Jason, I'm not mad at you, or condemning you. Please don't get all defensive with me. I just want to know what happened, in your own words. Then I'll decide what, if anything, I think you did wrong. I'm on your side no matter what. That doesn't mean if you did something wrong, I'm going to condone it. It means we will talk about it, and learn what could have, or should have been done, so the same mistake isn't repeated in the future."

Jeff ran the seat back as far as it would go, and stretched his long legs. His face was emotionless as he listened carefully to every word that came out of Jason's fifteen year old mouth. His beloved son nervously told his side of the story about the church bus incident. *The poor kid,* he thought, *I was twenty six years old, and didn't know what happened, when it happened to me.* He lit a cigarette, and started to smoke. He almost felt like offering one to the kid, he was still so nervous.

Jason side glanced his dad wondering what his reaction would be when he heard his side of the story. He knew when they were playing, his dad was quick and sharp with remarks, but when it was serious, Dad took his time and chose his words carefully. The silent seconds ticked on by. He figured he was in for it.

Jeff finished his cigarette, opened another root beer, took a swallow, then lit another cigarette. "Jason, I understand better than you think I do. I'm not smarter, I'm just older. I want to ask you some questions, and all I want are honest answers. Do you understand? I can't help you if I don't know the truth. If there are any surprises for me when we face the panel, it'll look like I don't know what I'm talking about, then it'll only make things worse. Ready?"

Jason nodded yes.

"First question, Are you sexually active?" Jeff asked bluntly.

"I've kissed, I been touched, and then that thing on the bus. Does that count?"

"Yes, son, that counts. But, what I want to know is this, have you had sex? Do you know what I mean, all the way, intercourse?"

"Yes, I know what you mean." Jason blushed. "No, Dad, I haven't…"

"Don't be embarrassed. Sex is great, but it's never as good as when you're doing it with someone you love." Jeff lit another cigarette.

"The girl… is she sexually active?"

"The guys say so… She sure seemed like she knew what she was doing to me, but then what do I know… The guys call me Chaste instead of Jase."

"I know, son, I have ears. Don't worry about it, the guys aren't all that bright. Look, it's going to be all right, okay? Just relax. Okay, so you haven't had sex with her, or anyone else. Did you ask her to do that to you?"

"No, Dad."

"Has anyone else ever done to you what she was doing?"

"No, Dad."

"Did you start mouth kissing first?"

"Yes, Dad."

"Did you French kiss?"

"Yes, Dad."

"Did you touch her... any of her private parts?"

"I felt her up there. Dad, do you think I'm a social retard? I'm around your garage, and the women there just embarrass the crap out of me! Like all the guys have done so much more than me."

"Yeah, some of those gals should wash their mouths out with soap. My guess is, those guys aren't gettin' any either. Don't rush things, son. When the time is right, you'll do fine. Maybe it's my fault, I'm the one who told you not to even kiss a girl until you're married."

Jason finally smiled remembering a little blonde haired girl in kindergarten.

"Did you touch her?"

"Ummm... yeah... but just her boobs."

"Jason, did she touch, or fondle you... before she put her mouth on you?"

"Yes, Dad, she did. We were just kissing, and stuff and then I felt her hand on me. Just like in France when Colette touched me, it was like nothin' else in the whole world mattered. But, I never touched her, or any girl... down there. That's the truth, Dad."

"Son, I believe you. I don't think I have any more questions, do you?"

"Dad, can we go get something to eat? I don't want to go home hungry, and have to sit at that table listening to Tom going off on me about this one more night." His blue eyes met his dad's, and were practically begging.

"Sounds good to me. What are you up for?"

"There's a Burger Barn not too far from here. I'd like a Bad Dog, but that's too far away, or maybe it's not far enough. Besides, you never take me there anymore. How about we go to Paris, and get a bite? I really miss Colonel Pop and Grande-mère." Jason regained some of his sense of humor.

Jeff started the Camaro, and drove towards the Burger Barn. "Wise ass." Jeff grinned then asked, "How's Rianne? Any of this affecting her?"

"She's a pain in the a... armpit. She kinda knows what is going on. Since that Rocky, and the split lip thing. She just rolls her eyes when Tom starts chewing me out, and Mom starts crying. Tom acts like I should be crucified over this."

That statement gave Jeff an idea. The guys each ate a deluxe cheeseburger, a large order of fries, and drank a few root beers. Jeff thought it best not to go to church with beer on his breath. He wanted to be in full charge of all his senses when he sat in on that meeting.

"Beth. It's Jeff. Say listen, Jason and I will meet you at the church at 7:00… Every thing is fine… Yes, he ate. Rianne isn't going to be there is she? Okay, good. Tell her Daddy says hi and misses her. Thanks. See you in a couple of hours. Bye."

"Jason, how many people do you think are going to be there at that meeting?"

"Probably ten."

"Okay, now I'd like some nails, and some rocks, and a bag, so let's go to Discount Mart, then we'll go over to the river bank."

"Hey, Dad, do you need a beer or somethin'? What you're saying doesn't make much sense."

"Trust me, my son, trust me."

As they walked along the river bank, they picked up rocks and stones. Jeff had Jason hold each one, and decide if it was good for tossing, or not. If Jason liked the way it felt in his hand, Jeff had him drop it in the bag after rinsing it off at the rivers edge. Jason was relaxing a bit more now that he could see his dad wasn't calling him a warped, perverted sinner. He thought a moment, "Dad, everybody else is really upset with me for what happened. I'd like to ask you about something without getting in even more trouble just for wondering…"

"You know you can ask me anything, son. How, and what I answer will depend on the question. So, go ahead, ask away."

"Well, I was just sitting there kinda light headed like, not really knowing what was happening, but honestly, Dad, I was enjoying the hell out of what she was doing to me. Is that normal? And even if it's not normal, and it feels that darn good, why is it wrong?"

"I'm sure you did enjoy the hell out of it, Jason. It's very normal to feel pleasure with intimate physical contact. I've told you that before. Some feelings are darn good, but are best if enjoyed with God's blessing. Jason, I don't want to push any particular life style on you, nor do I want to go against what you've been taught about morals. But, I have to be right up front with you about this. I feel the worst thing about this situation is that you took a private part of your life, and put it right out on public display. This has to do with respect. Doing that in the back of the bus showed no respect for the girl, or the people around you, and ultimately no respect for yourself. Love making between a man and a woman that love each other inside the bond of marriage is special. It's the most incredible, gratifying, satisfying, fulfilling gift God ever gave to mankind. I'd love to still be married to your mother, but that isn't the way the cards fell. Life doesn't always deal us the hand we would like to play. That urge, and that pleasure you felt, son, it doesn't go away. Remember our talk in the tree house a few years ago? Unlike animals, people choose to do intimate things in private. That's why my bedroom door is shut when I'm not alone."

Jason blushed remembering interrupting his dad having sex when Karen accidentally left the door open. He nodded his head, fully understanding what his dad was talking about. They walked on, still selecting rocks. "Jason, I loved being married. It was the only time in my life I really felt like a man."

Jeff walked into the meeting room with Jason a little early to get a feel for the place, and to form his battle plan. Shades of Colonel Vincent Madison were coming through. The only person there was Tony, who politely introduced himself. He gave Jason a reassuring pat on the back, and told him that he thought he was a good boy irregardless of the outcome. Jeff eyed him suspiciously with a stone cold look on his face, but did shake his hand. They sat down, and Jeff opened two root beers that he'd brought in for them.

Jeff opened up a conversation with Jason about the body work he planned on doing to the split window 1963 Corvette that he had just picked up at an auction. Jason mentioned that working with fiber glass was something he wanted to learn about, and get into. He then asked if there was any major body damage. Jeff said it wasn't anything they couldn't do a top notch job on, if they followed all the steps, didn't take short cuts, and took the time to do it right. Jason asked if it was mechanically sound. Jeff assured him that it was, but said the interior was ragged out. Jason mentioned the names of several auto supply catalogs that carried genuine GM parts that could be purchased and installed, that wouldn't depreciate the cars stock value. They talked about how many previous owners the car had had, and how many cars of that body style had been manufactured. Jason asked for the Camaro as soon as the Vette was road ready. Jeff told him to wish in one hand and spit in the other, then see which got filled the fastest. Jason was laughing with his dad, forgetting what they were there for. Jeff looked long at his son's maturing face, and just loved the boy.

After several minutes of listening to them, Tony mentally noted the ease of discussion, and fond looks between the father and son. He began to doubt the extent of truth behind the wild stories he'd heard over the years about the Madison children's father. It appeared to him that Jason and Mr. Madison had a rapport that most men would love to have with their sons.

The teenage girl, her foster parents, and a social worker arrived next. She seemed much more upset than Jason. Jeff wondered if she had anyone that she could trust to talk to. She made eye contact with no one. Jeff stood up when Beth entered the room, and shook her hand. He nodded, said "Tom", and sat down when Tom offered his hand. Everyone sat down. The pastor, and deacons all filed in, then took their seats.

The head deacon read from a paper that stated all acts of sexual misconduct, and other various charges against the children. The little teenaged girl burst into tears, and ran out of the room. The social worker followed her out. Her foster parents resigned from the church, and left right behind them.

Tom stood up, then apologized for what he perceived as Jason's wrong doing, "I assure each of you here tonight that my son, stepson," he corrected himself, "has been raised in a better environment than most children. The home that I provide for Beth, and her children does not lend itself to an atmosphere that would encourage low life's, and derelict people to hang around. My, our home is not contributory to children having the morals of barnyard animals."

The pastor and deacons all nodded their heads.

When Jeff was sure everyone there had their turn to speak, and they were finished slinging all the mud they were going to sling, he stood up. Beth felt both kinds of butterflies, nerves and flutters. He looked regal standing there, tall and statuesque like his father the Colonel, and composed and in control, like his mother. Jeff sure had changed from when they first met. She had no idea what to expect from him in this situation. He put the bag on the table. He'd found a Bible, and placed it at his fingertips. He cleared his throat, and glanced eye to eye at everyone left sitting around the table.

"Hello, I would like to introduce myself to those of you who don't know me. My name is Jeffrey Madison, and I am very proud to say that I am Jason Madison's father. I am the sole owner of a successful custom auto shop. I have three full time employees, not including myself, and several part time assistants. We do major and minor work on American made automobiles, and select foreign vehicles. I mention this only because I wouldn't want to be confused with a fly by night, here today gone tomorrow scam operation. My business is stable and reputable. My son has worked with me as my assistant since he could stand on a high chair, his mother can verify that fact. I trust him.

"There has been accusation after accusation charged here tonight, however neither child was asked one question. I questioned my son extensively before coming to this meeting. I repeat, I trust him, and I don't believe he is a liar. There is no doubt that what happened, happened, for that I apologize. I'm sure he will apologize, too, if given the opportunity. I want to assure you that Jason understands the seriousness of this situation, and he realizes now that it never should have happened.

"I now have a few questions for you people. Where was the supervision on that bus? Where were they? And, how did the situation escalate to the point that it did without a responsible adult stopping it at the kissing stage? The way I see it, my son is a victim. When my little Marianne is on that church bus in a few years, can I trust her virtue to you people? Or, will she be condemned in the same manner as my son has been, if she's caught with a boy that has his face between her legs?"

Beth gasped. Tom put his hands over his face. Eyes were wide open. Mouths were agape.

"I'm not finished yet." Jeff continued on…

"I have something in this bag for the little girl that obviously needs love and attention more than anyone here realizes." He reached in the bag, and pulled out a patch with a large red, capital "A", and flung it on the table before shoving it in the direction of the pastor. "She needs this like she needs a hole in the head, as you've already tagged her with the invisible scarlet letter. She'll wear it the rest of her life, unless someone decent comes along that can convince her that she's worth something more than a piece of meat. Quite obviously she didn't find that person at this church." He then pulled out a second identical patch, and tossed it toward Tom. "Here you go, pal, you might want to make my wife wear this. You see, in my religion, which happens to worship the same God that you do, we don't believe in divorce." Jeff turned to the Pastor. "The way we see it, every time Mr. Ericsen climbs into bed with *my* wife, *they* are committing adultery. When your good friend here, brother Tom made reference to morals of barnyard animals, he actually confirmed what the Book of Romans, Chapter 2 verse 1 says, " …for at whatever point you judge the other, you are condemning yourself, because you who pass judgment do the same things." Jeff passed the opened Bible in front of all of their faces as he pointed to the scripture. From the bag, he pulled out six barbed spikes, and placed them on the table. Then he dumped out the bag completely, emptying it of a dozen or so rocks. Turning in the Bible to the Old Testament, he began to read Deuteronomy 21:18 "If a man has a stubborn and rebellious son who does not obey his father and mother and who will not listen to them when they discipline him, his father and mother shall take hold of him and bring him to the elders at the gate of his town… …Then all the men of his town shall stone him to death." Jeff closed the Bible, glanced around the table again, and continued, "I've given you a choice here. You could crucify my son for his misconduct as was the Roman's method of punishment, or you could stone him to death. I thought stoning would be much more appropriate personally. That way we all can have an active role," he said as he placed a rock in front of each person including Beth and Tom. He also kept a rock for himself. He ordered, "Jason, stand up. NOW!"

His son obeyed, and was shaking scared. This was quite obviously unrehearsed. Jason realized that his dad kept the biggest rock for himself.

Jeff made reference to the Gospel of John, Chapter 8 and quoted, "If any one of you is without sin, let him be the first to throw a stone…"

Jason pulled his arms up around his head when his dad aimed at him with the stone in his hand. Jeff swung his arm as if to throw it, but dropped the stone on the table, stating, "I have sinned. I can't go first."

The look of shear terror on Jason's face, made Beth shriek before she realized that Jeff had set the rock down. Jeff quickly rushed to Jason, put his hands on his sons shoulders, to steady his boy. He kissed him on the forehead, then embraced him tightly. With his strong hand around the boys head, he pressed it firmly to his heart, and kept whispering, "It's okay Jason, it's okay. It's okay. Your Father loves you, and your daddy loves you, too. It's okay, son. It's okay."

Jason's heart was still pounding, but he knew what his dad had done. Much the same as Isaac, who carried his own kindling, Jason had chosen his own rocks. "I love you, Dad," he barely whispered. But, everyone heard.

Jeff released his boy. He pointed to the stones, as if to say there they are, pick them up. Hugging Jason again, he solemnly stated, "Dominus vobiscum. My beloved son, good luck." Jeff walked out.

The meeting was eerily silent after Jeff left the room. One by one, all filed out without saying another word. Following the pastors lead, they walked toward the bench where Jeff was sitting. Extending his hand, the pastor began to speak, "Mr. Madison, we are all sorry, and embarrassed-"

"Well, you're not half as sorry and embarrassed as my teenager is." Jeff said as he rose to his feet, and put his hands in his pockets. "When I was a boy, my father and I visited a church of this denomination near a base in the mid west a few times. Good pastor, he really could preach a great sermon. One sticks in my mind, he named it, 'Beware of Snakes in the Garden'. There are many snakes in the garden, Pastor."

"Mr. Madison, I really don't think-"

"That's obvious. If you don't think there are snakes in the garden, Pastor, we'd all be standing here in the nude, wouldn't we? Don't look at me like that. There is plenty of sin in this old world. It's in the Book. Read it, Genesis, Chapter 3." He turned his back, and stood gazing out the window.

Tom, Beth and Jason remained in the conference room. Beth ran her fingers through her darling son's curls. She hugged him tenderly, but his eyes were still downcast. "Jason, Mommy loves you very much. I pray that you, and God forgive me for what I've failed to do for you." She kissed him, and left the room next. She saw Jeff in the foyer with his forehead resting on the window. She walked up behind him, and put her hand on his upper left arm. He shrugged it off. "Jeff, I'm so sorry."

"So why tell me? I'm not hurting for myself at the moment, I hurt for my son. Jason was exploited, and no one was willing to help him. I'm very disappointed... Beth, I will love you until the day I die, but right now, at this moment, I don't like you, or anyone else associated with this church very much. Just go away." Jeff never turned to look at her.

"Okay, I understand, Jeff. But I'd like to say one more thing before I leave. You are brilliant. You handled this situation perfectly. I'm very proud to be the mother of your children." Beth turned, and found herself face to face with Tom and Jason.

Jason spoke, "Mom, if it's okay with you, I'd like to skip school tomorrow, and go spend an extra night with my dad tonight, if it's okay with him, too. I'll give up a night another weekend if you want. My grades are good, it won't kill me to miss one day. I really need a break."

Beth tearfully nodded her head yes, and broke into gushing tears when Jason hugged her, and said, "I love you, Mom. I know you're submissive, and you have to do what... you feel is right for the family. Tom says he cares about me, and he just doesn't want me to mess up my life. I forgave him when he asked."

"Dad, please can I go home with you?"

Jeff nodded yes, and smiled for the first time since the meeting. "Only if you go wash your face." The two guys headed for the mens room. "I don't want anyone to think it was me that put that lipstick all over your cheeks. It's not my color." Jeff made exaggerated kissing noises.

Jason hollered, "Dad! Yuk! Stop it! That's gross!" He socked his dad, and Jeff pretended it hurt him.

Beth stood watching Jeff, and their son walking away. Jason was getting so tall. If he'd get a hair cut, it wouldn't be any time at all before it would be hard to tell them apart from the back. A tear rolled down her cheek.

"Come on, Babe, let's go. I don't want to be gone too long after the babysitter puts Marianne to bed." Tom said softly. He slipped his arm around Beth's shoulder, and walked toward the door. Once outside he paused, "Beth, I'm sorry. I worry about the kids getting in trouble like I did. Kids can make mistakes before they even know they've made them."

Tony was waiting for the father and son to leave before he locked up the church. He stood smiling at the Madison men still carrying on.

"Dad! Speaking of color what color is the Vette? Are you gonna fix it up before it goes on the road, or are you gonna drive it as is for awhile? Did you tell me what size the engine is? I was just wondering, tomorrow after the shop closes, can I drive it around the lot? I bet it makes the Camaro feel like a mud puppy. This summer I get my learners permit, then I can take it out on the road with you, or one of the guys."

"Oh, yeah? Says who? How do you think you can drive with all that hair hanging in your eyes? Now that Candy's in the Air Force, she can't use all those hair bows and ribbons. Maybe I can get her to send you a few purses full of them. You said you wanted to do body work on the Vette, now all you talk about is driving it. Hmmm, I should uh known you were just scammin' me again!"

Tony only hoped he could be half that successful raising his own children.

Chapter 19

1978

"Jeff, do you ever think about getting married?" Jodi asked as she sat with Jeff one morning for coffee. She looked at him wondering what his answer would be.

"Jodi, it depends on how you meant the question. Yes, I think about getting married. I think about putting on my dress uniform, and going to the Chapel, and being nervous about my parents reaction. I think about seeing Beth walk up the aisle wearing her mother's gown, looking beautiful on her dad's arm. I knew she was going to be in my arms that night, and how I believed she'd be there forever. Yes, I think about getting married often. I don't think about getting remarried."

"I guess that's not how I meant the question. I'm sorry. It's just we've been together off and on for nearly ten years. I thought maybe you thought about… us."

Jeff rubbed his hand over his face, and let out a long breath. "Jodi, come on… You are such a free spirit. You're right it has been ten years, but I wouldn't hardly call us exclusive. There are nights I think you're with me, and I turn around, and you're gone. I don't know where you're coming from most of the time. One minute you act like you are vying for the homemaker of the year award, and the next you're wanting to take on the Navy. I like you very much. It's always a happier time when you're around. When there's a party you're always in the center of it. When it came to a 'maybe' and a 'sure thing', I'd always go with the 'sure thing'. Even with all our history, I still feel that you're a 'maybe' sometimes."

"Jeff, that hurts." Jodi took a swallow of coffee.

"Jodi, you're a great companion, you're fun, a real party doll, but it's like you're always looking for the next thrill." Jeff reached over to light her cigarette.

"People always make assumptions about me that aren't necessarily true."

"And, what kind of assumptions would you be referring to Ms. Jodi? I think I know you pretty well by now. Care to elaborate?"

"You know, things aren't always what they seem. My landlady used to tease me, jokingly, but I think half seriously, that my apartment was the 'Hot Pillow Motel'. She seemed to get such a kick out of it, that I played along. It appeared that I was popular, because of all the 'boyfriends' that hung around."

Jeff laughed, "Ten years together, and this is the first I've heard the hippie pad called the Hot Pillow Motel? You must've had a revolving door to earn a name like that for your apartment. Was it like a commune or something?"

"No! Geez, just assume the worst, Jeff. I ought to smack you. The guys were just friends. I knew I was cute, I knew I was funny, they knew I always had pot, they knew I always shared my pot. I was never fooled by their intentions for a minute. The truth about the Hot Pillow Motel is quite a let down. Wanna hear my life story?" Jodi got the coffee and freshened up their cups.

"Okay, I'm up for it, but not from the time you were born. Start from when you first started liking boys. Were you one of those little teases that we had to buy French fries, and cherry cokes for, hoping they'd man handle us out of gratitude?" Jeff laughed as he teased her.

"Neither, when I first noticed that boys weren't disgusting, I was thirteen and a half years old, and in the eighth grade. I had the cutest, thirteen year old boyfriend. He had black hair, and blue eyes. A very rare combination indeed. Odd, I should end up with you!"

"Jodi, we haven't ended, or ended up either. So you were thirteen and a half?" Jeff opened a new pack of cigarettes and lit one.

"Yeah, but we were just kids. He gave me my first kiss, and asked me to go steady, but not at the same time. We were in love. Puppy Love. It was 1963, and good girls didn't put out, you know, go all the way. I was a good girl, so I didn't. I got dumped."

"Okay, here it comes, all men are jerks. So skip that part. What happened next?" Jeff rolled his eyeballs.

"I had two more 'steady' boyfriends after him over the next couple of years. I didn't put out, and I got dumped. I kept my virginity all through high school. I was saving myself for the man I married. Shortly after graduation, I met the 'man' that stirred up my hormones. He kissed me, and thunder rumbled in my soul. We'd kiss, and kiss, and kiss, until I would ache with longing." Jodi pressed on her stomach.

"That was dumb. Why didn't you just 'do it'?"

"Jeff, I was a good girl. I don't remember when in the relationship, his hands started to wander, and I quit saying don't touch. I enjoyed his touch. He went away to college, to dodge Vietnam. He would come home every few weeks. He said he wanted to marry me. I believed him. I was really in love with him. By the time Christmas came, my virginity was gone."

"Did you cry?" Jeff asked remembering Beth's tears when they did it the first time.

"You bet I did. The jack ass was more concerned about the car seat being messed up than he was about me. But, I 'loved' him. He wanted to marry me. I did the typical eighteen year old girl thing, I started to gather. My hope chest wasn't so hopeless after all, until February when he dumped me. I cried my eyes out. He dumped me because he got another girl pregnant. I was devastated. It made no sense to me. I didn't put out, I got dumped. I put out, I got dumped."

"Sounds to me like he was a total jerk. You were better off without him. Did he marry the other girl? Have you ever seen him again?" Jeff asked sympathetically.

"Months later, I ran into him someplace. He took one look at me, and his jaw dropped. I was so darn cute, and I drove a red GTO. He asked me out. I asked him about the 'pregnant girlfriend'. He was ashamed to tell me. He made no eye contact. Seems before he met her at college, she had a baby, and gave it up for adoption. She miscarried his baby, dumped him, then went back to her child's father." Jodi's eyes looked off in space.

"You went back with him, didn't ya?" Jeff knew.

"I went out with him. I hadn't had sex since the last time I was with him, probably around ten months prior. I can't remember if I had sex with him on our first date back together, or not. He turned me on to smoking marijuana. We were together a few times, and I ended up pregnant. We bought rings, we had our blood tests, we bought our license. I had a miscarriage. My parents never found out." Jodi's eyes looked bitter now.

Jeff could see the change in Jodi's demeanor. He lit a cigarette, and handed to her.

"Thanks. He dumped me. Somehow I finished beauty school. I got a job and moved out of my parents house. I got the apartment with Marci and Jenny."

"Marci the fucking dog." Jeff still hated her as much at that Hanoi Hollywood traitor slut. "Well, Jodi those were a couple of positive moves. You were on your way. That had to be a while before I met you at the Alibi. What happened to the beauty career?"

"I needed extra money. I took a part time job as a... dancer. It paid much better, but I wasn't prepared at that age for what that was all about."

"What do you mean?"

"My 'first' and I were the same age, and of course all the boys I'd dated in high school, and got dumped by, had been my own age, also. I had so little experience. I met a man at the strip club. We dated, we smoked pot. At barely twenty years old, I was no match for a twenty six year old, divorced man, with two children. In the Hot Pillow Motel, I was date raped. After the initial fright of, 'can you karate a bullet?' it wasn't a vicious rape. But, it still wasn't a pleasant experience. The incident occurred because a few of the old neighborhood boys that I had never even dated, were bragging that I had put out to them, all of them. The man was twenty six, he should have known the school boys were liars. He figured if I did it with them, I should do it with him. Of course after he'd done the deed, he knew I wasn't a virgin. To him, one was the same as a thousand. He convinced me I was a cheap piece of white trash, and I was lucky that I had him. I kept clinging to him because I felt so useless, and dirty. I felt I was lucky to have anyone. I started to smoke pot heavy. I guess it was heavy. What's heavy? I smoked in the morning, and I smoked in the evening, every weekday. I smoked all day, and all night on weekends. I quit working at the club. I was a functional user though, I had a job at a busy shop, and didn't miss any days. I came home from work one day because I had cramps, and found him in bed with Jenny."

"Jodi, you deserved better than that. Did you throw his ass out?"

"No, I got dumped. That was a good thing, but it didn't seem so at the time. She moved out, and in with him. I quit the shop, and got a job full time as a dancer. I'd come home from work, and I'd smoke up. I had a bottle full of prescription drugs that I'd accumulated. I would hold it in my hand, and I'd think, 'will this be the night?' I'd smoke myself out, and usually end up on the couch, I didn't want to sleep in that bed anyway. One night, I opened the bottle, and poured all the pills in my hand. Before I popped them in my mouth, I decided I'd call a shrink in the morning. If he could give me one good reason to live, I'd try to go on. I put the pills back in the bottle, smoked another joint, and drifted off into dreamland. The next morning I looked in the phone book, and called Dr. Young. He asked why I needed to see him. I told him people were always telling me I was crazy. He asked why I believed them. I told him that many people couldn't be wrong. He said to come right in."

"Jodi, I've told you no strings, no promises, and no commitment. I hope I've never hurt you like that."

"Jeff, it hurt so much to walk in, and find you with your ex-wife. I cried both times. But, I knew we weren't exclusive, and I knew you would always love her. I was able to deal with it because of the help I received after the abuse. If you had ever lied to me about 'us' it would have been bad, but I keep reminding myself that you've always been honest. Stupid, and inconsiderate sometimes, but honest."

"Nice to know I have some redeeming qualities. How long did you see him? The shrink that is?"

"I saw him for several months. We cleared up a number of issues that had plagued me for years. Then the big one came up, the horrible guilt that I felt over my sexual activity. He asked me who paid my rent. I told him I did. He asked if anyone bought my food, or paid my utilities. I told him no. I was twenty one, and self supporting. He said what I did was my business. Nobody owned me, and I owed no one any explanation as to how I lived my life. If I wanted to get 'familiar' with any man of my choosing, it was my business, and my business alone."

"Wow, powerful words. Were you like a free spirit from that point in time?" Jeff wondered.

'Well, yes and no. I could do what I wanted, and with whom ever I wanted, but still didn't feel worthy of the air I breathed."

"Jodi, everybody has a right to the air. Even us smokers. Why did you feel that way? Well, never mind, let me rephrase that question. How did you get over feeling that way?"

"The landlady had a husband. He was kind to me, and never was disrespectful. He saw something in me that perhaps no one else did, and I still don't know what it was. He made me feel good about myself without asking any questions about what I'd done, or who I'd been with. He told me I was more than just cute, and funny. He told me I was smart, and I had a lot to offer the world. I just needed to find myself. He was what I needed in my life to help me on that journey to self discovery."

"So, Jodi, you were twenty one, and how old was this guy?"

"Forty seven."

"Oh, Jodi! Your landlord?"

"Oh, Jeff! It wasn't like that at all. He was a mentor to me."

"What did his wife say? I mean, you're so cute, wasn't she intimidated by a young uninhibited chick like yourself?"

"Nah, he was totally devoted to her. She knew I just needed a 'dad'. I've talked to her over the years, and also have thanked her for the help she gave me."

"Calling your apartment the Hot Pillow Motel helped?" He chuckled playfully.

Jodi laughed. "Yes, in a way it did. It became such a joke over the years, that it always brought us laughs I'd never talked about the rape. Not to her husband, or even to the shrink.

She attended a rape seminar, then questioned me about what I'd do if I was ever in a dangerous situation. I froze. I didn't want to talk. She told me, and I quote, 'Submit. It isn't worth losing your life.' Those words freed me from the guilt that I'd been carrying around believing I was responsible for what had happened. He ended up in jail, someone else was braver than me. I didn't press charges, basically I couldn't. I'd gone out with him, and invited him inside. A good lawyer would have twisted it to the point of me looking like the guilty party. After all, I was a dancer…"

"It doesn't seem fair though, does it? Life stinks sometimes. So, the shrink got you to believe that you could be intimate with whomever, the landlord got you to believe that you were a person worthy of air. How did your apartment earn the title of Hot Pillow Motel? Doesn't sound like you were gettin' it that much to me."

"They had a son, he had a lot of friends. We all smoked pot. I shared. They shared. I met new friends at my new job. We all smoked pot. I shared. They shared. I still had my old friends at my old job. We all smoked pot. I shared. They shared. Like I said before, it appeared that I was popular because of all the 'boyfriends' that hung around. I was never fooled by their intentions for a minute. I knew I was cute, I knew I was funny, they knew I always had pot, they knew I always shared my pot. Out of that whole group of friends, I got 'familiar' with two men. Not at the same time, not even in the same months. They didn't know each other. I did what I wanted to do, with whom I wanted to do it. Neither fling worked out. They both dumped me. They were both Vietnam vets. Both of them had big time drug problems beyond mine. I was still no where near being 'experienced'. I learned a little from one, and a lot from the other. I shed a tear over one, but none for the other. Neither breakup was devastating. My apartment was the party house. Just because the guys came over, didn't mean I was sleeping with them. But, we sure smoked a lot of grass."

"Was Rocky's dad one of the guys you just mentioned?"

"No, we hadn't met yet. There was this guy that hung around named Billy. Nicest dang fellow you ever wanted to meet. He must've fixed up half the marriages in the county. He was so insecure that he always brought a buddy with him whenever he'd go visit a girl. The buddy always got the girl. Too bad too, because he was a real good kisser!"

"Did you do it with him?" Jeff smirked.

"Nope, just kissed him. He brought Stan over early one evening. I wasn't working at the club any more. Well, just for parties, no more dancing every night. I was so embarrassed the night you showed up for that party, and you recognized me from the Alibi. That was my last party jumping out of cakes."

"So, what happened when Stan came over?"

"I had just bought my stereo, and didn't know where all the wires went. He just jumped right in there, and started hooking things up. I didn't know this guy from Adam, and here he was messing with my brand new equipment. Without thinking, or knowing what he did for a living, I said to him, 'If you don't know what the hell you are doing, keep your goddam fucking hands off my stereo.' He shot me a look. His eyes were as blue as yours, and they went right through to my soul. I soon ended up pregnant, he went to Nam. There was no way in hell I was gonna give up his baby."

"Feisty little vixen, weren't you? So was it love at first sight for him? You are cute Jodi."

"Stan wouldn't turn it down, but I don't know about love at first sight, or love at all. He came back from Nam all strung out on heroin, and he smoked marijuana non stop. He couldn't hold a job for more than a week. He cheated left and right, right in front of me basically, but I loved him so much, that I didn't care. He kept saying they meant nothing to him,

I was the one he loved. His comment, 'if it feels good, do it'. It was just free love. Rent wasn't free, and groceries weren't free, and Rocky needed diapers, they weren't free either. I had to work. He told me he'd been with Marci. Reminded me of the other jerk, but I got through it. I figured I'd show him, so I had sex with Larry. Stan got so mad. I reminded him that he was the one who was always pushing free love, and if it feels good, do it. It must've felt awfully good to him because next thing I knew he's in the sack with Jenny. I didn't want to fight any more so I just got in with them. I'm not real proud of that, but life gets sick when there are too many drugs, and not enough self esteem in your life. Stan got busted for dealing, and got sent up right before I met you the first time."

"Jodi, Jodi, Jodi... Sounds like neither of us had our life turn out the way we'd planned. Would you marry him now?"

"I don't know. All I have to do is think about him, and my heart flip flops a dozen times. It would never work out. Never. I just wish Rocky had a dad. Jeff, you are awfully good with him considering what a pain in the ass he can be, but I see how you are with Jason. I wish that Rocky had that in his life. Stan loves him. He really does, he's just so messed up."

"Jodi, I bet he loves you, too. A man's life is meaningless if there isn't a woman that truly cares about him in it. Jodi, we could get married. I could be happy with you, but Jodi, if something happened to Tom, like if he died, or she ever smartens up and dumps his arrogant ass, I'd be outta here in a heartbeat if she wanted me back. I'm afraid I'll never be totally free. You mean a lot to me, but I can't give you what you want. Want to try living together?"

Jodi and Rocky moved in with Jeff, and she did the best she could. Life was actually going better than Jeff ever thought that it would. Rocky went to the employee lounge at the Alibi Inn after school, so Jeff didn't have to be worried about him getting in the mens way. Jodi fed them, and since

Rocky already did his homework, he didn't have to listen to any fighting over lessons. They'd watch TV, their favorite was the new sit com about the '50's. Day to day life wasn't bad at all.

Jason had always liked Jodi, and they continually teased each other. Rocky was an annoyance to him now though. When Rocky was little he was fun to play tricks on, but now Jason was sixteen, and was getting into things he hadn't ought to be getting into. Rocky was a thorn in his side most of the time. It did help though that just before her tenth birthday, Rocky had kissed Marianne. She socked him in the face, and split his lip. Tom had such a fit over that, he was doing even more to keep Marianne from going to her dad's, and that suited Jason just fine. It suited Jodi just fine also. She really liked Marianne, but when she was there, sleeping arrangements were such a mess. She and Marianne slept in the room that Jeff and she shared during the week. Jeff, and the boys slept in the living room, and carried on rough housing throughout the night. Usually, Marianne pulled her curtain, and Jodi could hear her crying. It was fun being with her mom and Tom, because Tom cared and fussed over her so much, she never lacked for attention at their home. Nobody knew how much Marianne hurt that she never had time alone with her daddy. Jeff didn't know what to do. She shared none of the same interests that he had, and she didn't share with him what she did like other than horses. She wasn't interested in dolls anymore, and they had passed the playing in the tub stage a long time ago. He considered teaching her how to drive, but she was only ten, Jason would have a fit, since he wasn't allowed to drive until he was thirteen.

Marianne asked if Jeff would build her a barn. Of course he said yes, he couldn't say no to his little girl any more than Tom could. Then she asked if she could bring over a pony since there was plenty of room on the property for one.

Jason went off the wall, "Just who do you think is going take care of that thing when you aren't around Rianne? Those animals take up too much space, they take up too much time, and they stink. Dad's got enough to do around here without spending half his life grooming your disgusting animal. He doesn't have the time to go running across five acres twice a day just to feed a critter that's gonna fill the yard up with horse sh-"

"ALRIGHT! That's enough! Thank you very much for your brilliant observations Jason Madison, but if you recall, I'M the dad around here. Rianne, sweetie, Daddy loves you very much. I'd love to say yes to you about the pony. Maybe we can work it out, Baby Cakes. You know since Daddy expanded the garage it's busier than ever around here, if you could stay during the week to take care of the pony, I would be willing to care for it on the weekend, since I take a half a day Saturday, and all day Sunday off. Do you think your mom and Tom would let you live here with me, and visit them on the weekends?"

Marianne tearfully shook her head no.

"I think you're right, your mother would never agree for you to live here. A little girl needs to be with her mother more than she needs to be living with her dad just to have a pony."

"Daddy? Can I come every other month? I love you, Dad, but I never get to see, or ride my pony when there is school."

Jeff knew he couldn't compete. "Sure, Marianne, every other month would be fine. I'll talk to your mother, and see if we can agree on this, or if I need to go through court again." He felt like one more crack in the foundation their relationship had begun.

Jodi noticed changes in Jason's behavior. Jeff didn't see it, he blamed it on puberty. As far as he could see, the only problem that boy had was his smart mouth, and his refusal to get a haircut. Both Jeff and Jodi noticed that they were constantly running out of cigarettes. It became obvious that the thief was

Rocky. No amount of lecturing, screaming, or threatening, or grounding stopped his pilfering. Unfortunately, they had to start locking up their cigarettes. They also noticed that the condoms were disappearing. They decided not to put a stop to that. More than likely it was Jason taking them. They both felt if he needed them, it was better that he took them, than to go unprotected. They weren't wrong, but little did they know, Rocky still thought they were water balloons.

"Jodi, did you watch the news today?" Jeff asked as he came in.

"No, I don't pay any attention to what's going on in the world. I can't do anything about it, so why bother?"

Jeff shook his head at how vacuous Jodi could be at times. "There was a mass suicide in Jonestown. More than 900 people have died, including 276 children." He kicked off his work boots, and headed for the TV.

"Kids? Man, that's a bummer. Who were they? And how do kids commit suicide?" She asked sounding a bit interested.

"Kids usually do what they're told. Their parents were members of a religious cult called the People's Temple. Seems a California Congressman went there to investigate them. Ryan, was the Congressman, and four other people with him were shot by the cult security guards. Their leader, Reverend Jim Jones then ordered the entire group to commit suicide by drinking cyanide-laced fruit juice. What's this world coming to?" Jeff found the report on TV just as they were cutting to a commercial break.

"Reminds me of the time Jenny put acid in the Kool-Aid, and I walked in just in time before Rocky was gonna take a swallow."

"I don't recall that." Jeff looked at her blankly.

"Happened that week back in 68 or 69 when you went back to your wife." Jodi really couldn't remember what year it happened.

"That's exactly why I always had a fit when you, or your friends had drugs in the house. I guess pot isn't all that bad, but still, it isn't legal."

"Jeff, that reminds me, did you smoke up without me?"

"Huh?" Jeff looked like she'd spoken in an unknown tongue.

"Did you take one of my numbers? I know I had three joints in my jewelry box at the beginning of the weekend, and now there are only two."

"No, Jodi, I don't like it that much to smoke alone. Are you sure you didn't take one to smoke up when the boys got on your nerves fighting over the TV last Friday night?"

"Yes, I'm sure. Remember, I found the bottle of scotch in the back of the cupboard? I fixed me a scotch and soda. You drank a shot, and a couple of beers. I didn't make any excuses to go outside for anything. I'd like to know what the hell happened to it. Seems like everything needs to be locked up around here." Jodi hoped he'd catch on.

"You don't think Rocky took it since we're being more careful about the cigarettes do you?"

Jodi just looked at him. He wouldn't take the hint.

Jason called and asked his Dad if he could start staying overnight on Sunday, too. He was in a garage band now, and they needed to practice on Saturday, and hopefully get a gig for Saturday nights. He was excited about being the lead singer, and girls were noticing him. He knew that would clinch the deal with his dad. The girls really were starting to like him, the church bus incident had humiliated him past the point of wanting sex. He'd earned himself a reputation of being a tease, but he didn't mind. His new band member friends liked him just fine. He was good looking enough to attract the girls they wanted, and he usually showed up with a joint to share, and condoms to donate, if anyone needed them.

Having a free Saturday night, Jeff asked Jodi if she wanted to go to the Alibi. She was all for the idea. Rocky was at a sleepover with some boys his own age from school, and he'd be gone until Sunday afternoon.

"Look who's here on a Saturday night. You two are looking happy. Still shacking up?" Mack asked rather weakly.

"Yes, Mack we are. Jeff and I have been talking about getting married." Jodi announced with a big smile.

Jeff kind of blushed, and cast his eyes down. He nodded his head yes. It was the truth, they had talked about it. He truly hoped she didn't take him up on his offer of 'we could get married' prior to moving in with him. He cared about her, but he didn't know... he needed to talk to his priest.

"Well, congratulations! A round of drinks on the house to celebrate the future Mr. and Mrs. Madison." Mack announced while Deana seethed.

All the waitresses that knew Jodi came running up to see if she had a ring. She didn't. She told them, she wasn't into materialism. It was an old hippie thing. They asked if they'd set a date. They hadn't, Jeff needed to get a religious issue taken care of first.

Jodi didn't know if she was in love, or in love with the idea of being married. She knew she cared for Jeff a lot, and that he really rolled in the sack, but marriage was so serious. She was almost sorry she'd ever brought up the subject. Jeff would never tolerate her being unfaithful once they were married. She knew she had a weakness for smoke, and for men when she smoked. One of the waitresses wanted Jodi to have her picture taken with Jeff. They posed for the camera facing each other with his hands on her shoulders, and hers on his waist. They were looking in each others eyes when the camera flashed.

Before they let go, Jodi's eyes drifted, and she shouted, "Oh, My GOD!" Her arms dropped from his waist, as she focused her eyes across the bar at a long haired hippie freak that was walking toward her. She had one hand over her mouth as she walked swiftly toward him with tears streaming down her cheeks.

"Jodi baby! How's my little woman? Comin' home with Poppa tonight?" He asked with a great big huge grin.

"Stan, Stan, yes, yes, yes!" Jodi turned to look at Jeff, and shook her head no. She walked out of the bar with her head snuggled against Stan's shoulder, and both of her arms gripping around his waist.

Jeff was stunned. He let out a long sigh of relief, then stated loudly, "A round of drinks to celebrate the confirmed bachelorhood of Jeffrey Madison. Cheers!"

Chapter 20

1979

Stan, Jodi's true love, had painted the outside of Madison Motors after the new bays were added. Jeff took one look at it, and refused to keep it painted with swirls, flowers, psychedelic lettering, and colors. Jodi, Jason, and Jason's new friends, all thought it was pretty far out looking. But, it wasn't the image Jeff wanted to portray, especially with the massive expansion he had added to his place of business. Stan seemed to be in a drug induced time warp. Jeff explained, "Stan, it's not the '60's anymore. It's almost the '80's. The War is long over, the hippies have become yuppies." Within days, the building was repainted a popular conservative avocado green with harvest gold trim.

Other than the improvements he'd made to the garage, life was moving along with no major events. At the Alibi Inn, Deana was constantly complaining to anyone that would listen, about Mack being sick all the time, and the responsibility of running the Inn was being heaped on her. Silently, she wasn't crazy about Stan being back in Jodi and Rocky's life, but she might find a use for him some day, so she tolerated his presence. At nearly twelve years old, Rocky was very helpful, he was easy, and cheap to buy off with cigarettes, and favors.

Jodi was still trying to work it out with Stan. She still found him more difficult to live with than he was before Nam. Even when he wasn't abusing drugs and, or alcohol, a good mood could turn dark at the sound of a car backfiring, or fire crackers blasting, or thunder, or even the sound of a garbage truck.

Jeff missed Jodi more than he imagined he would. But, he understood where she was coming from, after all, Stan was Rocky's father. Stan couldn't have cared less that Jodi and Jeff had been intimate. Jeff had the feeling Stan wouldn't care if they still were, he certainly did his own thing, whether Jodi was aware of it or not. Jeff wasn't celibate, but it wouldn't be right to fool around with Jodi, since Stan was living with her again.

Jeff was sitting alone when Shauna walked into the Alibi Inn. As usual, all the men's testosterone levels started to rise as she strolled through the bar. Jeff had felt the strong attraction between Shauna and himself the first time he'd seen her there. He was still with Jodi then. When they were introduced, and lightly shook hands, Shauna looked at him with the "I'd like to play with you someday" look in her eye. Shauna seemed to be another free spirit, a much younger cross between Jodi, and Karen. He smiled to himself thinking how upset Karen was the first time he saw her again after being "caught in the act" by his kid. When it came to "your place or mine" with Karen, after that incident, it was always her place.

Jeff didn't want to be alone, but even though the attraction was strong, Shauna looked young. He knew she was legal since she was carded, and allowed into the bar. She was wearing the most perfectly fitting pair of designer jeans that any of the men had ever seen. A pair of stiletto heeled, strappy sandals made her look tall enough to be a runway model. The finishing touch was her white, fillet crocheted halter top. She was definitely braless. With a body like Shauna's, she spent most of her time on the dance floor. Each man was hoping he would be the one to get lucky. Just for kicks and giggles, Sam and Stan started a chick pool, taking bets on who would get the girl. Sam wasn't participating, seems he had picked up an infestation of phthirus pubis that had him a little crabby in more ways than one. And, Stan backed out, too, since he was in the dog house with Jodi, for once again sleeping with a bitch. Both of them put their 'nickel' on Jeff, while most of the others bet on one of the younger guys that was making a reputation for himself as the rising new Alibi Inn stud. Rather than his usual "your place or mine" line that he usually used, Jeff played it cool with Shauna. He danced with others, and winked at her as they crossed on the floor. She would glance at him, pucker her lips, and grin, as her partner would lead totally unaware. Jeff finally danced with her, and they made small talk as his eyes worked the room. Shauna knew he was playing a game, and even though she was barely twenty-one, she figured she could beat him at his own game. Playing cat and mouse, they carefully avoided each other for the rest of the evening, however there wasn't a moment in time when each didn't know where the other one was. Shauna stood alone in the crowded bar as she watched Jeff walk toward the door to leave. She had a small smile on her face that grew into a wide grin as he predictably turned around, and met her gaze. She flirtingly waved at him. He smiled, and walked back her way. He offered his hand, and she giggled as she slipped her arms around his neck. She stared up into his deep blue eyes, and again gave him the "I want to play with you" look. He leaned down, and kissed her with lightly parted lips. Shauna met his kiss, and circled her mouth across his as she gently caught his bottom lip between hers. She gave his lip sucking movements as she fluttered her tongue against it. She felt his breath quicken. She softly let go, took his upper lip between hers, and did the same thing. Jeff tightened his grip around her back as he slowly pulled his lips away from hers, then again kissed her fully, as he swirlingly moved his tongue into her mouth. His hands slipped down her back, firmly grasping her bottom, as he pulled her toward himself. She could feel he wanted her as much as she wanted him. Before they ended up being thrown out for lewd and lascivious behavior, they left together.

"Gimme five!" Sam and Stan were both all grins as they collected the take.

"Alright!" They gave each other the high five as they split the jackpot on chick pool.

Meanwhile, back at Versailles, it was a passion filled, steamy, rocking the night away evening in the apartment up over Madison Motors. Jeff only knew one woman that loved sex as much as Shauna did, and he dearly loved that woman. He didn't love Shauna, but he sure enjoyed boning her tight, sensuous, unbridled body again, and again. Jeff and Shauna knew that they'd be together again. Hedonistic pleasure was all either of them was interested in. Morning sunshine came much too soon.

Jeff's face lit up like the 4th of July, when they entered his garage, and unexpectedly saw his son sitting in the customer service lounge with Todd and Phil. They were being entertained by Sam's stories about Bike Week in Daytona Beach, shooting the Keys, and biking across Alligator Alley on Roxanne, his favorite motorcycle.

"Isn't that Jason Madison?" Shauna asked.

"Uh huh. That's my boy."

"Boy? What boy? Are you blind? That guy's a hunk." Shauna blew Jason a kiss and waved.

"Uh huh. See you later, baby doll." Jeff barely said good bye to Shauna. As he patted her rear, he gave her a peck on the cheek.

"Hey, guys! What's going on?"

"Hey, Mad. Geez, she was gorgeous, what a bod! She could be in show business. You Dog you! What's the deal? The older you get the younger they get." Phil was watching Shauna walk to her car.

Jason mumbled to Todd, "She's practically my age. She was a senior when I was a freshman." The boys rolled their eyes, as Sam hummed *Rock-a-Bye Baby*. Jeff flipped him the bird.

The old friends shook hands. Jeff blushed, side glancing Jason. "Yeah, well, uh what can I say? She's of age. So, what brings ya this way, pal?"

"Just dropped in to say good-bye. Trina and I sold the house. We're moving near to a Base in Florida."

"Wow! What a shock. When, and how did this come about?"

"Well, ya know I've been here for quite a while, and now it's time to move on."

"I thought you were retiring."

"Yep, sure am. Base Supply at Patrick where we were stationed in the 60's just went contractor."

"What?" Jeff wasn't sure he understood.

"Instead of Supply being manned by the Air Force, they've contracted it out. I can collect my military pension, and do an easier job than being a Major for a decent wage, and a lot less stress. Living in Florida again seems like a dream."

"Beth and I liked it there. Jason, do you still remember running after your mom with sand fleas on the beach?"

"I remember holding some kind of bugs that we picked up, and chasing Mom. We were laughing, and she was yelling at us. What did you do there, Dad?"

"I worked on the flight line. I was basically doing the same thing I do now, except on airplanes instead of cars. I've loved the smell of engines since I was a boy."

"How come you left airplane mechanics, Dad?" Todd asked Phil.

"Todd, haven't you listened to your mother harp about dirt?"

"Oh, yeah, she can go on about it, can't she? I was thirteen before I realized lemon scented furniture polish wasn't her perfume."

"Phillips, are you kidding me? I can't imagine switching from aircraft maintenance, to Base Supply. I always figured once you retired, you'd come to work for me. Then I could let Sam's ugly ass go." Jeff lit a cigarette, and laughed.

Sam looked at Jeff with a smirk, and rolled his cigarette around in his fingers, and across his lips. "Dog, you always were a REMF!"

"What's a REMF, Dad?" Todd looked from Sam to Phil.

Before Phil could answer, Sam laughed his raspy chuckle, and stated, "Rear Echelon Mother Fuc-"

"Sam! Shut the hell up!" Jeff grinned, put his hand up, and nodded toward the boys.

Todd and Jason looked sideways at each other, surprised that the old people knew that word.

Sam stopped what he was saying, and laughed harder, "You guys looked at those 'boys' lately? They're way past puberty, Mad."

"Phil, you relocated prior to the Cuban Missile Crisis, didn't ya?" Jeff turned to Phil

"Yeah, we went to Offutt straight from our honeymoon. Bet Patrick was hoppin' during that mess."

"Yeah, poor Beth nearly lost it again… She finally got her head together after having the baby. Her mother ragged all over her one night, and she started to sleep again. Anyway, things were finally back to normal, then the recon planes started going over. I didn't know exactly what the hell was happening, but growing up an Air Force brat, I knew when Dad was gone, something was happening somewhere. Dad had been hanging around a lot, so I figured this time it was near us. I figured right, 24/7 you could hear the planes, then barbed wire went up over night. Beth sat up all night, night after night with the baby in her arms. Thank God it was settled in days. I wasn't sleeping much myself, but I took some time off when it was over so I could take care of Jason. She was a mess again until she felt safe and secure enough to get some sleep."

"When did that happen, Dad? Where were we?" Todd asked.

"Summer of 1962, before you were born. We were still at Offutt in the mid west."

"Oh, that sounds boring." Todd not only looked disappointed, he sounded it, too.

"Not boring at all, Todd. As an airman first class, I was working in the priority section of Base Supply where all items that were needed in a hurry were ordered. It could get pretty fast paced in there."

"You made rank pretty fast, there Clarence. Who's ass did you kiss?" Jeff made kissing noises.

"Watch what you call me, REMF! Unlike flight mechanics who only had to crank a wrench, in Supply we actually had to know how to read. 67-1 was the Bible of Supply, and I had it memorized." Phil laughed, but shot him the look. He hated his first name. "I had been in the section about one year, and knew my job quite well. It was late in the day when my supervisor called me into the office, told me to shut the door and sit down."

"Why? Did you screw up?" Todd grinned as he poked at his dad.

"Todd, your dad never screwed up. That's why I made rank so fast. But, it was very unusual to be called in like that. He then told me he had a very important job for me to do. He felt that I was the only one there that was qualified, and had the experience to do the job." Phil looked proud of himself.

"Really? The *only* one?" Todd looked doubtful. "What was the very important job?"

"My job was to make calls through out the world to locate parts for aircraft that were 'AOCP'."

Jason repeated the initials, A-O-C-P, and stated, "Any Old Coot- "

"Geez, Mad, ever wonder where your kid got his mouth? Boys, it means Aircraft Out of Commission for Parts. This job would require me to be on call any hour of the day or night. It required me to leave contact numbers plus have immediate access back to base if necessary. Before telling me what the job was, he asked if I was able to do the above. I told him I was. He proceeded to tell me that my security clearance was being elevated to Top Secret, and I was not to tell anyone anything of this job."

"Cool, Dad. So how come you're spillin' yer guts now? Retiring, so you're turning traitor?" Todd smirked.

"Another wise ass. Forget it. I don't need to talk. You'll just tell your mother, then she'll sell the story so she can buy another figurine to collect more dust that she can complain about. So, Mad, I like the addition, and the new lounge area. Are you still thinking about- "

"Dad, come on! What did he say?"

"Who?" Phil laughed, then continued without any more prompting. "He proceeded to tell me about the Russians, and the situation they were creating in Cuba."

"The thing my dad was just talking about when I was a baby, when Colonel Pop was there?"

"One and the same. I was to be the main contact person in Base Supply to get all the film necessary for the recon flights made by the U-2 aircraft over Cuba. The job entailed a special password code for telephone communications that allowed me immediate Priority One status. Not even Generals could get me disconnected. I was able to call the flight control officer, and have a pilot and T-39 aircraft available in ten minutes, to go any place in the U.S. to pick up the special film, and fly it where necessary."

"Not even a General? Wow, my grandfather was only a Colonel."

"Jason, never say 'only' when referring to a colonel. Especially, when talking about your grandfather. He is the finest example of a military man that I've ever had the pleasure of knowing."

"Phil, that's a nice thing to say about my dad. I guess he took you under his wing when I got out." Jeff's blue eyes drifted off wondering how his meaningless life would have turned out if only…

"It was a very exciting time for me, being a lowly airman first class, to be needed, and used for this very special purpose. At the time I didn't realize how important the job was until I started to follow exactly what was going on. I did receive a letter of commendation, but more important to me was that I got to the top of the promotion list first. In addition to that they selected me to go to OCS… Officer Candidate School."

Hank and Clark came in from lunch, and Jeff waved for the guys to come join them in the customer lounge.

"You do Nam?" Sam wondered looking at Phil.

"Yeah." Phil said.

Sam nodded. He crushed out his cigarette, and lit another, dragging off it deeply. "Supply?"

"Uh, huh. Da Nang, 1966. When we first got there we were assigned sleeping quarters in several tents. Well, being Supply people, and knowing the ropes, and able to pull a lot of strings, we found an abandoned blockhouse that just happened to be big enough for the twelve of us. We commandeered it, and used influence to get electricity to the building. Then we installed a window AC unit, got new lockers, and installed lights in the lockers to keep the moisture out. We even had a refrigerator to keep the beer cold."

"Phil, you gotta lotta freakin' nerve calling me a REMF with pansy ass duty like that." Jeff picked at him.

"Yeah, well, it's nice to be a supply person with so much pull. We returned the favors by having parties on the weekends. We supplied the drinks, the mess hall supplied the steaks. We had a great life for the first six months." Phil smiled.

The boys chanted, "Par-tee! Par-tee! Par-tee!"

Phil grinned back, "While we were partying, the civil engineers were building new barracks for ALL the troops. They were wooden two story buildings all lined up in a row, seven barracks in all. We were forced to move to the second building, ground floor. We did manage to keep our lockers and lamps, but the AC, and refrigerator were history. No more parties, but at least we were going to be protected from the heavy monsoon rains that would come in the next few weeks."

Clark asked, "Figure God got the idea for Noah's flood watching the monsoons over there? I didn't think it would ever quit pouring. We wanted to build an ark, but we didn't have a damn thing Supply wanted, so there was no chance of asking their sorry asses for any favors."

"I don't believe we've met. I'm Major Phillips, my friends call me Phil. What did you do in Nam?"

"Just call me Clark. I was an MP, K9 Unit, 1967, in Da Nang."

"If it hadn't been for you MP's and your dogs we would have gotten our asses blown to hell one night."

"What did you do? You didn't just sit there watching, did you?" Todd asked wide eyed.

"Hell, no. We ran through the barracks to get to the sand bag bunkers. They were in front of the barracks, and were big enough to handle everybody from one building. If they had ever scored a hit on one of the bunkers, they would have killed a whole bunch of us. By the time the dogs got through the tall grass, about a hundred yards, and were attacking the VC, the backup MP's were mobilized, and came around the ends of barracks with weapons drawn."

"Did any Americans get killed that time, Phil?" Jason asked.

"Nope. Only one rocket managed to hit the barracks. It hit Building One, first floor, first bunk inside the door. I was in Building Two, first floor, first bunk inside the door. The guards, and dogs were watching out for the Base. God definitely was watching out for me."

Jeff watched how intently the teenaged boys were listening to Phil talk. Sam crushed his empty pack of cigarettes, and tossed it in the trash before walking out to his bike to get another pack. He was gone several minutes, and came back smelling like Jodi after a head party. Jeff noticed how quiet Sam had gotten, and wondered if he would talk. Instead he lit up another cigarette, staring off into space as the others continued to answer the boys questions.

"Hey, Dad, do ya think now that you're getting out of the military, maybe you'll grow some hair?" Todd asked, jesting with his dad again.

"You think it's short now? You should've seen me in Nam. I got a buzz cut every two weeks! I was one of the first computer operators for the new UNIVAC 1050 system being installed at several bases. It was June 1966, midday when I arrived in Saigon. We were told to board buses that would take us to our new units. All buses were stopping at the same places so it didn't make any difference which one we got on. Upon arrival at Base Supply I departed, and went to the Orderly Room to report in. The First Sergeant told me where I was to stay, and where every thing was, Base Exchange, Mess Hall, Hospital, etc. He said that I was the first operator in country, and I'd have to wait for the rest of the crew to get in country before we were shipped to Da Nang, AFB, about 300 miles north. He said I could go into town, Saigon, but to stay on the main streets, and only eat at the better restaurants. I also had to report in once a week for head count, then I was free to go again till the next week."

"Is this going to be another party animal story?" Jason asked, as Todd absentmindedly reached across the table for one of Jeff's cigarettes. Jeff swatted him, and Phil nodded his head in approval.

"You boys haven't been to a barber shop in so long, you don't realize how lucky you are to be able to walk into one, and walk out alive, without giving it a second thought." Hank kidded the boys.

"I don't know about that Hank. There's been a couple uh times Dad said if I didn't get a haircut he was gonna kill me."

"That's not what I said, Jason. I said if you didn't get a haircut, you were gonna kill yourself. I don't know how you see to drive with that wild mane hangin' in your eyes. You look worse than Tom's steeds." Jeff grabbed a hand full of Jason's hair, and made whinnying noises.

"Thanks a lot Pops, but I'm still not getting it cut."

When the laughter died down, Phil continued, "I'd been in country about two weeks, and needed a haircut so I went to the barbershop on base. I was still very leery about going anywhere by myself because only one person in Vietnam knew I was there. When I got to the barbershop I was surprised to see there were eight barbers. Also, the building was more like a bamboo hut, floors and all. I was the only GI in the place at the time, it was about 1300 hours, most everyone else was at their jobs. The barbers spoke broken English, just enough to understand how you wanted your haircut. While this guy was cutting my hair, a realization came to me. *What would happen if these guys were VC?* They could slit my throat, dump me under the floor, and no one would know I was gone for at least a week. This really scared the crap out of me. Fortunately, I got my haircut, and got out of there. As it turned out I was in Saigon longer than expected. About ten days later, the VC hit the East gate with satchel charges, and mortars. The guards repelled them, killing nine of the ten. Soon after the attack, it was time for another hair cut. I went back to the barbershop, this time only two barbers were there. The other six were in fact VC, and had been killed in the attack days prior. Finally the rest of the crew arrived in country. We were given a few days to check the equipment, get it ready to ship to Da Nang, and we were out of there by the end of the week."

"Got a buddy named Slick that stops by once in a while. He was in Phu Bai, he shared a similar incident about his barber being VC, and was killed in a sapper attack." Jeff stated.

"Upon arriving in Da Nang, we all checked in, and were again told to stay on base unless we went to protected areas, then to only use military vehicles. Well, here again, it was time for another hair cut. By this time, I was very leery about going to another barbershop run by the Vietnamese, but there was no where else to go to. This time there were only two barbers, but I still wasn't comfortable being there. Got the haircut done, and I was out of there in a heartbeat. It was about three weeks later we were attacked by the VC. This time they came in from the north. The Army and Marines repelled them killing at least forty. Guess what?" Phil asked.

"What?" Both guys answered together.

"Two of them were the barbers from the base. The first barber was the one that really sacred me. Anyway, at this point the Base Commander asked if anyone on base knew how to cut hair. There were three volunteers. All were given special privileges, as long as they were in country cutting hair. Two were promoted, which gave them more money."

Jodi, Stan and Rocky walked in with Doug, and nodded hello while Phil was still talking. Doug, Jodi and Stan sat down. As soon as Rocky heard the words "cutting hair" he left, and went outside to mess around in the woods. Todd knew he'd have cigarettes, but decided to stay and listen to more of Phil's story.

"As I told you earlier, I was one of the first computer operators in country so that meant I would be one of the first to leave. I was never so glad when my departure date came. I think I was ready a whole week ahead of time. I was going home for a short leave, then up to Bangor, Maine. They had an old RAMAC 305 computer system, and naturally I was the only one left in the Air Force that had any training on this machine. I had been there only a few days when I got a call from Da Nang saying that the VC had marched mortar rounds down the flight line. They managed to hit eighteen of the twenty aircraft parked in the revetment areas. One came down in the middle of the supply building where I had worked. Had I still been there you would not be listening to this today. Of all the people that worked midnight shift, only one survived. That was only because he had to go outside to take a piss. When the mortars started coming in, he headed for the nearest ditch. When I heard the news I was so upset they gave me time off. I finally got my self under control, and went back to work."

"I guess even in Supply, it was no walk in the park. One day I was on my motorcycle on my way to work, and just kept going. Was gone for three weeks. Didn't call the wife, or anything. I'd been on the job for seventeen months... tour of duty... It was over, never went back. When I, uh finally walked in the door, I pointed my finger at the ol' lady 'n told her, 'don't start'. I went tuh bed, and slept for two days." Sam said as he sat in his chair straddled backwards with his arms folded across it's back, swinging back and forth.

"If you were a medic, how did you end up in Motor Pool, Hank?" Jeff asked.

"A Thud crew I knew went down, I only remember two names. I've zipped a lotta body bags, but don't remember any names. Mostly only had greenies in country when I was there, thankfully. I was there early enough, didn't see enough of it to still bother me much. Only flashback I have is of the time our beer got warm. I met Connie in Nam. She's a nurse. She couldn't cut it, and came back home as soon as possible. I looked her up when I got back stateside. We married, and the twins came along ten months later. It was a few months after that they called me in for a retention interview. They told me if I re-enlisted, I had thirty days R & R, then was being sent back to Vietnam. Told them 'no thanks', and got out. No regrets. I had a wife and two little girls to support. Working in a walk in clinic, I was going out of my mind, I couldn't stand being cooped up in a building eight to twelve hours a day. I settled down when I met Seth and started to work for him."

"Clark, are the stories true about booby trapping babies?" Jason asked, as he caught a look from his dad.

"It's okay, Jeff, if he's old enough to ask, he's old enough to know." Clark answered. "I also worked the midnight shift, 12 a.m. to 0800. The rest of the day we had off. There weren't a lot of places to go. We could walk to the local village to buy fresh fruits, or trinkets, or just look around. We were always on alert, never went by ourselves, and were careful where we went. Never went down any side streets unless we were with someone who was familiar with the area. On this particular day, we were called into town, some grunts had spotted a baby lying in a gully. It was crying, and it needed attention. This raised a major red flag. It was one of the things they had been warned about. Not under any condition were they to approach the baby, or touch it in any way. They were to notify the MP's, and let the bomb squad handle the situation. They were told in all probability, the baby had a satchel charge under it. And, it most certainly did. It was guaranteed to kill all around. The Viet Cong had a very low value on the lives of babies. They felt babies were expendable as long as they took one, or more GI's out with it."

Jason was going to ask the obvious question, when he saw Jeff just shake his head no. He understood, and shut up. It was quiet for a few moments. Jodi got up to go look for Rocky.

Clark continued with his story, "They didn't have much respect for women either. While living in country the U.S. Government wanted us to use as many local people as we could to help their economy. We had a housekeeper who came in every day to clean, and keep things halfway straight. She had a friend who came with her once a week to get the dirty laundry, and bring back the clean pressed uniforms. One week the laundry lady didn't come with her. We asked where she was. One of the other MP's had stopped her at the main gate. She was searched with a metal detector, and they found she was carrying live grenades inside her vagina." One could see the sickened look on Clark's face as he related that story.

"A lot of MP's become cops when they get out of the Military, what's the deal? I've always wondered why you went to work for Seth." Jeff asked curiously.

"I used to skeet shoot with my dad when I was a kid. I got a job at a service station to keep me in shotgun shells. I liked working on the vehicles, and I was an expert rifleman. Government put me up in the towers where they figured I could do the most damage, or good, depending on how ya wanna look at it. Time I did in Nam made me never want to pick up a weapon again. When I got back stateside, I went to work for Seth, we grew up together. I'd just as soon stay under a car hood, and mind my own business. Saw too much sitting in that tower. I still like dogs though."

After a few minutes of silence, Doug mentioned, "I had a mighty close call myself.".

"I didn't know you were in Nam, Doug." Jeff remarked casually.

"Well, Mad, we haven't exactly been conversing lately. But, yeah, I did my duty in Nam. I spent as much time as I could get away with in the EM Club."

"What's EM Club?" Todd asked.

"Enlisted Mens Club, the bar. Once I dodged a bullet, I spent even more time there. I really liked the atmosphere, and listening to other peoples stories helped me to forget my own."

"You look young to be a Nam vet," Hank stated.

"I got drafted in the Army in the fall of 1969 right out of high school. My Base Camp was at Binh Thuy. I arrived in country 1970, but I lived in Can Tho. I was 4th Corps, Generator Repair. I was always on Temporary Duty Assignment status, so I pretty much had to be field ready to go any place in the 4th Corps to repair generators. I was sent out to a village where they had a small support site. It was a Vietnamese signal battalion. They supplied the power for a signal van that was used to relay messages from the infantry, to the air strikes. There were a couple uh generators on a flat bed trailer that weren't working. Nearby, was cement mountain, the VC would hide in a hollow space inside. They would shoot at anybody that tried to work on the generators. I didn't know about it, so I walked out with my tools, and a voltage regulator all ready to work on the generator. The canvas had been removed from the wooden bows that normally covered the trailer. It was so hot, they needed air. I was standing next to the generator, I bent down to remove the engine cover then I heard the bow snap above my head. I never heard the shot. The hole in the bow was in line where my head had been. I'd uh been a goner had I not bent down at that specific moment. I was armed with an M-79 grenade launcher. It didn't do me any good as it couldn't shoot far enough to hit the enemy. I got the part put on, and called for a helicopter to get me the hell out of there. Got back to base camp, and went straight to the EM Club to knock back a few to try and forget the day."

"Did they ever get the VC out of there Doug?" Jason asked.

"No we never did get them out. We had incoming from the mountain, and called for an air strike. The cargo plane came by and dumped all the used rubber tires on the cement mountain. A fighter came in and dumped napalm on the tires, and then shot Willie Pete, incendiary rounds at the napalm to set them on fire. Seemed like it burned forever. After it burned out, we didn't have any problems with incoming for a while. So, the ARVN's- Army of the Republic of Vietnam, went to search the caves for VC. They were shot and killed at the mouth of the caves. With all the heat, the decaying bodies began to stink to high heaven. The VC sent message through the farmers to come remove the dead bodies from the caves, and promised they wouldn't shoot at any body. That was the only time they honored their word."

Jodi came back in a snit, "I caught your brat out in the treehouse smoking again. I don't know what to do with him. I haven't had any control over that boy since he started cutting his teeth."

"Yeah? And what makes ya think you had any control over him before then, Jodi baby?" Stan had a great big grin on his face, and laughed his unmistakable chortle.

Jeff couldn't help but grin himself as he remembered Jodi handing her baby one Popsicle after another as he teethed. Figuring that everyone that had anything worth while to say, had already said it, Todd stood up to leave when he realized Rocky did have cigarettes. Jeff grabbed his shirttail, and pulled him back to his seat. He also picked his cigarettes up off the table, and stuffed them in his pocket. His skyrocketing cigarette costs might not be completely due to himself, he was beginning to realize.

"So, what are we talking about now?" Jodi inquired.

"Been talkin' about Nam, Jodi." Sam dryly replied. "Just about Nam."

"Stan was in Nam. He got me pregnant, then went off playing war games. He got to miss all the fun I had barfing and gagging every morning. He missed out on the thirty six hours I had to spend in labor before they finally figured out I wasn't big enough to deliver an eight and a half pound drill sergeant, so they cut him out of me. Stan came home to a three month old who took one look at him, and cooed."

"Geez, Jodi, shut up. Look around, do you see any other chicks here that wanna listen to that stuff? Why don't you go bake us some magic brownies? We'll toke up a few joints, and talk about less gory stuff, like bombing orphanages, okay?" Stan barked at her.

Sam reached inside his boot. Jeff growled, "Forget it!" The boys once again side glanced each other.

"Well, I know where I'm not wanted. See ya!" Jodi took off again for places unknown. Stan stayed with the men, he didn't need to smoke up, he'd had enough since lunch to keep him stoked the rest of the day.

Clark spoke up, "Well, we have the Supply Chief over there. Hank was a Medic, I was an MP, Doug was a generator man, Madison was a REMF, Sam ain't talkin', what about you Stan? Jodi said you were in Nam, any war stories to share?"

"Yeah, my battle axe just walked out the door. War's over." Stan was laughing again. "Ahhh… It don't mean nuthin'."

Another laugh came from the doorway. "Hey, Mad. Just came by to pick up my truck."

"Bob, hello. How long ya been waiting? I apologize, man."

"Not a problem, Mad… been listening to the war stories… hope ya don't mind… couldn't talk 'bout it myself for years… but then there's nothin' much to speak of... just working with the Army at Tan Son Nhut near Saigon... we were inspectors of the candy that came in country... broken boxes mainly... we were working with a Medic who would decide if they should be disposed of or not… those that were rejected, we took to the dump to burn... Vietnamese would watch until we torched it, then run in to the flames to get the candy to sell on the black market... we tried to keep them out as much as we could... but, then we would go downtown, and see them selling it... When I went back to my home base, which was

Bien Hoa, twenty miles north, we would truck salvage parts to Tan Son Nhut once a week on a tractor and trailer... I was driver... we were armed with side arms and rifles, .45's and M-16's... there was myself, a copilot, and a guard on the back... we would get shot at going, and coming on Highway One... and try to keep the locals from jumping on the truck... and stealing everything before we got it to the dump... when there was about sixty days to go in country before I PCS'd back to the States and we got shelled every night... lived in the bunkers those last days... we'd hit the bunkers until the gun ships would get airborne... then sit on top of our barracks... and watch them blow the hell out of Charlie..."

It was very quiet in the shop.

"Boys know what Charlie means?"

Jason shook his head no.

"Viet Cong... VC... Victor Charlie... Charlie."

"What's PCS?"

"Permanent Change of Station."

"Did we lose any men?" Jason wondered.

"Lost some... we had the 101st Airborne on the other side of the base and got to know them well... we would party with them and trade items they needed for what we needed... and then they would go on recon and some did not come back... you didn't ask what happened, you just mourned their loss... we, Air Force, had it good compared to the Army, except for our pilots... and our pj's... the pararescue guys that flew in the choppers to pick up and attend to the wounded til they got them to base camp hospital... that's about it..."

"How 'bout you, Sam?" Jason asked.

"Army. 1970. Combat. Cambodia. Lead tank. Hit villages, whacked hospitals." Sam drew in, then blew out a long breath of smoke. His eyes were spaced way off in the distance. About the War, he remained silent.

Jeff took care of business with Bob. Jodi, Stan, and Rocky left, but Doug stayed behind. He asked Jeff if they'd had time to look over Mack's van.

"Yeah, Doug, each one of us went over it individually, and then we went over it together. Can't find a damn thing wrong with it. What does he think is the problem?"

"Well, he says it runs fine. He's just been so sick lately, and the doctors can't find anything wrong with him. He's dizzy and nauseous. He has head aches, and is weak. Some times he can hardly walk. He thought maybe the van had an exhaust leak, or some other problem."

"None that we could find." Jeff said. Hank and Clark nodded in agreement. They each said good bye, and went back to work.

"Well, I drove it for a while before I dropped it off here for him, and I didn't get sick. I had my doubts, but it's never wrong to check out all possibilities. Thanks Jeff." Doug took the van, and left for the Alibi Inn. Sam followed behind him on his Harley.

Phil and Todd were outside while Jason hung back to say good bye to his dad. "Hey, uh, Dad, would it be okay if I stayed? It's not easy sayin' good-bye to Todd. Tom is being a pain in the ass again over me, and the guys garage band. They kicked Nathan out of the band so he isn't returning my calls…"

"Sure, you can stay. I'm sure you can find something to do."

They walked outside together, and said farewell to Phil and Todd. They wished them the best for their move, and vowed that they would all stay friends. They waved good-bye as Phil's car drove out of the yard.

Father and son went back inside the shop.

"Ya got another date with Shauna tonight, Dad?" Jason wondered as he leaned against the wall watching his father light a cigarette.

Jeff looked stunned, and answered, "Not really... How did you know her name?" He flicked the ashes on the garage floor, and took another drag.

"Dad, she was on the dance squad at school. She's the only girl ever to make the team as a freshman. She stayed on it all four years. She won every local talent show there was. Mainly for interpretive dance, but she also won for tap, ballet and jazz. Then, too, she always got the lead in every school play, whether it was a musical or not. Shauna's really talented. She never went out with high school boys, though. Rumor had it she was sleeping with the Psychology teacher, but nobody ever seen 'em together. Geez Dad, even he isn't as old as you."

"I'm only thirty-six, Jason. I've still got a lot of fuel in my tank, plenty of tread on my tires, and a lot of miles to go. How come you never asked her out?" Jeff reached in the refrigerator for a beer.

"Oh, yeah right. Like a senior would've even noticed a freshman."

"She did." He said with a smile as he snapped open the can.

"And you know that for a fact?" Jason looked doubtful.

"Uh huh. She noticed enough to recognize you and remember your name." He knocked back half a can in one gulp.

Jason thought a few moments. "Well, for one thing, she isn't blonde. For two, with that auburn hair, and those green eyes, I'd uh thought I was makin' it with my mother, and that's sick."

The boy was obviously more observant than Jeff thought. He finished the beer and tossed the can in the trash.

"Don't you date, son?" Jeff lit another cigarette.

Jason dropped his eyes. "Nah, women... ya can't trust 'em, they can't keep their mouths shut. Since you don't have a date, and I don't have a gig, do you care if I hang out with you tonight?"

"It's okay with me so long as you don't smoke my cigarettes."

"Not me, Dad. It's not my thing." He fanned Jeff's smoke away.

"Sorry about that. Glad you never picked up this filthy habit." He blew his smoke the other direction, and flicked the ashes on the floor again.

"Dad," Jason paused. "Dad, I'm glad you came back from Nam okay. Some guys came back pretty messed up. You may be FUBF, but ya know what? I love ya anyway Dad." He gave Jeff a hug for the first time in a long, long time.

"And, just what is FUBF?"

Jason grinned, "Fucked up but functional."

"You know what, boy? Even though you have a sassy mouth, and you're a royal pain in the ass, I love you too, Jason. Want to look over the Vette with me before we go grab a bite to eat?"

"Yeah, but I think first I'd like to take a quick look through the woods to make sure Rocky didn't leave any cigarette butts burning."

"Good idea, thanks, Jase."

Into the woods, across the stream, and up into the tree house Jason went. He reached deep in his pocket, and pulled out the hashish Stan had slipped him while Jeff was tugging on Todd's shirttail. He placed it in his hash pipe, and drew it's poignant smoke deep into his lungs.

Chapter 21

1980

"Hello, Mack?"

"Yeah... Who is this?" Mack answered weakly.

"Mack, it's Jodi. Doug said you are sicker. What's the matter?"

"Who?" Mack searched his mind.

"Jodi... I work for you at the Alibi Inn. Mack are you okay? My goodness, I've worked for you for years.

"Um, short, blonde, big boobs?" Mack mumbled.

Jodi didn't like the frail voice she was hearing on the other end of the phone. "That's right, Mack." She could hear the TV in the background. "Mack, I can hardly hear you. Can you speak louder? What's wrong? Is there anything I can do to help you?"

Raising his voice a little louder he began, "Everything is wrong. My stomach is sick, and my head is dizzy..."

Jodi heard the TV go up a notch.

"When I try to walk, the room begins to whirl..." He spoke louder, and the TV went up another notch. "My legs are shaky, and I've been walking with a cane. Who is this again?" The TV went up another notch.

"Jodi, it's Jodi, Mack. Have you seen a doctor?"

"Yes, they find nothing."

"Mack, I can't hear you."

"YES, THEY FIND NOTHING."

Jodi heard the TV go up full volume. "I think you need a second opinion. You've been sick for a long time."

"DeeDee! Dammit! Turn that thing down."

"Mack you're so loud on the telephone, I can't hear my program."

"DeeDee, I don't use the phone that much, is it okay if I talk to Jodi a few minutes, please?"

The volume went down to near nothing in seconds. "Sweetheart, why didn't you say you were talking to Jodi? I'm so sorry, honey. I'd like to talk to Jodi, too. When you're done of course, okay darling?"

Jodi heard every word. She was suspicious of Deana because she was such a hypocrite. Mack went on to tell Jodi different treatments the doctors had given him, but he continually grew worse. He excused himself so he could go back to bed. Mack handed the phone to Deana.

"Jodi, I just don't know… He keeps getting sicker and sicker. All he does is complain, complain, complain. I'm sorry about the TV thing. He's just so loud, and I was trying to see the end of that program. He knows I really enjoy it, so it seems he talks louder just to annoy me. Men! What are ya gonna do? You can't live with 'em, and you can't kill 'em!"

Jodi only half laughed at her attempt at making a joke. Mack's illness didn't seem to be a laughing matter. "Well, listen DeeDee, I'm sure we could talk girl talk, and bash Mack and Stan all night long, but what the hey? I've got to wash up the dishes, and check Rocky's homework. Catch you another time, okay? Bye."

Several days later, Rocky looked lustily at DeeDee, and smiled as she entered the employee break room. He recalled when he first started waiting for his mom at the Alibi Inn. He was insulted that they thought he was too young to stay at home without supervision. Then one day as he stood in front of the pop machine, he could sense that someone was standing close behind him. He turned around and found he was face to face with DeeDee. She put both hands on the machine on either side of Rocky's young shoulders, she licked her lips and began to speak, "Rocky, honey, you don't have to buy soda's while you're here. You just tell DeeDee what you want, and it's yours. Anything you want, Rocky, anything."

He smirked to himself remembering how young and stupid he was at the time. He would be sitting at the table reading whatever assignment he was given. She would come up behind him, lean over, and read over his shoulder. He could feel the swell of her breasts pressing into his back. She had to be the most beautiful creature on earth... or so Rocky thought.

DeeDee was fixing a cup of coffee, and smiled back at Rocky. "Hey there big boy," she spoke in a throaty voice, "Wanna bring this coffee out to Mack, then meet me in my office?"

She knew he did. She'd groomed that boy since he was nine. He shadowed her like a puppy trying to please her every whim in hopes that she'd touch him again... down there. He handed Mack the coffee, and wasted no time getting to her office. DeeDee had her back to the door as she sat in her big chair swaying side to side, while she was talking on the phone.

"Listen to me and listen to me closely you limp dicked, panty waste. I'm not paying you for second rate product. Got that? I thought you were on to something big when you called me from the City. Then I find out you stole a couple bottles of pills from your family. What kind of a low life does that? Your family?!? You talked like you were Mr. Big, and come to find out you are nothing. NOTHING!!!"

DeeDee listened to the voice on the other end, then shot back, "Don't you *dare* call me a whore. I'm a fire breathing, cock sucking bitch, but I'm no whore, and don't you ever forget it. Got that? Look I know dealers that use mules like you for target practice. Either you produce by the weekend, or suffer the consequences. This is no joke."

DeeDee turned around, and was startled to see Rocky sitting on the couch, wide eyed and shocked. "Well, Rocky, what did you think of my performance? Those were some lines I learned for a play I was in a few years ago. What do you think? Was I good?" She walked over to the door, turned the lock then sat down next to the enamored thirteen year old. "Don't mention the play to anyone, okay, honey? People might get jealous if they knew I've been on stage, and well, I really don't like all the attention that performers always attract. Rocky, quit staring… that's rude. Would you like to take pictures?"

DeeDee took him another step further into the world of sexual exploitation.

Jeff slowly drove through the parking lot of the Alibi Inn. Sure enough, Deana's car was still in the parking lot; he decided to move on. That wasn't the only drinking establishment in town, but it was the local favorite. He noticed the light in Deana's office switch off as he rounded the curve in the driveway to leave. He also noticed there was still the flickering of a candle reflecting in the window. "Bitch," he thought out loud as he recalled how the vile creature contributed to messing up his life. Just before giving it the gas to leave, he heard a light tap on the Corvette's passenger window.

"Hey, tall, dark and handsome! Why don't ya watch where you're going?" The voice didn't sound angry.

Jeff turned his head to see who it was, and a big smile broke out across his face as he recognized Shauna. He ran down the automatic window. "Hi, Shauna. Where have you been keeping yourself?"

"I might ask you the same thing. I've been coming here every night for nearly two weeks. This is the first trace I've seen of you, your hot car, and your gorgeous body... or should that be your gorgeous car, and hot body?" Shauna laughed playfully.

Jeff laughed back. "So have you eaten?"

"Yeah. If you have, what do you say we skip the preliminaries, and just go to your place?"

"Hop in. I haven't, but I've got plenty of food at home. So where have you been? It's been a year since I've seen you around."

"I'm going to school in the City studying dance. Hey I'm built for it, I love it, and I'm a natural. I'm more talented than what's in the dance clubs, so why not get a degree, and shoot for the stars?"

Jeff looked at her beauty closely. "Shauna, if anyone can make the cut, you can. Promise you won't forget me when you make it big?"

"How could I forget you? You are the only man that can dance the night away, and not pressure me for a commitment. No Jeff, I'll never forget you. So, how are your kids?" She said, changing the subject.

"My daughter's still distant. I try my best, but I can't compete with all her stepfather can provide. Once in a while, when I hug her good-bye, I see tears in her eyes. She is so non communicative, I don't know how to read her. She still sings beautifully. When I know she's going to be singing a solo at her church, I go over and sit in the back just to hear her. I realize she doesn't even know I'm there, but that's okay."

"I don't know her. I do remember Jason. He was the cutest freshman in his class. He was very popular. But, if it wasn't for his eyes, I'd never guess that he was your son! What's he doing now?"

"Jason, well, he's another story. Since his buddy Todd moved away, he's been in and out of minor trouble. Actually, it started before that with some sexual misconduct on a church bus a few years back. His other buddy, Nathan, distanced himself from him over it. He felt out of place at church, so he quit going. He started hanging out with a couple of losers who have a garage band, and he got involved with them, then Nathan cut ties altogether. His stepfather has him seeing a psychiatrist because of his rebellious nature, and his drug use."

"DRUG USE?" Shauna was appalled.

"Yes, sorry to say. Like too many of the kids these days, he started blowing a little weed with the band. Most eighteen year old boys are naturally rebellious at that age. I don't know what Tom is so upset about. The kid has a brain. He's always spoken his mind. But, it seems if his mind isn't lined up with what Tom has in his mind, my kid is naturally wrong, in *his* opinion. Not in mine. I know my boy. I do not approve at all about the pot use, but what the hell? He's a good kid, he'll out grow it. We've all tried it."

"I haven't."

"Are you kidding me?" Jeff looked at Shauna shake her head no. "Okay, I stand corrected."

"I'm very serious about being a professional dancer. I want to be on Broadway, or on a Las Vegas stage. I won't let anything, or anybody get in my way. It's in my blood. So who are the guys in the garage band?"

"All I know them by is Jesse and Andy."

"Hmmm, Jason needs some new friends. Losers is being too kind describing that duo."

"What d'ya mean?"

"Jesse's older brother was the major connection for kids getting weed at school. He was just a sophomore when I was a senior, but everybody knew. Nobody talked. Andy's mother is a street-walker who'd sell her own son for a fix."

254

"Ya don't say?" Jeff believed her, but thought she was probably exaggerating. He thought of his own high school reputation being likened to a local James Dean.

Jeff parked the car and opened the door for Shauna. She looped her arm through Jeff's as they walked up the stairs. He heard her stomach growl. "Young lady, are you sure you've eaten?" Jeff almost sounded like he was scolding Marianne.

"Oh, I guess it has been a few hours since lunch."

"Lunch? That's the last time you ate? Well, let me fix you my famous omelette avec jambon et fromage." Jeff unlocked the door.

"Sounds intriguing, but what is it?" Shauna wondered.

"A ham and cheese omelet." He put some ready to bake croissants in the oven. He quickly went to work dicing ham, and slicing cheese. In no time at all it seemed, they were enjoying a quickie supper. He noticed Shauna ate very lady like, and relished every bite. She cleaned her plate, and ate most of the croissants, saturating them in butter. He figured she hadn't eaten in a very long time, or she truly enjoyed food. Either way, he was happy. He offered her a cigarette, she nodded no.

"Jeff, I don't know when I've enjoyed an omelet so much. That was really good. And those croissants… yum!" Shauna watched him inhale.

"I don't remember the last time I enjoyed watching someone enjoy my cooking this much. How about a glass of wine? Or would you prefer milk?" He exhaled and asked with a grin.

"Wine sounds great. I'm over twenty-one you know. Jeff, um, I need to use the restroom. Excuse me just a minute, okay?"

"Of course Shauna, you remember where it is I'm sure." Jeff was picking up the dishes, and rinsing them when he heard the sound of gagging and retching coming from the bathroom. He heard rinsing and sloshing noises. Oh, no, he thought, fearing the worst.

"Shauna, are you in trouble?" Jeff asked kindly, when she returned.

"Trouble? No, not at all. Why do you ask?"

"I heard you get sick in the bathroom. When my wife was pregnant, she couldn't eat some foods without getting sick… I just wondered if…"

"The answer's still no. I'm not in trouble, and I'm not pregnant… It's how I control my weight. Hey, it's okay, I take a fist full of vitamins every morning with a diet cola. I pig out at meals, then I barf it. Works like a charm." Shauna patted her very flat stomach. "I even use sugar free mouth wash. So what do you say? Wanna help me burn up a few more calories, big guy?" She was pressing her abdomen against his as his back leaned against the sink.

Before Jeff could think of how dangerous what she was doing was for her health, they were in his bed. She was all over his body. *If sex was all there was to a relationship,* he thought, *I might just consider making a commitment with this girl.* He felt safe in that department, since she'd said herself she wasn't interested in anything but her career. *What an appetite,* was all he could think as she hungered for him again and again. Each time he easily arose to the occasion. He was beginning to think she was insatiable, when her heaving, pounding flesh finally rested against his firm, sweat covered body.

"Jeff, if sex was all there was to a relationship, I might just consider making a commitment with you…" Her lips playfully pulled the hairs on his chest.

"Shauna, I feel the same way, but neither of us deserves to be second." Jeff slid out from under her, and reached for his cigarettes.

"What do you mean?"

"Shauna, I'd always be second to your career. You'd always be second to my first, and only wife." Jeff pointed to his first tattoo. "There's only room in my heart for one." He drew in a long breath of smoke.

"I'm so glad that we understand each other." Shauna yawned. "Know what, big guy? I'm really, really tired. You are incredible." She fell asleep.

"Yeah, thanks, baby doll. You're pretty amazing yourself." Jeff knew he couldn't go another round even if it was going to be the last piece he ever got in his life, but how he longed for his wife. With the exception of the first time they'd had sex, and the night he left her, after a night of passionate lovemaking, they'd always fallen asleep in each others arms. Usually, they woke up still in a tender embrace. He missed being loved. He crushed out his cigarette, and went to sleep… with Shauna, but alone.

Chapter 22

1981

My Dearest Beth...

It's one of those long sleepless nights, when my mind won't let you go. My soul is tired, and my head pounds, but my body longs for your touch.

Darling, I still don't understand what went wrong. Whenever I look into your eyes, I know you love me, too...

It was time to go for the hard stuff. Jeff knew it. The bevy of women he'd sent away from the shop were continually on his nerves. He needed some space tonight. Everyone seemed to be getting ready to celebrate the Christmas season. Thanksgiving was only yesterday. It seemed like every so often he needed to get a good old fashioned cry out of his system. The only way he could do that was to be alone. He had chugged back more beer than he could count, and the pain in the pit of his stomach wouldn't be dulled. He poured himself a shot of scotch, and knocked it back without a blink. *Screw the shot glass*, he thought. He was alone; he drank straight from the bottle. He started to cry as he prayed...

"Dear God, Why can't the way be cleared for her to come back? If she can't come back, why can't this longing go away? I've tried so hard, and I just can't get over her. I still want her back in my arms. I adored her, I still adore her."

He kept swallowing from the bottle until his tears flowed like a river. Jeff knew he could quit drinking. He knew he could. He only drank to dull the pain in his head, and in his heart. His stomach still churned thinking of another man touching his virgin angel. Most of the time he didn't think about it. It was just the way it was. But, tonight he thought hard about it. It hurt to think about it, and tonight it hurt bad. He'd always had hunger for women and there were always women to fill his needs, but only she fulfilled the passion in his soul. She was something special. She was beautiful. He never expected to fall in love, or to even touch her that night long ago...

"I love you Jeff Madison... Jeff, we can stop. Just not yet. Kiss me... Yes... I'm sure." Her voice echoed.

Jeff squeezed his eyes tight, just the way he did when she first spoke those words to him. He remembered how she cried. Only this night, he was the one crying. The tears flowed, long, hard, and heavy. "I want my wife back." He sobbed out loud, and took another long swallow of scotch. Again, he prayed.

"Dear God, I never wanted to let her go. Never. Not then, not now. God, I loved her. She would stop whatever she was doing to fuss over me whenever I came in the door. She would sing to our kids while she rocked them to sleep. God, I adore that woman. Why, why, why did I have to let her go? What went wrong? I want my wife back. Please, please send her home."

Jeff finished off the pint of scotch. The tears wouldn't stop. He picked up the pen, and finished writing:

I know I still want you, just as much now as I did twenty years ago tonight when we conceived our baby boy. Please come

*home to me. You are always in my heart. I will love you until
the day I die.*

*Your adoring husband,
Jeff*

Jeff passed out.

He didn't know how long he'd slept. It wasn't long
enough. He didn't feel any better, and couldn't feel any worse.
Jeff made his way into the bathroom, then caught a glimpse
of himself in the mirror. He saw the face of a nearly forty
year old man, that was hollow, sad, and broken. He washed
his hands. and splashed cold water on his face. He went to
the kitchen, opened the refrigerator, cracked open a beer, and
downed it before grabbing two more, and going back to his
couch. He didn't want to go to his bed. There had been others,
many others in that bed, but memories of her haunted it still.
He remembered their life in Florida. He remembered long
walks and laughter in Okinawa, before… He remembered
how beautiful their time was each time they tried to make it
work again. He brought the second can to his lips, and found
it empty. He prayed once again.

"Dear God, I remember the first night I looked deeply
into her angel eyes, and told her I'd like to melt right into her,
but was afraid You would get me for it if I did. Is it because I
didn't honor her virtue that she was taken from me? If I wake
up tomorrow, I will hope for one more day that my beloved
Beth will come home to me. I love you, Lord. Please bless my
children, and their mother, my beautiful bride. I love her so
much. Amen"

Jeff pinched his lips together as he crushed the beer can
and heaved it across the room, totally missing the trash can
like a dozen others.

Jeff passed out again in a drunken stupor. He wasn't sure
if it was the telephone, or a dream, but the ringing wouldn't

stop. He pulled the pillow over his head, but it rang on and on. The only thing to do was answer, and ask whomever it was what the hell was wrong with them calling in the middle of the night, and not getting the hint when he didn't answer, that he didn't want to be bothered.

"Yeah?" Jeff answered in a raspy voice.

"Jeff… Ummm… It's, it's me… Ummm, Jeff… I ummm, I just called to say… …I love you."

Disconnecting the telephone, she prayed, "Thank you Lord for the courage and strength to call him."

Beth cried alone wondering if Jeff remembered… wondering… what went wrong?

Printed in the United States
131997LV00001B/1/P

9 781438 923451